Becky's Rebel

A sadness overcame her. Why was she the one breaking these horses? The war had been over for a month. She knew Joe wasn't coming back, but what about her brothers? Why weren't they the ones doing the man's work she'd been forced to do?

Suddenly the war, the inequality of war, the fact she'd been left behind to take over, became too much for her. Burying her face against the horse's neck, she began to cry.

"Damn them!" she screamed. "Damn them all to hell!"

She couldn't believe it when she felt someone's hands on her shoulders. Who could it be? When she'd started breaking the mare, she'd been alone. Her father was finishing the last of the planting, her mother was in the house. Who could have invaded her privacy?

"Ladies in Texas don't break horses, and they don't damn anyone to hell," a man drawled.

Becky's head spun, her heart beat faster and the ground seemed to drop out from under her feet. She could hardly dare to believe the voice belonged to Joe. To confirm her hopes, to see the materialization of her prayers, she turned to face him.

"Joe, is it you? Is it really you? The war's been over for so long and..."

What They Are Saying About

Becky's Rebel

Ms. Derr-Wille brings the spirit of understanding to the plight of the Civil War survivors. Becky Larson and her Rebel, Joe Kemmerman, reminds us that love and faith overcome all obstacles. A must read for those who still need to understand there is no difference in the hearts of people, North or South. *Becky's Rebel* will make you laugh, shed a tear or two and have you falling in love, once again, with a time and it's people that is uniquely America's... the Civil War era.

—Debbie Fritter
The Perfect Match
Whippoorwill Press

Sherry Derr-Wille has penned another winner. Becky's Rebel is truly an entertaining story, involving a colorful period of history, myriad characters and a story full of surprises. Picture the land, the sky, the smells, the feelings... Ms. Derr-Wille's writing style is so descriptive, you can. Becky's Rebel is not the first book by this author that I have read, nor will it be my last. My only problem is putting her books down once I pick them up. 4½ Roses

—Brett Scott
Crystal Reviews
http://www.crystalreviews.com/

Becky's Rebel

by

Sherry Derr-Wille

A Wings ePress, Inc.

Historical Romance Novel

Wings ePress, Inc.

Edited by: Crystal Laver
Copy Edited by: Gina Marie Cadorette
Senior Editor: Sara V. Olds
Managing Editor: Ann K. Oortman
Executive Editor: Lorraine Stephens
Cover Artist: Pam Ripling

Wings ePress Books
http://www.wings-press.com

Copyright © 2003 by Sherry Wille
ISBN 1-59088-774-3

Published In the United States Of America

August 2003

Wings ePress Inc.
403 Wallace Court
Richmond, KY 40475

Dedication

To Vicki:

Thanks for keeping me
on the straight and narrow.
Without your help
none of my books
would have ever been written

Prologue

The wind blew across the Illinois prairie, as only a January wind could blow. Snow, mixed with filtered sunlight, sifted through the cracks of the makeshift prison, only recently converted from a corncrib.

Through his fevered haze, Joe Kemmerman wished some of the flakes would fall on him, to quench the fire that burned just below the surface of his skin.

Beneath him, the thin mattress did little to cushion his body against the hardness of the floor. He'd gotten used to sharing his living space with not only the five other gray clad prisoners, but also with the rats who were free to come and go as they pleased.

A chill raced through his body. For days now the fever had alternated with the chills to accelerate the extent of his illness.

"It's numonie, Paul, I tell you, it's numonie," he heard Backwoods say.

Joe mustered all the strength he could find to open his eyes and look at his brother. "Am I going to die, Paul?"

"Of course you're not. Pa sent me along to protect you, remember?"

"You can't." A fit of coughing cut off his words.

"Lay still," Paul cautioned. "You need to save your strength. The guard said he was sending for a doctor."

Joe closed his eyes and listened to the conversation going on around him.

"Don't get yer hopes up, Paul," Backwoods warned. "They ain't gonna send no doctor."

"But he said..."

"They say a lot of things. When are you goin' to learn you can't believe anything they say? They told us they'd ship us East, but they didn't. They let us believe we'd get enough food and warm blankets. Have you seen any of it? They're nothing' but lying' blue belly Yankees."

Joe agreed with everything Backwoods said, he just didn't want to believe it.

How had all of this happened? Less than a year ago, he'd been nothing more than the youngest son of Mark Kemmerman. It was the war, this damnable war that had done this to him.

In his ramblings, he recalled his oldest brother, Luke. At the beginning of the war, he had enlisted. Letters were infrequent. Then, one day, they'd received word he'd been killed at Vicksburg.

Have faith, Joe Luke's voice echoed in his mind. *Paul knows Pa will make his life a living hell if you die. There's no love lost between the two of them. He's not like us.*

Tears filled Joe's eyes at the sound of Luke's voice. How many months had passed since he could recall Luke's face?

He turned his thoughts to the five other men who shared this nightmare with him. They had met just a week prior to being captured. At the time, only Backwoods was a seasoned veteran of many campaigns. His long dark hair and heavy beard hid his angular features in the same way his dirt and sweat stained uniform did his thin body. The other three men were as new to the business of war as Joe and Paul. He remembered them, not as they looked now, but the way he saw them when they first met. Billy Bob and Jimmy Roy Hastings came from a plantation in Virginia. Instead of standard issue, their uniforms were of fine quality material lovingly made by their mother. Even their hats carried a flare with a dark gray plume stuck into the band. In contrast, Bret Collier wore an expertly tailored uniform he said he had made by a tailor in New Orleans. He claimed to be a gambler, who enjoyed plying his trade on the riverboats that traveled the Mississippi River. With his means of livelihood temporarily gone, he decided to fight rather than starve.

We're all so different, Joe thought, *and yet here we're all equal. Hard working, pampered, illiterate, none of it makes any difference. To these Yankees, we're no better than animals.*

He couldn't help but remember their first military encounter. From that battle, there were only six men who weren't killed. The memory of bodies which had, hours earlier, been his friends made him sick. The Mississippi field had been soaked in blood from gaping wounds and missing limbs turning everything red with the spillage of life.

Another coughing spasm wracked his body. His coughing brought up phlegm. To his surprise, it tasted salty and he realized his mouth was filled with blood.

Someone turned him onto his side, so the blood could run to the ground rather than down his throat. *It would be better if I choked to death and died quickly,* he thought to himself.

"What can we do for him, Backwoods?" he heard Paul ask.

"Nothin', all we can do is try to make him comfortable and pray the good Lord don't let him suffer too long."

Pray, the word echoed in Joe's mind. His mother and Maria were the ones who prayed. Even Paul took his religion seriously. Joe knew he was more like his father. Mark

Kemmerman shunned traditional religion. With death inevitable, Joe wished he'd paid more attention to Maria when she insisted he accompany her to church.

A blast of cold air indicated the door to the enclosure had been opened. Joe couldn't stop the coughing. To his horror, he couldn't catch his breath.

Dear Lord, he thought as panic set in, *I'm dying.*

One

Dr. Tom Morgan finished his breakfast. After setting his dishes on the drain board by the sink, he checked the contents of his bag. Pleased he had everything he would need, he steeled himself to go out into the bitter January cold and begin his day.

Someone pounding at the door startled him. It was early, too early for most people to be out and about. Whoever was on the other side of the door must have real trouble. To Tom's surprise, a Union soldier stood on the porch.

"Can I help you?" Tom asked the young man.

"There's a prisoner who's sick. You need to come."

"Prisoner? Where?"

"The captain calls it the Marrow Place."

"The Marrow Place?" Tom echoed. "I thought the last prisoners left there in October."

"They did, but another bunch came in right after the others left. No one ever authorized us to send them out, so they're still here."

"No matter, it doesn't make any difference now. What did you say about one of the prisoners being sick?"

"He's not much more than a kid. If he doesn't get help soon, I'm afraid he won't last much longer."

"Why did you wait so long?"

"I—I didn't know. Corporal Talons usually checks on the prisoners. My job is to tend the horses."

"Then, why did you check on them today?"

"It's cold. Corporal Talons didn't want to go outside of the barracks. Look, my pa is a doctor. I know a sick kid when I see one. Are you going to help me?"

"Of course, I am. Give me a few minutes to get my bag and I'll be ready to leave."

Tom rechecked the supplies in his bag then added more from his medicine cabinet, before he put on his coat and muffler.

"Tie your horse on behind my carriage. It will be warmer if you ride inside with me."

The soldier agreed and insisted on hitching Tom's horse to the traces. Before they left, Tom spread a buffalo robe over their laps. He watched as the young man ran his hand over the robe.

"I certainly didn't expect to see a robe of this quality so far east. The buffalo have been gone from Illinois for years."

Tom smiled at the comment. "It was payment for services I rendered to a man who got sick while traveling North from St. Louis. I usually receive this type of barter, in lieu of money, from my patients."

The young man next to him said nothing further, leaving a silent void between them.

Tom realized the cold morning air penetrated not only the closed carriage, but the robe as well. The soldier must be even colder, considering he'd ridden the distance earlier and not taken time to warm himself before beginning the return trip.

"You must be freezing," Tom said.

"I'm used to the cold. My home is in northern Minnesota."

"I've lived in this part of the country for a good part of my life, and I'm still not used to it," Tom confessed.

The young man nodded. "With all the urgency, I never even asked your name, Doc."

"It's Morgan, Tom Morgan. What's yours?"

"Alexander Pometere, Private Alexander Pometere, but my friends call me Alex."

Tom allowed Alex to ramble on about the town where he grew up and the family he left behind. The young man's monologue helped to pass the time on the nearly hour ride to the Marrow Place.

He couldn't help but remember the last time he'd visited Burt and Amy Marrow. They'd been the type of couple who did everything together. You didn't think of one of them without thinking of the other. Even in death, they hadn't been parted long. Tom sat with them as Amy quietly slipped away, after a long illness, only to have Burt collapse and die minutes later. He couldn't prove it, but Tom knew Burt died of a broken heart.

"I really miss my folks," Alex said, bringing Tom back to the present. "We live in a farming community like this. Most of my friends live on farms. I guess I could have pulled worse duty. At least I don't have to fight the Rebs, just guard them."

Tom looked up to see the buildings of the farm coming into view. The house stood as evidence of the neglect the property experienced ever since Burt and Amy's deaths. It certainly needed a coat of paint. As for the outbuildings, they all looked like they were ready to fall down.

"Where do they keep the prisoners?"

"In the corncrib, it doesn't seem right to me, but my opinion doesn't carry much weight around here."

Tom swallowed the bile rising in his throat. What were these people thinking of? This was no place for prisoners. He had little time to dwell on his dark thoughts, as he noticed two blue clad men warming themselves by a fire built just outside the barn.

Tom stopped the carriage. To his surprise, one of the men approached the buggy.

"Just where in the hell have you been, Pometere? I thought you ran off somewhere. I was going to give you another hour then I was going to tell the captain you deserted. Get your scrawny ass into the barracks. I'll deal with you later."

"I see nothing to deal with," Tom commented. "This young man came to town to tell me one of your prisoners is sick. I've come to treat him."

"Treat him? What are you some kind of a Doc?"

"I'm Dr. Thomas Morgan, and if you'll excuse me, I have a patient to see."

"Patient? Hell, there ain't no patients here. These ain't men, they're animals. I should have put a bullet in his head when he first got himself sick. I was foolish enough to allow nature to take its course rather than waste ammunition."

Tom held his tongue. To say anything would put him on the same level as the man he assumed to be Corporal Talons.

"What's going on here?"

Tom turned to see a man wearing the uniform of a Union officer, striding toward them.

"Just who are you?" he demanded, pointing at Tom.

For the second time since his arrival, Tom repeated his name, as well as his reason for leaving the warmth of his house to travel for an hour to get here.

"A prisoner is sick?" the man, who identified himself as Captain Delos Courtney, asked. "Why was I not made aware of this before now?"

"Beggin' your pardon, Captain, but I saw no reason to bother you with something so trivial," Corporal Talons said.

"Trivial!" Tom spat. "I don't call a sick man something trivial. I'm certain the officials in Washington will agree with me."

Tom wondered if he imagined it or if Captain Courtney paled at his threat. "No one in Washington gives a damn. If they did, these prisoners would have been sent east months ago, and we would be out of this hellhole."

"At least your description of this place is correct. I want to see the prisoner."

"Take Dr. Morgan to see the boy, Corporal. When he's finished, report to me." Captain Courtney turned on his heel and returned to the house, leaving Tom alone with Talons.

The man said nothing audible, only grumbled under his breath, as he led the way to the makeshift prison.

Once the door opened, Tom blinked against the darkness. The smell of human waste combined with that of unwashed bodies, made him want to retch. To his right, he noticed a pail filled with the waste of these men.

"When does this get emptied?" he demanded.

"At supper," Talons growled.

"It should be done more often. It's no wonder one of these men is sick. The smell is enough to turn your stomach, to say nothing of the cold."

Talons made no comment.

"Who's in charge here?" Tom finally asked.

"Reckon thets me."

Tom assessed the tall thin man who approached him. "Who are you?"

"I'm Sergeant Nicodemus Langtree, but the boys here call me Backwoods. Captain Wallace got hisself shot. He died the day after we was captured."

He pointed to the rag clad man lying on the pallet then continued. "Joe here, he's got numonie. From what I can see, he ain't got a snowball's chance in hell. I know a death rattle when I hear one and he's got it."

Tom brushed past the man and knelt beside the inert form on the mattress. Alex had described him as a boy and now Tom understood why. While the others stared at him with haunted eyes from behind full beards, this boy had only a few scraggly whiskers.

"What is this young man's name?"

"Joe Kemmerman," one of the other men said. "He's my..."

The man's words were cut short as Talons shoved the butt of his rifle into the man's stomach then lifted it. Tom could hear the young man groan in pain as he sunk to his knees doubled over.

"The Doc ain't talkin' to you, Reb. Someone should teach you to respect your betters."

Tom turned his attention from the sick man to the injured one.

"Joe and Paul is brothers," Backwoods advised him.

Tom heard what Backwoods said and merely nodded, as he did a quick examination of the man called Paul. His fingers barely touched the man's stomach before Tom noticed pain radiating from his eyes.

He listened as Paul gasped for breath. "I'll be all right, Doc. Joe needs you more."

"I'll take care of your brother. I'm taking him to a hospital. He will be well cared for there. As soon as I can, I'll be back."

Turning to Talons, he said, "Help me get the boy out to my carriage."

"Why, Doc?" Talons questioned. "Let him die. He's nothin' more than Reb scum."

Tom wanted to hit the man. For the second time, he'd been tempted to lower himself to be an equal with Talons. "I said, take him out to my carriage. I didn't ask for your opinion and I'll thank you not to give it so freely."

"We'll help you, Doc," Backwoods offered.

"You animals stand back," Talons ordered. "I'll take the boy out to the carriage."

Tom followed Talons out of the enclosure. He felt as though someone had punched him in the stomach when he heard the door close, and the lock click into place behind him.

Once Joe had been placed in the carriage, Tom doubled the buffalo robe and tucked it around the unconscious young man.

The cold bit at Tom's fingers, as he slapped the reins against the back of his horse. Once headed away from the farm, he allowed his mind to focus on the hospital where he would take Joe.

How would the Larson family accept the young Confederate soldier who rode beside him? With three sons fighting for the Union and a fourth killed only months earlier, could they find it in their hearts to care for Joe?

He couldn't think about that now. If he'd left Joe in the prison, the boy would be dead by nightfall. There was no use in questioning his actions. As a doctor, he needed to do everything in his power to save Joe's life.

~ * ~

Becky Larson gathered the eggs from the hen house. This had been her first job on the farm. She remembered the day her mother allowed her to do it, while she watched to be certain Becky did it right.

How simple things had been then. The word WAR had not yet entered their vocabulary. Becky's brothers did the barn chores, help plant and harvest the crops, and broke the horses to saddle so they could be sold. Why had everything changed?

When the war pitting North against South first broke out, her three oldest brothers immediately enlisted. Ralph was assigned to a medic unit, while Herman and Edmund were given positions in the cavalry.

After a year of complaining of being left behind, Becky's youngest brother, Teddy, lied about his age and joined the infantry.

The thought of Teddy caused tears to well up in her eyes. Letters from all of the boys were slow in coming, especially from Teddy. His last letter had been delivered on Christmas Eve, two weeks after they'd learned of his death,

If it hadn't been for the recovery hospital Dr. Morgan insisted they open in the rambling farmhouse, she knew Teddy's death would have destroyed her mother.

Thoughts of the hospital brought to mind the faces of numerous men who had occupied the upstairs bedrooms over the past two years. Each came with different problems. Each seemed to thrive under her mother's expert care.

If the hospital gave her mother a reason for living, it had the opposite effect on Becky. In addition to helping her father with the barn chores and the farm work, she assisted her mother with the hospital. Every day there were beds to make and sheets to wash. She also helped with the cooking and cleaning, and often wrote letters for the men who were unable to do so for themselves.

Becky closed her eyes and saw herself as a young girl, begging her mother to allow her to help with the housework. How could she have been so foolish as to beg to help? Why hadn't she been content to be a carefree child, loved and protected by her parents, as well as her brothers? What she wouldn't give to turn back time, to once again become the innocent little girl she'd been.

She reached her hand under the last hen in the coop, only to have the bird peck at her in anger. The pain of the sharp beak piercing her skin brought her back to the reality of the moment.

"You think I'm stealing your babies, don't you?" she asked aloud. "I suppose I am, but we need your eggs to feed all of our patients. Someday, when this war is over, you'll be allowed the luxury of raising a family. If that someday ever comes, I'm afraid none of us will ever be the same."

With the last of the eggs gathered, Becky opened the door to the hen house and stepped out of the enclosure. A gust of cold wind took her breath away. Ahead of her, the wind caused snow devils to swirl about the yard like smaller versions of summer twisters.

I hope this cold doesn't stop the hens from laying, she thought. *We certainly couldn't do without all these eggs, considering the number of patients we have upstairs.*

The jingle of horses' harnesses caused her to turn. She smiled when she saw Tom Morgan's carriage pull into the dooryard.

"You're late this morning," she said, when he got out of the carriage.

"I had a stop to make. Is your Pa in the house? I've brought another patient for you."

"You can't be bringing another patient? You know we're full up. There isn't any more room."

"Sorry, Becky, but somehow, your folks will have to find room for this one. Now, will you go in and get your pa? I need help getting this boy into the house."

Becky glanced toward the carriage. With the cold, the isinglass window had frosted over so she couldn't see inside. Where would he have gotten another patient at this time of the morning? The riverboat didn't dock until closer to noon, and with the weather, it might not dock at all.

The warmth of her mother's kitchen embraced Becky, as soon as she opened the door.

"Come over by the stove," her mother said. "You look like you're chilled to the bone."

"I am. Tom is outside. He wants Papa to come out and help him with another patient."

"Another patient?" her father echoed, as she had moments earlier.

"I told him we didn't have the room, but he was insistent."

Her father grumbled as he pulled on his heavy jacket. "We should have never agreed to this. Tom is working you into the ground, Emma."

"Never mind, John. Just go out and help him bring in this patient. Becky and I will make up a bed in the summer kitchen. There's certainly no more room upstairs. It's the only place left."

Becky followed her mother into the room that in winter doubled as a storeroom. A day bed from the upstairs hall had been placed there when the last batch of patients came.

From the pile of sheets and blankets on the top shelf, Becky selected bedding to fit the single mattress and deftly made up the bed.

In the summer months, the windows brought in cool southerly breezes. Now they were shuttered against the cold and snow. Even though the cold blasts from outside could not penetrate the shutters, the room felt chilled.

Once she finished making up the bed, Becky turned to see her mother building a fire in the cook stove.

"This should warm it up in here," Emma said, once the kindling caught fire.

"I certainly hope so," Tom said, as he and Becky's father entered the room.

Between the two of them, they carried a man with long brown hair, wrapped in the buffalo robe Becky knew Tom used in his carriage.

Once they placed their burden on the day bed, Tom unwrapped the robe, causing Becky to gasp.

"A Reb!" John shouted. "How in the name of God did you think you could bring a Reb into this house and expect us to care for him? Take him out of here and do it now!"

Becky watched in horror as her father's face turned red with anger. Never before had she ever heard him utter an angry word, to say nothing of taking the name of the Lord in vain.

"Calm down, John," Becky's mother said, as she placed her hand on her husband's arm. "I'm certain Tom gave this matter a lot of thought. This boy can't be much older than our Becky. How can we turn him away?"

"How can we keep him here? He could have been the one who killed Teddy. Can you honestly say you want him in this house?"

"I can understand your concern," Tom said. "At least hear me out before you make your decision."

Becky listened as Tom explained about the prisoners being held at the Marrow Place. She could hardly believe anyone in their right mind would keep prisoners in a corncrib throughout the winter.

"His name is Joe Kemmerman. I'm certain he has pneumonia. If I take him back to the Marrow Place, he'll be dead by the end of the day."

"We can't send him back there, John," Emma agreed. "What if it were one of our boys in a Confederate prison camp who got sick? What if a southern family turned him away? Could you live with yourself, knowing you'd turned away a dying boy?"

"Boy?" John shouted. "He was man enough to go to war, man enough to pick up a gun and fight boys like ours."

"So was Teddy," Emma reminded him. "He was only sixteen. Too young for such things, but he went anyway. Now he's dead. I won't allow this child to die as well. If you want no part in his care, so be it. Becky and I can see to his needs, as well as those of the others."

"This one will be the end of you. You're already doing too much. I won't allow it."

"Then I'll care for him, Papa," Becky said, coming forward to voice her opinion for the first time.

"I know when I'm outnumbered. He can stay, but the door will be bolted, from the kitchen side. I'll not have any murdering Reb killing us in our sleep."

Becky watched as her father stormed from the room. She understood his concern, even worried about caring for someone she considered the enemy, but she knew it must be done. Like her mother, she could not allow Joe Kemmerman to die when proper care was available.

"Bring some water in from the kitchen to heat on this stove then get me a clean nightshirt," Emma ordered.

Becky cast one last glance at the rag clad young man who lay on the day bed. Even wracked with fever and congestion, he appeared to be handsome. Her heart ached, as she realized her mother was right. He couldn't be much older than she was.

In the kitchen, she found her father sitting at the table, a cup of coffee in one hand and a freshly baked cinnamon roll in the other.

"What are you doing, Becky?" he asked.

"Mama wants me to bring in some water so she can heat it up to bathe Joe."

"I don't want you caring for the boy without his clothes on. I'll take the kettle of water from the stove. It's already warm. You go and get a nightshirt."

Becky was not surprised by her father's change of heart. No matter how he felt about the uniform, she knew he would not let the man in the summer kitchen die.

Leaving the room, she went to the downstairs closet and took a clean nightshirt from the shelf. By the time she returned, her father no longer sat at the table.

From the summer kitchen, she heard the hushed voices of her parents and Tom.

"How bad is he?" she heard her father ask.

"It doesn't look good. Those people out there consider these men little more than animals. This boy should have received treatment long before this. If that young guard, Alex, hadn't come into town this morning, Joe could have been dead by now."

"How can they call that a prison? In this weather, who in their right mind would keep men in a corncrib?"

A corncrib! Her father's words echoed in Becky's mind. A vision of their own corncrib, the one that sat beside the barn materialized before her eyes. It wasn't a tightly built structure. The boards were placed two inches apart. Her father had explained how the building was designed so the corn could breathe. She certainly understood what he meant, especially since one of their neighbors lost his barn when fresh hay burst into flames.

"Something has to be done," Tom declared, dissolving Becky's vision of the makeshift prison.

"Why do we have to be the ones to do it? You know we have our hands full here."

"I know you do, John. The problem is, I don't have time to contact the other families in the area."

"I suppose you don't. I guess I can make time. I'll go back there with you and assess what needs to be done then go to the neighbors and see what we can do.

Becky almost collided with her father as he hurried out of the summer kitchen.

17

"Where do you think you're going, young lady?" he demanded, once he regained his composure.

"I'm taking a nightshirt to Mama."

"I'll take it to her. You go to your room and change out of your barn clothes. I'll not have you going in that room and seeing a half naked boy."

Becky knew better than to argue with her father. It would have made sense to say she'd helped with every aspect of the care for the men upstairs. The only difference between Joe and the others was the color of his uniform.

Before going to her room, she set a kettle of water on the stove to heat. She would take this opportunity to clean up. Usually, there wasn't time to heat water for washing.

While she waited, she poured herself a cup of coffee and put a cinnamon roll on a plate. She savored the sweetness of the roll that was in direct contrast to the strong coffee laced with cream.

"I'm sorry I snapped at you earlier," her father said.

He had entered the room so silently the sound of his voice startled her. "It's all right, Papa. I understand how you must feel about having a Reb in the house, considering..."

"Like your mother says," John interrupted, "he's just a boy, even younger than your brothers. It's our Christian duty to care for him. I want you to remember, he's a Confederate soldier, not a Reb."

"But Papa, the patients call them Rebs, so did you."

"I know, but it isn't right. I'm sure the other patients would be upset if you called them Yankees, when they consider themselves Union soldiers. That's one of the problems with this war. Everyone uses labels that don't fit. Just because someone comes from a different part of the country doesn't mean they're any less human."

"Yes, Papa."

"Now go to your room and get changed. Your mother needs your help."

Becky nodded. She'd finished the roll and took her coffee, along with the warm water, to her room.

Once behind the closed door, she took off the shirt and pants she'd taken from Teddy's closet. They were much more practical for doing barn chores than her skirts and blouses.

As she rinsed her body with the warm water, she allowed her mind to wander to Joe Kemmerman. She'd seen him only for a moment, and yet she could not forget what she saw.

Throughout her life, she'd seen her brothers and father come in from the fields, their bodies crusted with dust. Never before had she seen someone she considered dirty. Dirt seemed to be a permanent part of Joe's skin. It made her wonder just how long it had been since their newest patient enjoyed the luxury of soap and water.

Two

"We have to set up a schedule," Tom said, as Becky entered the kitchen. Until Joe regains consciousness, I don't want him left alone. I realize it's an imposition..."

"You're damn right it's an imposition," John declared, his earlier concern seeming to disappear. "We're already over loaded here."

"I can understand Tom's concern," Emma added. "I can't allow that poor boy to wake up alone and frightened."

"Whatever it is, I want to be involved," Becky said, joining their conversation.

The three adults turned at the sound of her voice. "I don't know, Bek," her father said, getting to his feet. "This man could be dangerous."

"The men upstairs aren't? Do you have any idea how many of them have tried to take liberties with me? If I can handle them, what makes you think I won't be able to protect myself against someone as weak as Joe?"

The surprised expressions on the faces of Dr. Morgan and her father told her they had no idea what went on in the upstairs bedrooms.

"Becky's right," Emma explained. "She's become quite adept at avoiding the advances of the patients. She's a lovely girl and they're all young men who've been away from home far too long. She'll take good care of Joe."

"Then it's settled," Tom said. "We'll take two hour shifts, with the exception of nights. I plan to stay here until he's out of the woods, so I can sleep in the summer kitchen."

"That's not right," John said. "You can't function on lost sleep any more than we can. I'll spell you throughout the night, and Emma and Becky will have to handle the days. Just remember, once he comes around, everything is different."

Becky sighed with relief. She knew she'd promised her mother never to mention the way the patients treated her, but it just slipped out. She prayed her father wouldn't insist they shut down the hospital. It was evident that caring for these men had eased her mother's pain over her own sons being away. It even helped her overcome the grief of losing Teddy.

"The two of you will have to care for Joe right now," Emma declared, breaking into Becky's thoughts. Becky and I need to take this food up to the patients. By the time we get back, maybe you will have the schedule figured out."

Once they left the summer kitchen, Becky picked up the tray of bowls, while her mother carried a kettle of porridge and started upstairs. Behind her, she could hear her father grumbling to Tom about how much trouble the hospital had caused them.

"What was all the commotion about, Miss Becky?" Tad Martin asked, as she set a bowl and spoon on the table next to his bed.

She hesitated, unsure of how she should answer his question.

"Dr. Morgan brought in another patient," Emma replied, coming to Becky's rescue. "Without any more space up here, we had to make room for him in the summer kitchen."

"I've heard a lot of talk about Rebs down there," Tad continued. "Is this new patient a Reb?"

"Yes, Tad, he is," Emma answered.

Becky smiled as her mother explained about the makeshift prison and the forgotten prisoners. She marveled at how easily her mother chose her words so as to not show anger toward either Joe's presence or Tad's probing questions.

"I sure don't like it, Ma'am, and neither do the others," Tad commented, once Emma finished. "It ain't right, treatin' animals the same as fightin' men."

"I won't try to change your mind, Tad. Hate can't be erased overnight. I do want you to remember, this is our home and you are a guest here, just as the young man downstairs is a guest. Nothing about your care will change. I trust we won't speak of this again."

Becky watched as her mother turned from Tad to begin serving the others. Doing the same, she couldn't help the ache in her heart. By allowing Joe to be in the summer kitchen, were they being fair to the Union soldiers who were here first? This was, after all, a Union hospital. Would a Reb, a Confederate, contaminate her home?

Fear, apprehension, even uncertainty pulled her in several directions. They had promised to care for Joe. She knew she would do her best, but would it be enough? Could she make him comfortable? Could she, in all honesty, wish him well, knowing he could have easily met her own brothers in battle?

~ * ~

Tom cringed as he heard John putting the new lock on the door of the summer kitchen.

Beneath Tom's hand, Joe's head burned with fever, while his body involuntarily shook with chills. Tom had never seen anyone so sick survive, and yet he had promised Joe's brother, Paul, he would do his best.

"This one is in your hands, Lord," he whispered. "You've sent this boy here for a reason, but for the life of me, I don't know why."

"Did you say something?" John asked, making Tom realize John's pounding had ceased.

"I was just talking to myself."

John made no further comment, leaving Tom to his own troubled thoughts. While the Larsons were torn between their sons, who were fighting for the Union, and the Confederate patient he'd forced on them, his own emotions were in turmoil over other circumstances.

Coming from Ohio, he had a brother who remained on the family farm, and a sister who had married a young man from Virginia. His brother's sons wore blue and his sister's sons wore gray. It was doubly hard when those who should be the enemy were blood relatives.

"Papa says he's ready to go out to the Marrow Place. He sent me in to relieve you."

Tom turned at the sound of Becky's voice. Over the past few hours he had become painfully aware of exactly how young she was.

Seeing her standing in the doorway made him wish she'd had the luxury of youth, the time to be courted by young men, rather than nursing them.

"Are you ready to go?" John asked, as Tom entered the kitchen.

"Yes, but I thought you were going to some of the other farms in the area."

"Didn't you hear me say I wanted to assess the situation at the Marrow Place first?"

"I must have forgotten." Stepping into the cold, he couldn't help but think of the men in the corncrib. How could they ever hope to keep them warm?

During the drive to the Marrow Place, Tom allowed his mind to wander over the events of the morning.

He wished John had ridden with him in the carriage rather than on his horse. It certainly made more sense than riding in the cold.

Don't you mean it would have given you a chance to persuade him to accept Joe, his inner voice cautioned.

Before he could formulate an answer, the Marrow Place came into view. This time, he studied the corncrib more closely. Through the slats, he could see the silhouettes of the men inside. Closing his eyes, he could picture Paul Kemmerman and the others huddled around the small fire.

"What kind of a man would allow prisoners to be housed in a corncrib?" John asked, as soon as Tom got out of the carriage.

"I don't know, but I intend to find out. Before I go to see Captain Courtney, though, I want to cheek on Joe's brother."

"Did you bring back that prisoner, Doc?"

Both John and Tom looked up at the sound of Micha Talon's voice.

"Joe is being cared for at the hospital. I've come to check on the other prisoners."

"Does the captain know about this?"

"I doubt it. I'm certain he won't object."

"Who's he?" Micha questioned, pointing toward John.

"I'm John Larson. Joe is at my place. I couldn't believe what Tom told me, so I decided to come and see things for myself. I think I've seen enough. I'm going to talk with some of the neighbors. Between us, I'm certain we can come up with something to make this place more comfortable for these men."

John mounted his horse and turned back in the direction, from which they came. For some strange reason, Tom couldn't help the feeling of dread at being alone with Micha that was building inside him.

"You ain't packin' no gun, are you, Doc?" Micha asked.

"Why would you ask such a ridiculous question? My job is to save lives, not jeopardize them. Now, are you going to let me in to see these boys?"

Reluctantly, Micha led the way to the corncrib. Tom followed, listening to the man's mumbled curses.

"Bang on the door when you're done, Doc. I ain't takin' any chances. I'll be lockin' it behind you."

Tom's stomach churned as he heard the door slam behind him and then the lock click into place. How did these men stand it?

"Didn't know iffn you'd be back, Doc," the man who identified himself as Backwoods earlier said, as Tom approached them. "Thet rifle butt stove in Paul's ribs somethin' fierce."

"I'll take a look."

"It's not that bad," the young man who lay on the mattress gasped. "How is my brother?"

"Joe is being well cared for. It's more than I can say for you."

Paul made no comment in response. Instead, he allowed Tom to make his examination.

In the dim light filtering through the slats, Tom could see an ugly bruise across Paul's belly. He knew the slightest touch would generate great pain, but he realized it must be done. There was no other way to determine the extent of Paul's injuries.

Tom's probing fingers hardly touched the bruised area when Paul's scream of pain shattered the silence. "I'm sorry to have to hurt you further, but I have to assess your injury. I'm afraid Backwoods is right. You have at least three broken ribs. I'm going to bind you to help them heal. Guess I don't have to warn you about doing any heavy lifting."

The comment, meant as a joke, met with stony silence from the prisoners who stood in the semi circle around Paul.

Once the bindings were in place, he gave the boy some Laudlonum for the pain he was experiencing. Getting to his feet, Tom assessed the other prisoners.

Backwoods was tall and gangly. It was hard to judge his age. He could have been anywhere from twenty to forty. His questions gave Tom the information he sought. Backwoods hailed from the hills of Kentucky, was thirty-two years old and had left behind a wife and six children.

Billy Bob Hastings and his brother, Jimmy Roy, were from a Virginia plantation, where their parents owned slaves to do the hard work. It was certain the two brothers never endured any hardships to prepare them for the life of prisoners being housed in primitive conditions.

Bret Collier was as out of place as the others. A riverboat gambler, he called New Orleans home. As for wife and children, he admitted to having three of each scattered at various ports along the mighty river. At thirty-eight, he was indeed the oldest of the men.

To Tom's relief, none of them showed signs of pneumonia or any other illness. The biggest problem was malnutrition.

"I'll be back to check on you boys. Make sure Paul eats and when he's up to it gets up and about."

"I'll take care of the boy, Doc," Backwoods replied.

Tom made his way to the door and rapped to signal he was ready to leave. The stench from the slop bucket by the door caused him to gasp. Before the door opened, Tom picked up the pail.

"What do you think you're gonna do with that?" Micha asked.

"I plan on having you dump it. I thought I told you this morning, to have it emptied more often."

"Don't see why I should be takin' orders from you," Micha grumbled. "Since you got the damn thing, you might as well dump it. You're the only one it seems to bother."

Tom bit back the remarks he wanted to make. Instead, he went to the barnyard and dumped the contents of the bucket, using the snow as a cleansing agent. Once it was clean, he handed it back to Micha.

"What do you want me to do with this?"

"Take it back where it belongs. I'm going up to the house to talk to Captain Courtney. When I get back, I expect to see you've done as I asked."

Again Micha spat out a line of obscenities before going toward the corncrib.

Tom watched until Micha opened the door then made his way up to the house. He considered knocking at the door, but thought better of the idea. If Courtney was using the house as his office, the formality was unnecessary.

"Is there something I can do for you?" a young man in a blue uniform asked, when Tom entered the foyer. The man pointed a rifle at Tom, causing him to stop.

"I've come to see Captain Courtney," Tom replied, annoyed at having the man challenge him.

"Is he expecting you?"

"You know he isn't, so let's stop this nonsense. Where will I find him?"

"Are you looking for me, Dr. Morgan?" Captain Courtney's voice boomed, as he stepped from a doorway just to Tom's right.

"You're damned right I'm looking for you. How in the hell do you justify the conditions you're holding these men in?"

"I don't. They should have been shipped east months ago, but I've never received any such orders. If you want someone to blame, maybe you should start with the bureaucrats in

Washington. While you're at it, why don't you ask for more rations?"

Tom stared at the man in disbelief. "I don't see why you should think contacting Washington would be my obligation. As commander of this post, I would think it's your responsibility. In the meantime, John Larson is enlisting the help of some of the neighboring farmers. Hopefully, they can succeed in making these men more comfortable."

"I don't see where the comfort of these men is any concern of yours. They're prisoners of war. Whatever treatment they receive is more than they deserve. If Larson and the other do-gooders want to make some physical changes, I won't stop them, but that's as far as it goes."

"No one deserves to be held in a corncrib with no protection from the elements. It's a wonder they haven't frozen to death. Then there's the business of the slop pail. It should be emptied at least three times a day."

"Look, Dr. Morgan, this camp is my responsibility. I'll thank you not to concern yourself with what goes on here."

Tom knew if he said more, he would regret what he would say in anger. Instead of responding to Captain Courtney's comment, he turned and left the house.

Once he got into the carriage, he glanced over to the bonfire by the barn. To his surprise, he found Micha Talons studying him. From the look in the man's eyes, Tom realized Micha had the look of a man planning a murder.

~ * ~

"I've come to spell you, Mama," Becky said, as she entered the summer kitchen.

"Is it time, already? I was beginning to enjoy having time to sit with my sewing."

Becky watched as her mother got to her feet. "There's broth on the stove. If he comes around, try to get him to take some of it." With that parting comment, she left the room, closing the door and putting the bolt in place.

Becky dwelled on the fact she was locked in the room with a Reb. *Confederate,* she mentally corrected herself.

After stirring the broth, she seated herself in the chair next to the day bed. Her plans to concentrate on her reading were sidetracked by the man who slept beside her.

His long hair was a deep shade of brown, as were his heavy brows. She could only allow her imagination to run wild as to the color of his eyes.

"Maria—Maria, where are you?" Joe called out in his sleep.

Becky's heart ached to hear him call out a woman's name. She couldn't help but wonder what part Maria played in his life. Was she the sweetheart he left behind?

"I'm going, Pa, with or without your blessing," Joe said. He paused, as though listening to a reply Becky couldn't hear. "What can Paul do to protect me? He doesn't want to go. Why are you forcing him?"

Joe became restless, as though the fever that trapped his body and sent him into unconsciousness was consuming his entire being. In an attempt to soothe him, she dipped the washrag in cool water and bathed his face.

At the touch of her fingers on his face, he opened his eyes. A tremor of fear raced through her body. If Joe came to, what would she do?

Fighting the impulse to run from the room in fear of what he might be capable of, she picked up the bowl and ladled in some of her mother's broth.

After helping Joe to a sitting position, she forced the warm liquid into his mouth. By instinct, he swallowed two spoonfuls before his eyes closed and he lapsed back into unconsciousness.

Becky's hand shook as she lowered him back onto the pillows. The realization she had supported his body while he took the nourishment he needed made her feel weak.

She set the bowl on the floor and eased herself back into the chair. "Did I do the right thing?" she whispered. "I gave comfort to the enemy. Dear God, how can I live with this?"

Don't be so hard on yourself, little sister. Teddy's voice sounded in her mind. *I would have given anything to have a beautiful woman offer me comfort when I was dying.*

"Oh, Teddy," she said aloud, as hot tears flowed down her cheeks. She knew she should be frightened by the sound of her brother's voice, but she wasn't. Even though she'd never heard it before, she realized it gave her great comfort. Perhaps, it was only her overactive imagination, but whatever it was she didn't want it to stop.

Just remember, little sister, this young man is very sick. He needs your compassion, even if he is a Reb.

Hearing his voice for the second time, she wondered if she was going mad. She shook her head to rid herself of Teddy's voice. Her brother was dead. She knew she couldn't possibly be hearing his voice.

To take her mind from her imagined conversation with Teddy, she got to her feet and took the bowl back to the stove to put the uneaten broth back into the kettle.

The lock clicked and she looked up to see Dr. Morgan enter the room.

"Are you all right, Becky," he asked. "You're white as a sheet and you're trembling."

Becky choked back a sob at the thought of her brother dying alone in a muddy field. She knew Tom would never understand what she couldn't comprehend herself.

"It's nothing," she replied s she steadied herself against the cook stove. "I was just thinking of Teddy. I wonder if he was all alone or if someone gave him comfort in his final moments."

"I'd like to reassure you, but the letter your parents received said he died on the battlefield. I don't fault you for comparing him to Joe."

Tom turned from her and looked toward the day bed. "Speaking of Joe, has he been awake?"

Becky nodded. "He took a couple of spoonfuls of broth, but then he went back to sleep. I doubt if he was awake long enough to remember even looking at me."

"I'm certain you're right. Your mother needs you in the kitchen. I'll stay with him for a while."

Becky cast one last look at Joe. He was sleeping peacefully. She prayed his dreams were pleasant ones, rather than the nightmares he must have about fighting this war.

As soon as she stepped into the kitchen, she became aware of the conversation her parents were engaged in.

"I tell you, Emma, nothing Tom could have said would have prepared me for what I saw today. Those poor souls staring at me from between the slats was enough to break my heart. From what I saw, none of them had adequate clothing. I could see a small fire, but nothing else to keep them from freezing to death."

"Did you talk to any of the neighbors?"

"Yes. I stopped at several places. The general rule of thought is that we should pile hay and straw around three sides and hold it in place with corn shocks. Luckily we all had good harvests this past year."

"Why not cover all the sides, Papa?" Becky asked, after joining her parents at the table.

"We talked about it, but knew they would require sunlight and fresh air. We also decided to see if we could find some extra clothing for them to wear. I don't think I'll ever forget what I saw out there."

"If those men are about the same size as Joe," Emma began, "Teddy's clothes should fit them."

"But, Mama," Becky protested. "How can you give away Teddy's things?"

"Teddy won't be coming back. I've come to grips with his death and you should do the same."

"Your mother is right, Bek. I think your brother would be the first to want to help."

The folks are right, little sister. I would be the first to offer aid to these men. Just before I was killed, I shot a boy not much older than you. In his eyes I saw the same fear I was feeling.

Why are you talking to me, she silently implored.

I have been granted this privilege in order for you to understand what we've all been through. My duty, before I can be allowed into heaven, is to help you to understand what is happening in this world.

"Is something wrong, Becky?" Her mother's voice silenced Teddy's incessant monologue.

"I'm fine, it's just..." she left the rest of her reply unspoken. Her parents would never understand the strange goings on in her head.

"It's just what?" her father pressed.

"Nothing. I guess I'm overreacting to this whole thing."

"Tell them, little sister. I'm only allowed to speak to you. I want them to know there is no pain here.

But why me?

Because you and I have always been closer to each other than we were to our brothers.

Tears stung Becky's eyes.

"Why are you crying, Honey?" Emma asked.

"I think I'm losing my mind. I've been hearing Teddy's voice in my head. He says it's his duty to try and explain this war before he can get into heaven. He wants you to know there is no pain where he is and he's happy."

Her father shook his head. "This has all been too much for you. Maybe you shouldn't be caring for Joe."

Don't let them keep you away from Joe. He was sent to help you understand as well as to heal.

"Please, Papa, don't forbid me to care for him."

"What about this business of you hearing Teddy's voice?"

Becky looked up at her father. "I don't know. Maybe I'm just tired, but I do know I heard him. It's a comfort to believe he is going to a better place." She knew she should tell her parents everything Teddy revealed to her, but she couldn't.

Please understand, she silently pleaded. *Mama and Papa just wouldn't understand. I've relayed your message. Now leave me alone.*

Three

Joe awakened. He wondered how long he'd been sleeping. The bed supporting his body was soft, the room where he slept warm, and the scent of herbs filled the air.

He remembered dreams of a battle as well as being imprisoned by the Yankees. Thank goodness they were only dreams. Now that he was awake, Maria would be coming into the room to give him some broth and perhaps some juice.

A knock at the door startled him. Why would Maria knock? If she were caring for him, she would enter unannounced.

"I've come to relieve you, Papa." he heard a young woman say. Her voice did not carry the soft Texas drawl of anyone he knew. Instead, it sounded hard, more like that of the Yankee's in his dream.

"Be careful, Bek, Joe's fever broke during the night. It's entirely possible he will awaken soon."

Joe quit listening. The man's voice sounded with the same hard twang as the woman's. Even though he was already awake, he would not allow them to know of his condition. By remaining silent and pretending to sleep, he could learn more about where he was and why he'd been brought there.

"I'll tell your mother to bring in fresh linens as well as a clean nightshirt. I'm certain he has saturated everything."

Joe moved his hand only slightly to feel the garment that he wore. At home his nightshirt was made of linen and had short sleeves. The one he now wore was made of a much heavier material and had sleeves that reached his wrists.

To his horror, he realized he hadn't dreamed the events in his memory. He had lived them. If he was in a strange bed, surrounded by Yankees, what had happened to Paul?

The conversation between the man and woman ceased, as Joe heard the door close and a bolt lock click into place. The sound of the lock snapping shut made his stomach churn. He wanted to protest but held his tongue.

Within minutes the lock was slid open and someone entered the room. The soft rustle of a woman's skirts echoed in his ears as she moved closer to his bed.

"Papa says you could wake up today, Joe. What will you remember of the care you've received here?"

With her standing close to his bed, her voice sounded soft and soothing even if she pronounced the words in her hard and crisp tone. How did she know his name? What else did she know about him?

"Papa says your fever broke in the night, but I have to see for myself."

The feel of her hand on his forehead surprised him. Involuntarily, he opened his eyes. To his surprise, he looked into the face of an exceptionally beautiful young woman. In the light of the lamp, her blond hair gave her the look of an angel, like the one on the wall of Maria's room. Her blue eyes reminded him of the clear blue of the Texas sky in summer.

"You're awake," she said, as shocked by the opening of his eyes as he was by her hand caressing his forehead.

His mouth felt dry. As much as he wanted to speak, he found the words wouldn't come.

"Can you hear me, Joe?"

He nodded, trying to get the words past his lips. "How do you know my name?" Although he knew he spoke the words, he didn't recognize the sound of his voice.

"Dr. Morgan was called out to the Marrow Place and brought you here."

"Where is here?"

"Our farm."

"Did I hear you talking to someone?"

Joe looked up at the sound of another unfamiliar Yankee voice. The man touched the woman's shoulder and she moved away from Joe's side.

"I'm Dr. Morgan," the man said. "Becky and her parents have been caring for you."

"I must have been very sick, for those Yankee guards to send for you. How long have I been here?" With each passing moment, Joe could feel his strength return, his voice sound more normal.

"For a while, I didn't know if you were going to make it. You had pneumonia. I brought you to the Larson farm five days ago."

"Five days! I've been here for five days? What about my brother."

"For now, all you need to know is the men you were being held with are comfortable."

Comfortable, the word Dr. Morgan spoke echoed over and over again in Joe's mind.

"Did you hear me, Joe?" Dr. Morgan asked.

"I'm sorry, I guess my mind was wandering."

"It's no wonder. I don't know how I would react to waking up in a strange bed, not knowing how I got there."

"You said something about my brother being more comfortable. What did you mean?"

Dr. Morgan began to smile. "I'd like to think I had a hand in changing things out there. When I brought you here I told John Larson about the conditions you boys were being held in. He went with me and then met with the other neighbors. They put straw and hay around three sides of the building and secured it with corn shocks and twine. A lot of the families donated warm clothes for your friends."

Joe contemplated Dr. Morgan's words. "Why would Yankee families do that for us?"

"They all have boys fighting in this war. It didn't take much for them to imagine their own sons being held by the enemy in similar conditions. Folks aren't so different, no matter where they come from. They all love their children and can't stand the thought of them being kept in a corncrib, with no protection from the elements."

For Joe, the explanation was plausible, but was it believable? When he regained enough strength to return to be with his brother, would he find the changes Dr. Morgan described?

Before he could ponder his question further, the door to the room opened. Unwilling to show the girl Dr. Morgan called Becky, his weakness he closed his eyes and prayed for sleep.

"Becky tells me our patient is awake," he heard a woman say.

To Joe's surprise, the voice belonged to an older woman. He searched his mind to recall all Dr. Morgan said. He remembered something about Becky and her family. The woman must be the girl's mother.

"He was," Dr. Morgan replied. "I'm afraid the effort has been too much for him."

"It won't be the first time I've changed the nightshirt of a sleeping patient. I will need you to help me, though."

Joe could hardly believe his ears. This strange woman was intent on changing his nightshirt. It was one thing to think she may have been the one to change his clothes when he was unconscious, and quite another for her to perform the same act with him awake. No woman had seen him unclothed since he was a child.

He felt a chill as the covers were taken from his body. Realizing the woman meant to do what she said, he opened his eyes. "I can change my own nightshirt, Ma'am," he managed to say.

"Nonsense, you have nothing I haven't seen before. I've been married for over thirty years, raised four boys and cared for more patients than I can begin to count. Now, just let me do what must be done. You're far too weak to help yourself."

Joe tried to concentrate on thoughts of home, as the woman expertly removed his nightshirt and sponged his body with warm water. The lightness of her touch reminded him of Maria and brought tears of homesickness to his eyes.

"Are you in pain, Joe?" the woman asked.

He shook his head no, unable to say anything for fear of sobbing like a lost child.

Dr. Morgan's strong arms lifted him off the bed, as though he had no weight at all. When at last the bedding was changed, he was laid down again and clean blankets were drawn up around his neck.

"Becky will be in soon with some broth for you," Dr. Morgan said, once the woman left the room. "Try to eat all of it. It will help you regain your strength. Unfortunately, I will have to tell Captain Courtney of your improvement."

Joe nodded. Once he was well enough, he would have to go back to the prison camp. He would miss the comfort of being warm and lying on a soft mattress. Involuntarily, his body shuddered at the thought.

"That woman," he finally mustered the strength to say, "she said something about patients. What did she mean?"

"The Larsons have opened their home as a recovery hospital for Union soldiers."

The statement caused a fear to grow in Joe's mind. "A Yankee hospital? You brought me to a Yankee hospital? Why didn't you let me die?"

"You are in no danger from the other patients. They're far too weak to do you harm. Even if they were able to come downstairs, the door to this room is locked. For as long as you are here, you're safe and protected."

Joe again closed his eyes. Too exhausted to ask more questions, he drifted off to sleep.

~ * ~

Becky changed into her barn clothes. With Joe awake and no longer needing constant supervision, she could, once again, help her father with the chores.

As soon as she stepped out onto the porch, she took a deep breath of the crisp cold air. After five days of being in the overly warm summer kitchen, she relished the freshness of the early morning.

A southerly breeze promised a false spring. Her father called it the January thaw. It was a time she looked forward to each winter. Even though she knew February and March would bring more snow, she relished the few days of reprieve the wind promised.

She began to whistle as she crossed the dooryard. The act brought back a memory of the first time she'd imitated her brothers by whistling. Grandma Larson sat on the porch and scolded her for her actions.

"Rebecca Isabelle, don't you know better than to act like a boy? Just remember whistling girls and cackling hens, always come to no good ends." Her grandmother's words rang in her ears.

"Thank goodness you didn't live long enough to see me now," she said aloud. "If you didn't approve of my whistling, what would you think of me dressing in Teddy's clothes and helping with the chores?"

Her question hung in the morning air. Even though she expected no answer, she was disappointed to hear only the morning sounds of the farm.

"Good morning again, Papa," Becky chirped, as she entered the barn.

"Are you sure you should be out here, Bek? Doesn't your mother need your help?"

"It's too early to take breakfast to the men upstairs and Mama is with Joe. I needed to get out of the house for a while. I can go back in if you don't need my help."

"You know I always enjoy having you out here with me. The milking goes much slower when I have to do it alone."

Becky picked up a full pail of milk and took it to the milk house to put it in one of the waiting cans. When the milking was finished, her father would put the full cans into a tank filled with cold water. Sometime later this morning they would be picked up and taken to the dairy.

She stopped mid-stride and began to laugh. With all of the happenings at the house, she realized she thoroughly enjoyed thinking about more mundane things, if only for a few minutes.

All too soon the chores were done, and Becky reluctantly returned to the house with her father.

"These extra obligations have been too hard on you," John observed. "You should be thinking of young men and marriage."

"I suppose I should, but with everyone away because of the war, I might as well keep on helping you. Don't tell Mama, but I much prefer chores and fieldwork to cooking and sewing.

John put his arm around her shoulders and gave her a long hug. "You're right, Bek, your mother would be none too happy to hear you say such a thing. I'm just sorry you ever had to learn how to do all the things your brothers should be doing."

She enjoyed this moment of understanding with her father. Someday this war would end and her position in life would change. For now, she savored every minute she was allowed to do that which would be forbidden in the future.

"I wondered what happened to you," Emma greeted Becky when she entered the kitchen. "I should have known you'd be out in the barn with your father."

Becky cringed at her mother's words. She should have been more considerate of this woman who was so much more than a mother. "I'm sorry, Mama."

"Don't be sorry, Becky. If I had the opportunity, I think I'd like to run away to the barn and get away from all the sickness and suffering in this house. Unfortunately, the work here never ends. Now go up and get changed. Dr. Morgan and I are taking breakfast up to the patients. After you have something to eat, I want you to take some broth in for Joe. He should be awake by then."

Becky kissed her mother's cheek. "You really do understand, don't you, Mama? I won't be long."

After filling the pitcher from her room with warm water, Becky left the kitchen. As much as she wanted to linger, she hurried to wash up and change into a dress.

There's a young man in the summer kitchen that could use your companionship, little sister.

Teddy's voice, sounding in her mind, no longer upset her. *Aren't you forgetting he's a Reb?*

Aren't you forgetting he's a frightened young man? Oh, and as for Grandma being disappointed in you, you're wrong. She's very proud of what you've been doing.

Oh, Teddy, you always did know just what to say to make me happy. Please tell Grandma how very much I love her.

I don't have to, she already knows.

~ * ~

Joe awoke. This time he had no illusions about where he was. Even though he wasn't at the prison camp he still remained a prisoner, a Confederate soldier, the only Confederate soldier in this Yankee hospital. The bed was comfortable, the room warm, but he only had to listen to the lock clicking into place to remember who his jailers were.

The thought no more than crossed his mind, than he heard the bolt of the lock click. Looking up, he immediately recognized Becky. She appeared even more beautiful now that he was actually awake.

"I brought you some broth," she said. "Mama told me to bring it in and help you eat some."

"Thank you, Ma'am."

"I'd rather you called me Becky. Ma'am makes me sound as old as Mama."

After he'd taken all the broth he could hold, Joe put his hand over Becky's. "No more."

"Are you sure?"

"Positive. Why do you do this? Don't you have better things to do than care for sick men?"

"With the boys away at war, we had the room. Caring for the patients is Mama's way of coping, especially since we got word of Teddy's death."

"Who's this Teddy?" Joe asked, unable to help the twinge of jealousy nibbling at his mind.

To Joe's surprise tears pooled in Becky's eyes. Using the back of her hand, she wiped them away. "Teddy is—was the youngest of my brothers. He was killed in November, but we didn't know about it until he was gone for over two weeks."

Joe remembered hearing about Luke's death. Becky's tears for her brother brought back the memory of his own tears. Luke, older than Joe by seven years, had always been there for him. The thought of never seeing him again made his heart ache now, just as it had the day they received the letter about Luke being killed in action.

"How many brothers do you have?" he managed to ask.

"Three, not counting Teddy. The others are much older. Teddy and I were only a year apart. Ralph is thirty, Herman is twenty-six and Edmund is twenty-two. Do you have brothers?"

Joe lay quietly for a long moment. "My brother, Paul, is twenty-three. He's over at the prison camp. We lost my brother Luke at Vicksburg. He would have been twenty-four this year."

"How old are you?"

He pondered his answer. He knew his physical age and the age the war had made him were two different things. "I'm seventeen. I thought I was old enough to fight. Now I realize my pa was right. War is certainly not a game."

"I know what you mean. I'm seventeen, too. Since the war came and the boys left, I feel like I'm much older."

Joe found himself becoming increasingly tired. He could hardly keep his eyes open.

"I should have realized you're getting tired. I'll be back later, after you've had some rest."

~ * ~

"I should be going out to the Marrow Place," Tom said, as he pushed his chair away from the table.

"You aren't going to tell that terrible Captain about Joe, are you?" Emma questioned.

43

"I'm afraid I have to. He is a prisoner after all. Besides, I want to give his brother, Paul, some encouraging news for a change. Every time I tell him there's been no change, he seems to get more and more depressed. Considering the guards rarely allow me to see the men alone, Captain Courtney would certainly know if I deceived him."

"It still doesn't make it right," John commented. "The boy deserves better than being kept in that hellhole."

"What's changed your mind? When I first brought Joe here, you were dead set against letting him in your house."

"That was then, this is now. I had trouble looking past the uniform. After spending so much time watching him sleep and listening to him gasp for breath, I've seen the boy. Good God, Tom, he's not much older than Becky. What business did he have going to war? Where was his father? What kind of insanity has kept this war going?"

Tom placed his hand reassuringly on John's arm. "From what I can make out, Joe's father was dead set against the boy enlisting. Why else would he have forced Paul to enlist to protect his brother? As for why this war doesn't end, I have no more answers than you do."

"But can't you just not say anything to Captain Courtney for a few days?" Emma pleaded. "Couldn't you find a way to tell Paul privately about Joe?"

"Who are you telling about Joe?" Becky added, once she entered the kitchen.

Tom got to his feet and embraced Becky. He knew she would be the most hurt by what he had to do. "I have to put his brother's mind at ease and I do have to inform Captain Courtney about the change in his condition."

"I can understand your reasons for telling his brother, but why Captain Courtney?"

"Tom has explained it all to us already," John said, taking the burden of further explanation from Tom. "Joe is a prisoner of war. Captain Courtney is responsible for him. Therefore, we cannot withhold information from the man. I realize the conditions out there aren't the best, but being civilians, we can't change them."

Tom ached at the tears flowing down Becky's cheeks. Seeing her reaction, he knew what a mistake he'd made by bringing Joe to this house. The young man from Texas had managed to touch the hearts of each member of the Larson family, but no touch had been so great as the one to Becky.

"I'll walk you out, Tom," John's voice dissolved Tom's thoughts.

Once outside, Tom got into his carriage. With the change in the weather, he ignored the buffalo robe and wished he'd brought the open buggy.

After bidding John good-bye, he snapped the reins and turned his horse toward the west. For the first time, he wished the trip would take longer, wished he could put off the inevitable.

All too soon, the Marrow Place came into view. Instead of going directly to the makeshift prison, he drove up to the house.

This time, the young soldier in the foyer did not challenge him. Without knocking, he walked into the living room that now housed Captain Courtney's office.

"Dr. Morgan," Courtney said, getting to his feet. "I didn't expect to see you. Does your visit mean the prisoner's condition has changed?"

"Can't you call him by name?"

"I don't bother with names."

"You should. If you got to know these men, you'd find they are interesting people."

"I might, but I have my position. I can't afford to make friends of the prisoners. I'm certain you didn't come here to argue about what can't and won't be changed."

"You know I didn't," Tom said, the truth of Courtney's words burning like acid.

"Then why have you come, Doctor?"

"This morning, Joe's fever broke and he regained consciousness. I thought it was best if I advised you of his condition."

"When can you bring him back here, where he belongs?"

"Not until I am convinced he is well enough. I don't want him to suffer a relapse."

Captain Courtney sat for a moment, in silence, as if contemplating Tom's words. "If the prisoner is awake, he must be guarded."

"I doubt a guard will be necessary. Why don't you come back to the Larson's with me and see for yourself? Both John and I have assured you the entrance to the summer kitchen is locked and the windows are shuttered. Come to think of it, where could he go if he did escape? He's miles from Confederate territory, in the middle of winter, wearing nothing more than a borrowed nightshirt."

The man sitting across from Tom began to smile. "You draw an interesting picture, Dr. Morgan, interesting, but highly impractical. I must insist on an around the clock guard."

"You seem to forget you'd be putting an imposition on the Larson family."

"Perhaps you should have thought of that when you took him there in the first place. It's my responsibility..."

"Hang your responsibility," Tom shouted, pounding his fist on the desk to make his point. "If you had been responsible a few months ago, these men would have been shipped east. As far as I can tell, you created your own problem. All I see here is incompetence. I'm more convinced than ever to write a full report and send it to Washington. Even with a war to contend with, I'm certain someone will be interested to know what a hellhole you're running here."

If Courtney hadn't taken Tom's threat seriously the first time he made it, the expression on the man's face said he did now. "You've made your point, Dr. Morgan. I'm certain nothing I do will change your mind about writing to Washington, although it will do you no good. I will accompany you back to the Larson farm, though. I refuse to make any decision until I see the situation for myself."

Tom smiled to himself. He'd won a small victory. If he could somehow persuade the Captain to change his mind about posting a guard, he certainly had won a major battle.

"I have to go and check on the other men who are in your custody. When I'm finished, I'll come back and get you."

~ * ~

Micha Talons saw Dr. Morgan leave the Captain's quarters. Not wishing another confrontation with this do-gooder, he busied himself with the horses.

If he could have shot those men the Doc was catering to and got on with the war, none of this would be happening. He'd enlisted to fight Rebs, not guard them.

If it hadn't been for the fact the Kemmerman kid got himself sick, Micha could have tormented the prisoners enough to get them to try and escape. Then shooting them would have been the only choice open to him.

Now that the Captain was watching him more closely and not allowing him contact with the prisoners, he wouldn't get the chance to carry out his plans. He was certain the captain didn't give a rat's ass how he treated those animals who called themselves men. Damn Morgan for making the order mandatory.

All of his troubles were the fault of Morgan and those damn farmers. Whoever heard of coddling prisoners? Christian charity, brotherly love, it was all hogwash.

Anger overcame reason as Dr. Morgan again came into his line of vision. Picking up the pitchfork that lay at his feet, he walked slowly out of the barn to confront the man who had become more of an enemy than the men he'd been sent here to guard.

~ * ~

Tom crossed the frozen farmyard, heading toward the enclosure housing the Confederate prisoners. He didn't see Micha Talons until the man stood in front of him.

Micha held the pitchfork, ready to strike. His eyes were red with rage. Reason had left him and Tom realized the man had gone mad.

Before he could react, to show fear, he heard a shot and saw the big man fall at his feet, dead. Turning, Tom saw Captain Courtney lower his rifle.

"He meant to kill you, Doc," Courtney said. "It's evident he snapped. I've seen it coming."

Courtney crossed the yard to stand next to Tom. "His treatment of the prisoners came to my attention after you took the boy to the Larson's. I haven't allowed him further contact with them. If there had been a way to have him transferred to another unit, believe me, I would have done it."

Tom made no response to Courtney's comments. Instead, he turned from the morbid scene in front of him and walked to the corncrib.

The guard at the door looked shocked at what had just happened. Without saying a word, he unlocked the door and held it open.

Tom entered the enclosure, pleased with the warmth the straw and hay provided.

"What's goin' on out thar, Doc," Backwoods asked.

"Micha Talons is dead. He went mad and came at me with a pitchfork. Captain Courtney shot him, before he could carry out his murderous plans."

"The Lord does answer prayers," Backwoods commented. "That son of the devil got what he deserved. Maybe this is a sign that God will put an end to this war soon."

"I don't give a damn about Talons, Doc."

Tom looked toward Paul. The young man had propped himself up on one elbow.

"I just want to know about Joe."

"Of course you do," Tom replied, kneeling beside the pallet where Paul lay. "Today I have good news for you. Joe's fever broke in the night and he awakened this morning."

Paul laid back, the look on his face showed relief. Tom wished the rest of what he had to say would be as well received.

"It's only a matter of time until he regains his strength. Unfortunately, when he does, he will have to return here."

Paul made no comment. Tom decided it was just as well, as it gave him time to make his examination. He was pleased with how well Paul's injuries were healing.

"You don't need me anymore," he finally said. "I have other patients, including Joe to care for. Pray for an end to this war."

Without saying more, Tom got to his feet and left the prisoners to their own thoughts. He knew his words had generated a combination of joy and despair. How could he condemn Joe to return to this?

Once again outside, Tom made his way back to the house. There he found Captain Courtney standing next to his carriage. "Are you ready to leave, Captain?"

"I'll come along, directly. I must see to the burial of Corporal Talons."

"As well you should. I have some business to attend to in town. I will meet you at the farm later this afternoon."

Tom got back into his carriage and turned toward town. He could feel the same emotions he'd seen mirrored in the eyes of the prisoners.

All the events of this day made him want to vomit. Because of Courtney's inability to carry out his duty, Micha Talons was dead. The same inability kept the five men in the corncrib in inhumane conditions and the boy at the Larson farm would be condemned to return to this hellhole.

"Dear God," he prayed aloud, "why have you allowed this to happen?"

Four

When Joe again awakened, he hesitated before opening his eyes. Had it all been a dream? Would he be in his own room, with Maria nursing him? As he opened his eyes all illusions disappeared. All of it was true. He was in the same semi-darkened room.

He found himself praying for Becky to return to his side. If he weren't so weak, he would have laughed at the thought. Becky, as well as her parents, were nothing more than his jailers. True, he wasn't at the prison camp, but he wasn't free, either.

Who do you think you are, Joe Kemmerman, he asked himself. *You're no one special to these people. They probably aren't thrilled to have you here, taking up their time and disrupting their routine.*

The thought brought on a vision of Becky. She hadn't seemed annoyed with him, when she spooned the rich broth into his mouth. The way she spoke his name was not angry. Even with her harsh Mid-Western twang, he heard concern.

He wished she would return to the room, wished she would bring him more broth. It wasn't as though he was as hungry for the food as he was for her company. The scent of the soap she used was totally feminine. It had been so long since he'd enjoyed the company of a member of the opposite sex, he'd almost forgotten what it was like to be close to a beautiful woman.

The sound of the bolt to the lock opening sent a shiver of anticipation through his body.

Instead of the soft rustle of a woman's skirts, the sound of men's boots on the floor made his spirits drop. Either Dr. Morgan or Mr. Larson was coming into the room.

"So this is where you're keeping the prisoner," a vaguely familiar voice said.

"Yes, Captain, it is. Would you like to check outside?"

"That won't be necessary. I checked the outer entrance as well as the windows before I came in. It seems to be a secure room. Now, I want to check on the prisoner."

Joe stiffened. The voice was that of the captain from the prison camp. Since he was awake, had the man come to take him back?

The footsteps moved closer to the bed. He immediately recognized Dr. Morgan and Captain Courtney. He could only assume Mr. Larson was the third man in the group.

"You've made your point, Doctor," Captain Courtney said, as though Joe was invisible. "I'll send a man over daily to check on his progress. Should he try to escape, I will hold you and the Larson's responsible."

Joe wanted to scream, but remained silent. Even if he had enough strength to escape, where would he go? He wasn't a criminal, wasn't even a well-trained soldier. He was merely a boy enchanted with, and disenchanted by a war that was not of his making.

~ * ~

John closed and bolted the door to the summer kitchen. While Tom and Captain Courtney had been engaged in conversation, he watched Joe. It was evident the boy was awake. He marveled at Joe's restraint. He must certainly had been annoyed at being talked around. If John had been in Joe's place, he knew he wouldn't have remained silent.

"I don't want your men here on a daily basis," John finally commented.

"May I ask why not?" Captain Courtney questioned.

"I have a wife and daughter to consider here. If you were in my place, would you want your womenfolk subjected to soldiers who haven't seen a woman for far too long?"

"I can understand your concern, but the prisoner is my responsibility."

"I think I have a solution to this dilemma," Tom said. "When I took Joe away from your camp, I promised you I would let you know when he regained consciousness. As you can see, I've kept my end of the bargain. Now I'm asking you to trust me again. I give you my word, when Joe is ready to return to your custody, I will come out and personally let you know."

John could see the prudence in Tom's suggestion, but Captain Courtney remained silent, as though contemplating his response.

"It goes against my better judgment, but you've given me no reason to mistrust you."

John could hear Emma and Becky talking as they came downstairs. It was evident Captain Courtney heard them as well, since he turned his attention to the door where the two of them would appear.

"I don't think I've had the pleasure," Captain Courtney said, obviously taken with Becky.

"Captain Courtney, this is my wife, Emma, and my daughter Rebecca."

"It's a pleasure, Rebecca."

Becky cringed as Captain Courtney took her hand and pressed it to his lips. "I—I prefer to be called Becky," she stammered.

"What a shame, when Rebecca is such a beautiful name. Of course, if you insist on Becky, please call me Delos."

"It's nice to meet you, too. Now, I have work to do." She tried to remove her hand from his, but he tightened his grip. "Please, Captain Courtney, I said I have work to do."

"Delos, my dear, my name is Delos."

~ * ~

Fear gripped Becky as she realized the man who entrapped her was Joe's jailer. It took little imagination to visualize him as a cruel man. His increased pressure on her hand, coupled with the look of lust in his eyes, made her painfully aware of his intentions.

"Captain Courtney," she heard her father say. "My daughter said she has work to do. Now, I'll thank you to take your hands off her."

Delos released her hand, but did not alter his gaze. His green eyes reminded her of a cat on the prowl, looking for a mouse.

Becky quickly turned away from him and filled a bowl with broth for Joe. Even with her back turned, she could feel him staring intently at her.

Trying to ignore the feeling, she placed the bowl on a tray and made her way to the locked door leading to the summer kitchen.

"Do you mean to tell me you allow your daughter to tend to that animal?" Delos stormed.

"We are all treating a very sick young man," Becky declared. "Upstairs there are sixteen more very sick young men who we also treat. There is no difference. They all receive the same care."

Courtney's look of adoration turned to one of scorn. "Can't you see what has happened here, Larson? Your own daughter is giving aid and comfort to the enemy."

"The enemy!" John shouted. "How can you call that boy the enemy? Where is your compassion? Are you forgetting I saw the condition in which you are holding those men? I'll thank you to leave my house. When Joe has regained his strength, you will be advised."

Becky opened the door and stepped into the security of the room where Joe slept. When she closed the door, she leaned against the wood separating her from the bitter words in the kitchen.

"They're arguing about me, aren't they?"

The sound of Joe's voice startled her. She sat the tray down on the sideboard next to the stove and went to the chair beside his bed.

"I didn't know you were awake."

"I have been for a while." His soft Texas drawl made her feel comfortable.

"Captain Courtney is here."

"I know. I was awake when your pa and the doc brought him in to check on me. He wants to take me back there. Can't blame him none. It's where I belong."

Joe's words shocked her. "Don't ever say such a thing. No one belongs in conditions like that. You aren't well enough."

He reached out his hand to touch hers. The act caused her to look into his eyes.

"Please, I don't want to talk about it. I know what I am as well as what you are. Until this war is over, neither of our positions will change."

Becky swallowed the lump in her throat, but she couldn't stop the tears burning her eyes. Joe saw her as the enemy, just as Courtney had branded him earlier.

"What do you mean?" she finally managed to ask.

"Isn't it obvious? You're a Yankee and I'm a Confederate. We're at war. Don't you understand?"

"How can I understand when my brothers are fighting the Re—, Confederates?"

Joe's face relaxed and softened into a smile. "You were going to call us Reb's, weren't you?"

Becky nodded shamed by the fact she made the verbal slip. "Papa says you don't like being called a Reb anymore than I appreciate you calling me and my family Yankees. He said you are a Confederate and we are Union."

"Does that mean never the two shall meet? I'm sorry if I offended you, Miss Larson."

"Please, I wish you would call me Becky." She remembered saying almost the same words to Delos Courtney earlier. The difference between then and now being this time she meant the words.

"All right, Miss Becky, anything you say."

"For now, I say you need to eat something. Mama has the broth ready for you. If we keep on talking, it will get cold."

Becky got up from the chair, relieved to have a reason to end the conversation with Joe. She could feel a bond beginning to grow between the two of them and it frightened her. Having cared for many patients since they opened the hospital, she knew what she felt for Joe was different from anything she'd ever experienced in the past.

~ * ~

The door closed and the lock clicked into place. To Joe's surprise, he didn't panic. In fact, he relished the security of solitude.

He could use the time to consider his feelings for Becky. She certainly wasn't anything like the dark skinned girls of

Mexican descent who allowed him to steal kisses on warm summer nights.

This woman's blue eyes and blond hair reminded him of a mixture of summer and winter. In her he could see both the Texas blue skies of summer and the Illinois white of winter snow.

Sleep crept into the corners of his mind and with it promised dreams of Becky. Instead his dreams were filled with Luke.

"Becky's a pretty girl, Joe. Be certain of your feelings."

"I have no feelings. She's a Yankee."

"She's Union. Didn't you hear her say she dislikes being called a Yankee as much as you do the term Reb?"

"Of course I did, but..."

"But nothing, the only Yankees you know are at the prison. They aren't all like Courtney and the others. The Larson's are no different from the people back home. Give them a chance to show you what they're like."

"It sounds like you're pushing me at Becky."

"Not really, I only want you to see her with an open mind."

Joe's body jerked. The movement brought him to full awareness. His bedding was soaked with sweat and the dream remained vivid in his mind.

Why would I dream of Luke now, he questioned himself. *He's dead. What can he possibly know about Becky?*

More than you think.

Joe shook his head. If he hadn't known better, he would have sworn he heard Luke's voice.

"I know I've been sick, but has it affected my mind?" he whispered.

The spirit lives on Joe. I've been sent to guide you, just as Becky's brother, Teddy, has been sent to guide her. This war isn't about people. No war is. A few men in high positions that make all the decisions have destroyed many families.

Joe contemplated the thoughts running through his mind. Could he be hearing Luke's voice? If not, who was invading his mind? He preferred to believe his brother was trying to help him make sense of this situation.

Are you telling me I shouldn't have enlisted? It's nothing I haven't told myself ever since we got captured. My decision has affected both Paul and me. How can I ever make it up to him?

You will, but that isn't important now. It is no accident you have been brought into this home. Learn from these people and cherish the time you are here. You will find what is missing at the Lazy K.

Joe asked many more silent questions, but Luke ceased answering. The things Luke told him must have more meaning than he had gleaned. He would have to ponder Luke's words more completely.

Before he could dwell on them further, he fell into a deep dreamless sleep. This slumber was what he needed. It would leave him not only rested, but also hungry to understand the full meaning of his brother's message.

~ * ~

Tom finished his afternoon check on the patients in the Larson's upstairs bedrooms. With Joe passing the point of crisis, Tom would be going back to town to spend the night in his own home for the first time in several days. He knew it would feel good to sleep in his own bed. He certainly hadn't rested well on the divan in the Larson's parlor.

From the stairs, he became aware of the silence of this portion of the house. At this time of day, Emma would be resting, John would be getting ready for evening chores and Becky would be overseeing the cooking of the evening meal.

He hadn't realized what a hardship the hospital put on the Larson family until he spent the past few days here. The work began at four each morning, when John and Becky went out to milk and Emma started breakfast as well as heating water to wash bedding. He knew the day would not end until well after dark. He certainly couldn't fault Emma for resting when she got the chance.

Tom paused before entering the kitchen. The smell of roasting chicken made his mouth water. He was certainly glad he accepted Emma's invitation to stay for supper.

From his vantage point, just beyond the kitchen door, he silently watched Becky. She sat at the table, a book open in front of her. Tears ran down her cheeks and he knew she was unable to read the words on the page because of them. He wondered if he had the right to intrude on this private moment.

To his surprise, she looked up. He realized she was embarrassed to see him watching her. In haste, she wiped her tears with the back of her hand.

"Is there something I can do to help?" he asked, for lack of anything better to say.

Becky shook her head. "I doubt there is anything anyone can do. No one can make sense of this war. Why is someone as crude as Captain Courtney in charge, and a boy as young as Joe a prisoner?"

"Why do you call Captain Courtney crude?" he inquired, sitting down in the chair opposite Becky.

"He's old enough to be my father and yet he looked at me as though he were my suitor. He frightens me."

"You have good cause to be frightened. A man of his age should not be interested in a young girl. You also mentioned Joe. Does he frighten you as well?"

From the look on Becky's face, Tom knew the last thing Joe did was frighten her. If nothing else, he had become a fascination, the proverbial forbidden fruit.

"I—I don't know. He's so much like Teddy it worries me. Teddy wasn't much older than Joe when he ran away to fight and now he's dead. If Joe hadn't been captured, he might be dead, too."

Tom leaned across the table and put his hand over hers. "Be careful, Becky. Joe isn't Teddy."

"I know he isn't. He's a Reb. One of the men my brothers are fighting. I should hate him. He's the enemy."

"But you don't hate him, do you?"

She lowered her eyes to avoid him. "No, I don't. My emotions are in knots. Ever since Mama and Papa opened this hospital, I've been helping to care for the men. I've never had the feelings for them I have for Joe. I don't understand any of it."

"Give it time."

She nodded, fresh tears brimming in her eyes.

He wondered if she already knew what was happening to her. It was evident she'd begun to experience her first love. Why couldn't she have experienced this feeling for one of the men upstairs? Why was Joe the one to awaken her woman's feelings?

"Something certainly smells good," John said, as he entered the kitchen. "Those boys should be thankful they've been sent here. Not all of them get food like this, do they, Tom?"

"I'm certain they don't. The Union is lucky to have people like you who are willing to open their homes."

John continued to carry on the conversation, with Tom making comments when necessary. From the corner of his eye, Tom watched Becky. He wondered if John realized how confused Joe's presence in this house made his daughter.

~ * ~

Becky half listened to the conversation between her father and Tom, while she basted the chickens roasting in the oven. When she was pleased with the look of the birds in the pan, she continued preparing supper. She lifted the heavy kettle of peeled potatoes onto the stove, and then started mixing the dough for baking powder biscuits. Once she was pleased with the consistency of the mixture, she turned it out onto the flowered board.

While she rolled the dough, she allowed her mind to wander. How long ago had she ceased thinking of calling Tom, Dr. Morgan? When had he started treating her as an adult? She couldn't remember when it began, but she did appreciate his concern. Her own parents would never understand her concerns about Delos Courtney and Joe Kemmerman.

~ * ~

The click of the lock made Joe cringe. Since Becky had left earlier, he drifted in and out of sleep. He wondered who would be coming into his room now.

He silently laughed at himself for calling this his room. It belonged to the Larson family and they were using it as his prison.

He listened intently, pretending to be asleep. If Captain Courtney wanted to take him back now, he'd make a convincing case for leaving him here.

The soft rustle of a woman's skirt came as a comforting sound. He wouldn't have to face Captain Courtney, at least not tonight.

Opening his eyes, he saw Becky set down the tray she carried then turn up the wick on the lamp.

"You're awake," she observed. "I've brought you some chicken for supper."

"Now that's a pleasant surprise. I expected more broth."

"Tom, Dr. Morgan, said it was tender enough. You shouldn't have any trouble with it."

The fact she called Dr. Morgan by his given name, made Joe's mind prickle with jealousy. Did her affections revolve around the older man?

He allowed her to help him eat his supper. The chicken, as well as the mashed potatoes and gravy, tasted better than anything he could ever remember eating.

The last time he'd had real meat was before he enlisted. Maria made him a Sunday dinner of chicken. He remembered it tasting good, but not as delicious as this.

"What day is this?" he asked, after he finished eating.

"It's Wednesday. Why do you ask?"

"You brought me chicken. Isn't chicken for Sunday dinner?"

"I don't understand."

"At home, Maria only fixes chicken on Sunday. Through the week, our meals consist of beef."

"Maria?"

Joe wondered if he detected a hint of jealousy in her voice. When he made no comment, she repeated the question.

"You've mentioned her name before, when you were sick. She must be very special to you."

"She is. My ma was always sickly. I guess you could say Maria raised me and my brothers. She told me she came just after Ma and Pa moved to Texas, right after Paul was born, and never left. When Ma died, nothing really changed. Maria took care of the house, did the cooking and continued to raise us."

"She's your housekeeper?"

"I guess so, but she seems like so much more. I hardly remember my ma."

"How old were you when she died?"

"I was ten years old. About all I remember is her sitting on the porch, wrapped in a blanket, or being in bed."

"I'm sorry."

"Don't be. It all happened a long time ago. Kids heal easily. At least, that's what Pa says."

"They heal easily and they grow up too fast," she added.

He smiled at her concern. She couldn't be much older than himself. She'd certainly been forced to grow up because of this war. He couldn't help wondering when this was all over if she would marry Dr. Morgan. If not, did she wait for some lucky young man to return and claim her as his wife?

"Does it ever get warm here?" he asked, anxious to change the subject.

"Of course it does. In another couple of months, we'll be able to get into the fields, at least to do the plowing. By the end of April, we'll have the oats planted and be ready to start the corn. Of course, somewhere in between, we'll have to get the horses broken."

"Horses?" Her statement baffled him. Why would someone in Illinois be worried about breaking horses? If she were talking about the Lazy K, he would understand, but not Illinois.

"Yes, horses, Papa raises them. He has a contract with the army..." she stopped, as though she'd said something wrong.

"I don't blame you for supplying a need. They have to get horses from someone. It might as well be your pa. I guess I never thought people 'raised' horses."

"How else would you get them?"

He couldn't help but smile. Their lives were so different. "We raid the wild herd. We don't have time to breed horses, especially when they run wild so close to the ranch."

"I can't imagine such a thing. If they ran wild here, they would destroy the crops. Don't you have trouble with such things?"

"We don't plant crops. There's no need. We run the cattle on the open range. The only things we plant are Maria's garden and Ma's flowers."

Becky giggled and he wondered what she found so funny.

"I'm sorry," she finally said, when she regained her composure. "I shouldn't laugh, but you're right, a garden is definitely not the same as planting crops. Our farm covers two hundred acres. Of that we plant fifty acres of corn, fifty acres of oats, fifty acres of wheat and fifty acres of hay."

"It sounds like a lot of work."

"It is. How many acres does your ranch cover?"

She seemed so proud of their two hundred acres he debated telling her the size of the Lazy K.

"There I go again," she remarked, "being too nosy. Mama always says I shouldn't ask questions about things that are none of my business."

"You aren't being nosy. I was only trying to decide to tell you about the Lazy K. It covers two thousand acres, but the land is different. The only thing most of it is good for is grazing cattle."

The expression on her face said volumes. The size of the Lazy K surprised her.

"Two thousand acres?" she questioned. "That's ten times the size of our farm."

He simply nodded his head, suddenly too exhausted to carry on the conversation.

~ * ~

Becky wondered if the exhaustion she saw in Joe's eyes came from his physical condition or the memory of home she evoked with her probing questions. Without saying more, she finished helping him eat his supper. When he'd eaten enough to satisfy her, she watched him drift off to sleep.

For several minutes, she sat, watching him. As she did, a vision of a healthier Joe entered her mind. With it came a picture of him riding across a vast prairie in search of wild horses.

She shook her head to rid herself of such foolishness and got up from the chair. After turning down the lamp, she went over to the door and rapped on it lightly.

Footsteps sounded on the other side of the door, followed by the sound of the lock being opened. The brightness of the kitchen stood in direct contract to the semi-darkened area of the room where Joe slept.

"Is he still awake?" Tom asked.

Becky shook her head.

Her mother came over and took the tray from her hands. "He did eat a good meal."

"Are you all right, Becky?" Tom inquired.

"I'm just tired. If you'll excuse me, I'm going to bed."

No one questioned her decision to retire earlier than usual.

"I'm worried about Becky," she heard her mother say, once she left the room. The words made her stop to listen to the rest of the conversation.

"Have you considered she could be attracted to Joe?" Tom asked.

"Of course not," her father said. "This is Becky we're talking about. She's far too young for such nonsense."

Tears spring to her eyes. *Oh, Papa,* she silently shouted. *How can you say such a thing? Under normal circumstance, I would have been married by now. Mama was only fifteen when you married her. Why can't you see me as an adult, the way Tom does?*

Five

The howling of the wind caused Joe to shudder. Being fully aware of his surroundings for two days now, he knew he had no reason to fear the wind. The warmth of the room attested to that. His concern centered on Paul and the others.

Even as sick as he'd been, he remembered the bite of the cold. It penetrated so deeply, it chilled the very core of his being.

What kind of people lived in these conditions? How could a beautiful woman, like Becky, endure such a place?

The mere thought of Becky brought a vision of her to his mind. He could never remember seeing anyone with such beautiful blond hair. Although she wore it pinned up, he wondered what it would look like hanging loosely around her shoulders, what it would feel like if he ran his fingers through it.

He studied the vision more closely and focused on her blue eyes and the dimples in her cheeks when she smiled.

To his surprise, when he opened his eyes, Becky stood beside him, her hair down, the way he wanted to see it.

"Did I wake you?"

"No, I was just lying here thinking."

She smiled that smile which so disarmed him. "I was afraid I'd disturbed you."

Of course she disturbed him, but not from sleep. He'd been so engrossed in his vision of her he hadn't heard the real thing enter his room.

"How do you stand it?" he finally asked.

"Stand what?"

"The wind, the cold."

"On days like today, I wonder myself. It wasn't too many days ago when I thought we'd be having a false spring, the air felt much warmer. Now today we have this."

"What makes today so different?"

"Of course, you wouldn't know. We're having a blizzard."

The word blizzard puzzled him. Was she suddenly speaking a foreign language? "What is a blizzard?"

She began to smile, the laugh. "I can't believe you don't know what a blizzard is. It's snowing so hard we can't even see the barn and the wind is blowing so fiercely the whole house seems cold. Papa says we could get about a foot and a half of snow before it's all over."

The description of the storm seemed almost too ridiculous to be true. Since he'd been sent north he'd seen snowstorms, but nothing like what Becky just described.

"Don't you believe me?" she inquired, apparently noting the puzzled expression on his face.

"It's hard. Where I come from, we don't have snow and it's never cold."

"Never?"

Now it was his turn to laugh. "What I call cold at home and what you call cold here are two different things. Until I was sent North, I'd never seen snow, never even shivered. We ride the range every day, all year round."

Becky pulled the chair close to his bed and took his hand in hers. To his surprise, her hand felt cold against his skin.

"Tell me about Texas," she prompted. "Today, I want to hear about someplace warm."

Joe heard a hint of sadness in her voice. For a moment, he wondered if he should question her. It took only a moment of consideration for him to throw caution to the wind and probe into her pensive mood.

"Is something wrong?"

She shook her head.

"Why is it I have trouble believing you?"

Tears began to run down her cheeks. "I should be used to this. It's happened before, but..." A sob choked off her words.

He wished he had the strength to take her in his arms and comfort her, but he didn't. "But what?" he asked instead.

"I'll never be able to accept death. One of the patients upstairs died last night. He wasn't even sick."

Her statement bewildered him. "If he wasn't sick, why was he here? Didn't you tell me this is a hospital?"

"It's a recovery hospital. Sergeant Williams was due to go home to Wisconsin soon. Tom said it was his heart. He wasn't even twenty-five years old. It isn't fair. Why does God allow things like this to happen?"

"You're asking the wrong person about God. I'm more like Pa, I don't see God the way other folks do."

"But you have to believe in God!" she exclaimed, wiping her eyes with her apron.

"I didn't say I don't believe. It's just I don't do it the way other people do. God is all around us in nature. Men brought about this war, like all of the other wars since the beginning of time. God had nothing to do with it."

He watched her as his words sunk in. He wished he'd never brought up the subject of religion, especially since he saw her stiffen.

"Don't you go to church?"

"Paul goes with Maria, sometimes. Once or twice a year, Pa takes us to the other church in town."

"The other church? We only have one church. Is your town large enough for two?"

Joe began to smile. "Maria is Mexican. There are a lot of Mexicans in the area. They all go to the Catholic Church, white people, like Pa go to the Anglo church. At least the minister speaks English when he damns you to hell for cussing and drinking. The priest at Maria's church conducts the service in Latin. You'd think he'd speak Spanish so the people could understand him."

Talking about home caused a lump to form in Joe's throat. What if Dr. Morgan hadn't been summoned? Would he have died? If so, what would have become of Paul? Joe didn't have to be a genius to realize his father would blame Paul. There was no love lost between the two of them.

He remembered his father and their foreman, Don Parsons, talking. It had been shortly after they'd received word of Luke's death. Don had asked about his father's plans for the ranch. To Joe's horror, he heard his father say the ranch would go to Joe and Lydia's son would work for him. He hadn't even mentioned Paul by name. As Joe thought on it, his father never called Paul anything but Lydia's son.

Why did his father hate Paul? What had his brother ever done to deserve such scorn?

~ * ~

Becky watched as Joe's smile faded. From the far away look on his face, she knew the conversation had pained him. She waited to speak until he again turned toward her and made eye contact.

"You must be tired," she said, pushing back her chair.

His hand on her arm stopped her. "Don't go. I like your company."

"But you became so sad. It must have been my fault."

"It's no one's fault. I'm just not comfortable talking about home. It's so far away. Sometimes I wonder if I'll ever be allowed to go back there."

Becky experienced the ache of homesickness she knew he was feeling. She'd seen it often among the men in the upstairs bedrooms not to recognize it in Joe.

"I don't know how I'd feel being so far away from home. I'm afraid I'd miss my family terribly."

"It's not Pa I miss," Joe said.

His words surprised her. How could he so calmly confess to not missing his family?

"Don't look so shocked. My family and yours are two different things. Your parents love you as well as your brothers. My memory of my mother is that she was always in bed, sick. As for Pa, there's only one thing he loves and it's not his sons. He only wanted children so he could pass on the Lazy K when the time is right. Otherwise, we're an annoyance to him."

Becky's heart ached at Joe's words. How could a father not love his children?

~ * ~

John sat at the table. The death of Sergeant Philip Williams affected him more than he cared to admit. It was one thing to receive word your son had been killed in action and quite another to learn your son died while being cared for in a hospital.

Acceptance would have been easier if the young man hadn't died so suddenly. There had been no warning. Although his wounds were extensive, a full recovery was expected. How could any of them predict the man's weak heart?

"I finished cleaning up Phil's bed," Emma said, as she entered the kitchen.

John looked up to see her loaded down with bedding. "Were there many personal things?" he inquired, getting up to take the burden from her.

"There were hardly enough to fill a pillowcase." She held up the white linen pillow covering with only a few items inside. "It's sad to think his life was summed up by so few personal things."

"You know these men are only here for a short while. There's no reason for them to have a lot of things."

He placed the soiled linens in the bushel basket next to the stove and turned to the window.

"Thank God he died last night, while Tom was still here. At least he was able to take the body to town with him. If he'd died today, who knows when he could have been readied to be shipped home?"

"There's something else on your mind, isn't there?" Emma asked, coming to stand beside him.

John nodded. "It's that damned Reb in the summer kitchen. Tom thinks he's interested in Becky."

"I know, he spoke to me about it yesterday."

"Why didn't you say something to me before this?"

Because there is nothing to say. Becky's a young woman, she's..."

"She's a child, Emma. My God, that Reb is lusting after our child."

Emma took his hand and guided him toward the table. Once they were both seated, she pressed it to her lips. "Becky ceased being a child the day Teddy went to war. Because he left, she had to start doing the chores, helping in the fields and caring for the patients. She'll be seventeen years old soon. When I was her age, we'd been married for over a year and I was nursing Ralph. It's hard to accept, but she's a woman. If it weren't for this war she'd be married with a baby of her own by now."

John didn't want to accept the truth about his daughter, his baby, but he knew he must. "She may be a woman, but it still doesn't make this business with the Reb right."

"I don't think we have anything to worry about. As soon as he's well, Captain Courtney will be taking him back to the Marrow Place. Eventually, they'll ship him East and when the war is over, he'll go back to Texas. Becky will forget all about him, especially when the young men come back and one of them sweeps her off her feet."

John wished he could agree with his wife. He'd been against bringing this particular patient into his home and now knew why. If someone like Joe Kemmerman hurt Becky, he'd see the bastard paid for his actions.

~ * ~

Becky tossed and turned. For some reason, she'd been unable to sleep. Although she'd been exhausted when first going to bed, she awoke after only an hour of sleep. Since then, she'd remained awake.

About an hour ago, she'd heard the wind die down and knew the storm finally passed. There would be extra work to do, just to get to the barn to do the milking.

Seeing no reason to stay in bed any longer, she got up. The chill of the water in the pitcher on the washstand made her shiver. She could hardly wait until she finished dressing so she could start a fire in the cook stove.

Once in the kitchen, she struck a match and lit the lamp. A noise in the sleeping house caused her to freeze in her steps.

You're being silly, her inner voice scolded. *Everyone is asleep and with the storm, there is no one outside.*

She turned back to her task and filled the stove with kindling to bring the dying fire to life. The job finished, she heard another noise and then a crash from the summer kitchen.

Her heart pounded wildly as she hurried toward the locked door. Had one of the upstairs patients come down to do Joe harm?

Seeing the lock still securely in place, she breathed a bit easier. Wasting no time, she unbolted the door and stepped into the dimly lit room.

To her horror, she saw Joe lying on the floor, his breath coming in ragged gasps. She quickly turned up the lamp then knelt beside him. Her hand on his forehead assured her his fever hadn't returned.

Somehow, she would have to find a way to get him back to bed. Before she left her bedroom, she'd heard the clock in the parlor strike three. It would be at least two hours before her father would be getting up. She needed to get Joe off the drafty floor by herself.

She took a moment to compose her thoughts, to devise a plan. The first thing she did was pull back the covers. She knew getting him back into bed would be easier without having to contend with the sheet and blanket.

Once the bed was the way she wanted it, she again knelt beside Joe. When she turned him onto his back, she noticed a cut on his forehead. Looking around, she saw blood on the corner of the table.

Carefully, she moved him and put her arms under his armpits and around his chest, so she could drag him to the bed. With him being unconscious, he was dead weight. She could only move him a matter of inches, before she needed to rest. After several minutes, she finally felt the frame of the bed against her back.

She allowed herself a moment of rest then hoisted Joe up onto the mattress and covered him. Exhausted from the task, she sat down on the floor and cradled her head in her hands.

What if I hadn't been awake? What if I hadn't heard the noise? Would he have been dead by the time someone found him?

The thought of Joe dying and her never seeing him again caused tears to flow uncontrolled down her cheeks. Only his soft moan forced her to compose herself.

Knowing he was waking up brought to mind the cut on his forehead. It needed attention. She hoisted herself to her feet and then went to the kitchen for a basin of warm water as well as her mother's sewing box. She wasn't certain if the cut would require stitches, but she wanted to be prepared.

"What happened," Joe asked, when she reentered the room.

"I thought you could tell me. What were you doing out of bed?"

He looked at her with a blank expression on his face. After a moment of silence, she saw a change in his eyes as his memory came back.

"I've been trying to take a few steps whenever I'm certain no one would be coming in. I heard a noise in the kitchen. I guess I turned too quickly and lost my balance."

"It serves you right," Becky scolded. She dipped a piece of cloth into the water and began to sponge the blood from his forehead. "You had no business being out of bed."

"Ouch!" Joe yelped as he flinched in pain.

"If you hadn't gotten out of bed, you wouldn't be in pain. When you fell, you gashed open your head. It's going to need stitches."

"Who's going to do it?"

Becky laughed. "I am, of course. I've helped Mama, when the boys would get cut, since I was a little girl. Now hold still while I get you stitched up."

Each time the needle pierced his skin she cringed. The memory of her mother stitching up a gash in her leg last summer, allowed her to relive the pain. Although Joe didn't flinch, she knew it must hurt.

"Finished," she said, triumphantly, when she tied off the last stitch. "Now we have to change your nightshirt. This one is soaked in blood."

A look of disbelief spread across his face. "I'll change my own nightshirt, Miss Becky."

"Nonsense, you weren't even strong enough to get back into bed alone. Just lie still and let me do the work."

"It's not right. An unmarried woman shouldn't see..."

"Shouldn't see what, a naked man? You wouldn't be the first, I assure you. I have four older brothers and I've worked with Mama in the hospital since the first day we opened it. If it makes you uncomfortable, I suggest you close your eyes and let me get you cleaned up."

Becky carefully removed the soiled nightshirt and began to wash the blood from his upper body. Although he was painfully thin, she noticed his well-formed chest. It was evident his muscles had been hard at one time.

In order not to embarrass him further, she kept his lower body covered. She could only guess as to what the blanket hid from her view.

~ * ~

John woke up as the clock struck the half hour. The thought of getting out of his warm bed disturbed him. Rather than digging his way to the barn, he would prefer to stay here and make love to his wife.

"What time is it?" Emma whispered, snuggling closer to him.

"Time to get up; you should try to go back to sleep, though. I'll have Becky help me clear a path to the barn."

"Let me help you. Becky needs her rest."

"So do you. Becky will be able to rest later today. I'll help you with the patients and insist she take a nap. We'll be in for breakfast when we're done."

He kissed Emma's forehead then got out of bed. He pulled on his britches over his long underwear then added heavy socks and a warm flannel shirt. After putting on his work boots, he readjusted the blankets around Emma's shoulders and left the room.

Instead of going directly to Becky's bedroom, he made his way to the kitchen. A cup of coffee would be the best way to fortify himself for the task ahead of him. Emma would be pleasantly surprised to find he'd built up the fire.

He stopped short when he saw the kitchen lamp burring brightly. He shifted his gaze to the door leading to the summer kitchen. His heart stopped momentarily then beat so fast he was afraid it would jump from his chest, as he hurried toward the open door.

"What in the hell are you doing in here in the middle of the night, Bek?" he demanded.

She got up from the chair by Joe's bed, a bloodied nightshirt in her hands.

"Ssh," she whispered, putting her finger to her lips. "He just fell asleep. We can talk in the kitchen."

"Just what is going on?" John questioned, as soon as she closed the door and slipped the bolt in place.

He listened, in disbelief, as she described finding Joe lying on the floor, his head cut open.

"And the nightshirt, Bek? How did he get it off?"

"He didn't," she replied calmly. "I changed it for him."

"That does it. I want him out of here. Did he hurt you?"

"Stop it, Papa. I've changed the nightshirts of almost all the patients. What makes Joe so different?"

"He's a Reb! How do you know it wasn't his bullet that killed your brother?"

"I know he didn't kill Teddy."

"How?"

"Teddy was killed in November in Tennessee. Tom said Joe and the others were captured in Mississippi in October."

John could feel his anger at finding Joe and Becky alone in the middle of the night drain. Becky was right, he had no reason to be angry with the boy in the summer kitchen. Still, he couldn't help the premonition of upheaval nagging at the back of his mind whenever he thought of Joe Kemmerman.

"I'm going out and start shoveling," Becky announced, as she reached for her coat.

"I'll go with you."

"Please don't, Papa. I need some time alone."

John nodded, and watched his daughter go out the door. Before starting the coffee, he went to check on Joe. Why had this boy been brought here? Why did his thoughts turn dark at the mere mention of the boy's name?

~ * ~

Joe lay on the bed, his mind reeling. Becky's hands on his upper body while changing his nightshirt and washing off the blood, brought about feelings he'd forgotten existed.

Just remembering the feeling brought back memories of the girls at the cathouse in his hometown. He'd gone there the first time two years ago. His pa insisted it was time he found out what it was like to be a man.

His mind wandered back to the girls at Margarita's place. They knew exactly what to do to make his body respond. He never thought anyone like Becky could have the same effect on him. His father always told him you married nice girls and visited the whores for pleasure. Could he have been wrong? Was it possible for a nice girl to produce pleasure as well as marriage?

The lock again slid open. Joe took several deep breaths to calm his body as well as his mind. He wondered how he would respond to Becky.

As soon as the door opened, he knew he wouldn't have to worry about being alone with her. The footsteps, as well as the scent belonged to a man.

Mr. Larson made his way to the bed. Joe's calming breaths help him feign sleep. He had no desire to have to engage Mr. Larson in conversation.

"I never wanted you here," the man said, his voice no more than a whisper. "Why should I? My sons are fighting the like of you. My youngest boy is buried somewhere in Tennessee. He caught a Confederate bullet. I don't even know where they laid him. I'll never be able to visit his grave."

Joe could feel tears building behind his closed lids. The anguish in the man's voice was heartbreaking.

"Are you awake?"

John's question took Joe by surprise. He could only nod, unable to say anything.

"You weren't supposed to hear what I said. I thought you were asleep."

"It doesn't matter. It's how you feel, how I'd feel, if someone brought a Yankee into our house. The Yankees killed my brother. I never thought they were human."

John pulled the chair closer to where Joe lay. "What do you think now?"

Joe swallowed the lump in his throat. What did he think? "You're not much different from us. You run this farm, just like my pa runs the Lazy K."

"The Lazy K?" John repeated.

"Our ranch. Pa runs cattle over two thousand acres."

"He runs that much acreage alone?"

"No, he has twenty hands and his foreman, Don Parsons, to do the work. It's hard to do all of it alone when the ranch is so big."

"When the war is over, will you go back there?

Joe couldn't believe this man would ask such a question. "Of course I will. Someday, the Lazy K will belong to me."

"What about your brother? Isn't he older than you?"

Thoughts of Paul flooded Joe's mind. How could he ever explain his father's feelings for Paul to these people? Why his father hated his middle son had always remained a mystery. Pa always told Joe Paul was Lydia's son. As much as Joe loved Paul, he loved the Lazy K more. When Luke died, Joe was certain the ranch would, someday, pass to Paul. His father's announcement had been unexpected and exciting. He'd seen the look on Paul's face at their father's words. It had been a cross between disbelief and defiance.

"Joe," his father had said. "You'll be going to school. I want you to get a good education. Running the Lazy K will require a good head for business."

"What about me?" Paul had asked.

"You'll work for Joe, just as you would have worked for Luke."

"Did you hear me?" John asked.

"Yes I heard you. I guess I was just thinking about Pa and Paul. Being a rancher just isn't in the cards for Paul. He's more like Ma. He'd never be content to stay on the Lazy K. He's hungry for an education. Someday he'll be a lawyer and a good one at that."

John nodded, and Joe wondered why he so easily put voice to the things he and Paul only talked about since their capture.

He watched John's face and was relieved the man didn't push him further. He certainly couldn't envision a future on the Lazy K without Paul.

Damn it Pa, why can't things be different between you and Paul? Why do you hate him so much?

No one has the answer to your question, Luke's voice sounded in Joe's mind. *No one but Pa and maybe Don knows the answer. Life is strange. I've learned that much since my death. Pa has his reasons and they're valid. It's nothing Paul did, nothing I can explain. Someday Pa will tell you everything. Only then will you understand.*

Luke's intrusion into Joe's thoughts no longer frightened him. Instead, the comforting sound of his older brother's voice lulled him into a peaceful sleep.

~ * ~

John watched as Joe slipped from full awareness into a deep slumber. The boy hadn't said anything to arouse his suspicions, but something in his tone told John Joe didn't tell him everything about his family. What had he left out? What could have prompted the hurt he saw in Joe's eyes.

Still contemplating the questions with no answers, he pushed back the chair. He'd spent too much time in this room with the young Reb. He felt guilty about leaving Becky to do the backbreaking work of digging out after the storm.

Once he left the room and locked the door, he grabbed his coat and headed out to where Becky worked. Seeing his daughter doing the work of a man made him sick to his stomach.

This war, he thought, *this damnable war is to blame for all of this. My daughter is trying to take the place of my sons while the young man in the summer kitchen is confused, not only about why he's here, but who he is. Something is terribly wrong on that ranch in Texas. I just wish I knew what it was.*

Six

Becky followed Dr. Morgan as he made his rounds. Because of the storm, his last visit had been three days ago. As usual, she made notes, regarding the treatment these men would require until he could get back out to see them again.

"Good news, Tad," Tom said, as he stopped by the bed of a young man from Pennsylvania. "You've made such good progress, I'll be taking you with me today. Once we get to town, you'll be going home."

Tad's expression was one of joy. He'd lost his leg in a battle six months earlier. During his time at the Larson farm, he'd learned to walk using crutches. Becky and her parents had helped him to adjust to his new lifestyle and now he was leaving.

As usual, when a patient was finally able to go home, Becky felt a sadness tug at her heart. Tom had warned her not to become too close to the patients, but it still happened. These were men, like her own brothers, who were far away from home. They needed someone to talk to, someone to care.

Dr. Morgan went back downstairs while Becky remained behind to help Tad get ready to leave.

"I'm gonna miss you, Miss Becky," Tad said, as she gathered his belongings to put them into the box Dr. Morgan brought out to the farm.

"I'm certain there are a lot of girls back in Pennsylvania who will be excited to see you again."

Tad looked down at the pinned up leg of his pajamas. "What makes you think they'd want half a man?"

"You've lost a leg, but not the man you are on the inside. Believe me, the girls will be falling over themselves to get to be with you."

Tad shook his head. "You don't know them, Miss Becky. They ain't like you. You're different from anyone I've ever known. I think I'm in love with you."

"No, you aren't, Tad. I'm very flattered, really I am, but once you're home, you'll forget all about me. Someday the right girl will come along and you'll find out what love is all about."

She turned to leave, but his hand on her arm stopped her. "It's that Reb downstairs, ain't it? You've changed since he came."

"Maybe it is. Since Joe came, there's more work, but no more time. I'm sorry if any of you feel neglected."

She picked up the box from the bed and left the room. This time, Tad didn't try to stop her. As Becky hurried down the stairs, she thought about what he'd said. Had she changed since Joe came to the house? She knew the answer. Joe dominated her thoughts both when she was awake and asleep. Her grandmother would have called Joe forbidden fruit.

"What happened to Joe's head?" she heard Tom say, when she stepped into the kitchen.

"He was trying to get out of bed and fell," her father explained. "He hit his head on the corner of the table."

"That was a very foolish thing for him to do. Who stitched him up?"

"I did," Becky said, pulling out a chair to seat herself at the table.

"You did a good job. Maybe I should be recommending you for medical school, as well as Ralph, when this war is over."

Tom's mention of Ralph brought memories of her oldest brother to mind. Of her three remaining brothers, he was the one she didn't worry about. Instead of fighting on some unknown battlefield, like Herman and Edmund, he'd spent the war working beside the army doctors in a hospital just outside of Baltimore.

"I don't think Ralph would be very understanding about his baby sister going to medical school with him," John said.

"You don't have to worry about Ralph's feelings, Papa. Whoever heard of a woman doctor? I only stitched up Joe's head the way Mama taught me."

"Well, you certainly did a good job. You'll make some man a good wife. When this war is over your father will have to beat off the young men with a stick."

Becky smiled at Tom's comment. Inside, she wondered if the war would ever end. The longer it went on, the more likely it was they would receive word that another of her brothers was wounded, or maybe even dead.

Nothing will happen to them, little sister, Teddy's voice sounded in her mind. *My life was destined to end early. God knows the moment of your death, the instant you are born. Ralph, Herman, and Edmund are not going to die in this way. When they come home, it will be to lead long and prosperous lives.*

"You look tired, Bek," her father said, silencing Teddy's voice. "Why don't you go to your room and take a nap. I'll help your mother."

Becky nodded and pushed her chair away from the table. She wanted to protest, to tell her father this was the time she normally spent with Joe, but she didn't. Tad's words rang in her ears. She wouldn't let Joe's presence in the house interfere with the care she gave to the other patients, the Union soldiers.

~ * ~

It hadn't taken long for Joe to become accustomed to the routine of the Larson household. He knew morning came when he heard Becky and John go out to the barn to do the milking. Mrs. Larson always came into his room to inquire how he spent his night before she started breakfast. He knew she brought him his morning meal before she served the others, because she no more than left his room for a second time when he heard Becky and John return to the house.

Soon it would be time for Becky to come in and take away his dishes. This was the time he waited for all day. Although her voice carried a harsh Yankee accent, it sounded like beautiful music to his ears.

The bolt of the lock slid open and he held his breath in anticipation.

"Good morning, Joe."

He opened his eyes, surprised to see Dr. Morgan enter the room.

"Dr. Morgan? I didn't expect to see you so soon. The Larsons said you wouldn't be coming out for a few days because of the storm."

"It did keep me away for a while, but it was better today. I was in earlier, but you were asleep. Becky tells me you've been out of bed. I thought I told you not to get up."

"Can't you see I don't belong here? My brother and the others are out in that hellhole. That's where I belong, not here, not lying in a soft bed in a warm room. I know it, so does Mr. Larson."

"What do you mean John knows you don't belong here?"

"After I fell, he came into the room. He thought I was sleeping. He said he never wanted me here. I can't disagree with him. I'd feel the same about a Yankee."

"Have you been mistreated here?"

"You know I haven't. That's what makes being here so hard."

"Look Joe, there's no way you are going be able to go back to the Marrow Place until you're much stronger. Until I say you can be up and about, you will be staying in bed. Do I make myself clear?"

"Perfectly," Joe said, his tone one of dejection. "I'll be honest, I won't like it."

"You don't have to like anything, but you do have to do as I say or you'll never be able to go back to your brother."

~ * ~

Tom left the room, still unable to believe what Joe told him. How could John have voiced his opinions to Joe? The boy was sick enough without laying such a burden on him.

John sat alone in the kitchen. "How could you say such a thing to Joe?" Tom asked, unable to suppress his anger.

"What are you talking about?" John's expression denoted his bewilderment.

"How could you tell him you didn't want him here? It's no wonder he's been trying to get up when he needs to rest and regain his strength."

John looked down at the table as if in an attempt to evade Tom's gaze. "I didn't mean for him to hear me. I thought he was sleeping. His being here has changed everything. I found Becky in his room, in the middle of the night. I guess something snapped. The way she was caring for him, I can't put my finger on it, but it made me uneasy."

"Maybe it should. I've noticed the change in Becky since Joe came. He's the first patient you've had who is close to her own age. If things were different, she'd be married by now. What she's feeling is only natural. It doesn't excuse your actions, though."

"Of course, it doesn't. Have you had a chance to talk to either him or his brother about where they're from?"

"I've tried. It seems as though the subject is very painful for Paul. As for Joe, he seems to be anxious to return to Texas and work with his father."

"While we were talking, Joe told me he would inherit his father's ranch. It seems very strange to me, since Paul is the older of the two. I can't imagine a father passing over the older son for the younger one."

"Can't you? Knowing Ralph's desire to be a doctor, would you make him stay here and run this farm?"

"You know I wouldn't. It just that Joe told me his father plans to have Paul working as a hired hand, when he wants to be a lawyer. He sounded so sad when he spoke of it. I could feel a real anger building in that boy, against his father."

Tom could understand John's anger. The small bits and pieces of information he'd gleaned from the two Kemmerman boys helped him understand it. Joe portrayed Mark Kemmerman as a loving father, while Paul refused to talk about the man. It seemed, to Tom, as thought Paul was terrified of the man both he and Joe called Father.

~ * ~

A faceless man motioned for Becky to come to him. Hesitantly, she took a step toward him, and then another. The Becky in the dream began to smile as she recognized Joe and ran to his arms.

"You can't go to him!" she heard her brother, Ralph, say.

She turned to face him. "Why? Why can't I be with Joe?"

"He's a Reb, Bek. Who do you think we've been fighting? Who do you think killed Teddy?"

"Don't listen to him, little sister," Teddy said. "Follow your heart. Do what you feel is right. Joe is a man, just as we are men."

"Stop it! Both of you stop it!" she screamed, jolting herself to full awareness.

She blinked several times to decide where she was. The pale afternoon sun of winter shone through the window barely lighting the room because of the curtains at the window.

A light rap on the door surprised her. "Are you all right, Honey?" her mother asked, as she entered the room.

"I was dreaming. I guess I must have shouted out in my sleep. I woke myself up."

"Was it a terrible nightmare?"

Becky thought about the dream. Was it a nightmare? In the end it was. In the beginning it was what could only be an impossible dream. No matter what she thought she felt for Joe, it didn't mean he felt the same thing for her. Even if he did, her brothers would never accept her feelings for a Reb. If only Joe lived on a neighboring farm, if only this war had never happened.

"Did you hear me, Becky?"

"Oh, yes, Mama. I was just trying to remember my dream but I couldn't." She hoped her mother would believe the lie she told. How could she explain the joy she felt when Joe beckoned to her?

Her mother began to smile. "Somehow I think you do remember your dream. If it was a pleasant one, try not to forget it. If it was, indeed, a nightmare put it behind you. Dreams can't hurt you."

Becky nodded. She wanted to forget she ever had the dream. How could she possibly have feelings for Joe? The entire thought was foolish.

She allowed her mother to hold her and tell her dreams had no meaning.

Once her mother left the room, Becky got up and splashed her face with water from the pitcher.

"Mama's right," she said aloud. "Dreams are meaningless."

Are they? Teddy's voice sounded in her mind. *Sometimes they are small windows into the future. What you are feeling for Joe is normal. You are becoming a beautiful young woman. Don't let the opinions of others keep you from finding happiness.*

Oh, Teddy, if only it was as easy as you make it sound. Papa wants to blame Joe for your death. I can't allow myself to have feelings for him.

Teddy's only response was soft laughter. She remembered that laugh whenever he bested her or had information she wasn't privy to.

Instead of dwelling on what she decided was her overactive imagination, she dried her face and hands then went to the kitchen. She'd spent far too much time pampering herself by taking a nap. There was too much to do to dally any longer.

The kitchen smelled of roasting beef and freshly baked bread. Becky knew exactly what needed to be done. She wasted no time in going to the cellar for potatoes and two jars of the green beans she'd helped her mother put up last summer.

Although she knew the cellar was perfectly safe, she remembered how her brother's taunted her with stories of a monster lurking in the shadows. Something scurried across her feet, causing a scream to escape from her lips. Holding the lantern toward the direction the creature went she saw a field mouse disappear behind a row of shelves.

"Is everything all right, down there?"

Becky looked up to see Tom peering down at her from the trap door in the kitchen floor. "It was just a mouse, nothing to be concerned about. I was startled is all."

She picked up the jars of beans and tucked them under her arms then filled her apron with potatoes.

Tom met her at the top of the stairs. "You should have asked me to help you with this."

"Why? It's nothing I haven't done before. Why is everyone suddenly so concerned about my activities?"

"Maybe it's because I've been trying to convince your parents you work much too hard."

"No harder than Mama or Papa," she replied. Even though she said the words, she knew she didn't mean them. During the day she matched her mother's footsteps, while she did the same at chore time with her father. She did work harder than her parents, but then she was much younger.

~ * ~

With supper ended, Becky changed into her barn clothes. She was just getting ready to go out to help her father when Emma stopped her.

"Would you go get Joe's dishes before you go out to help your papa? I have to pick up the dishes from upstairs."

Becky nodded. She hoped the pounding of her heart wasn't audible to her mother. Her nap kept her from her late morning visit with Joe and she longed to see him.

"I thought you'd forgotten me," Joe said, when she entered the summer kitchen.

"I wouldn't forget you. Papa and Tom insisted I take a nap."

"That's good. I think you must have needed it or they wouldn't have made you do it."

She watched as he scrutinized her attire. "I've never seen a woman wearing britches before."

"I had them on when I stitched up your head," she countered.

"I didn't notice. Why do you have them on now?"

"When I finish here, I have to go out to help with the milking. These are much more comfortable than a dress."

"What else do you do when you wear britches?"

Becky couldn't help but laugh. "Not much in the winter. When spring comes, I'll help Papa in the fields and break the horses to saddle."

Joe became immediately alert. "Do you want me to believe you break horses?"

"Of course, I do. I'm good at it, too. Papa says it's because I'm so small."

"If you were in Texas, you'd never wear britches."

Becky wrinkled her nose. "Never?" she questioned, easing herself into the chair she sat in when Joe was unconscious.

"You sound as though you like dressing like a boy."

Becky thought about her answer. She did enjoy the freedom britches afforded her. "I guess I do. It's much easier to work without a skirt wrapping itself around my ankles."

"How hard do you work?"

Joe's question caught her off guard. In the past they'd had several conversations regarding the farm. Did he not remember them or worse yet, did he think she'd been lying?

"Like I told you, I help with the milking in the winter. Once summer comes, I'm out in the fields with Papa and I break the horses."

"You can't be serious. I know you've said this before, but I find it hard to believe. Your far too delicate to be breaking mustangs."

"What is a mustang?"

The smile that crossed his lips told her he thought her question foolish. "A mustang is a horse from the wild herd.

Once a year we raid it for fresh stock. It's a treat for the men to be able to take a day off to break them."

"I'd hardly call breaking a horse a treat. It's hard work."

"I suppose it would be if one person had to do it alone, but we have twenty men to do the job."

"It makes sense, but I'm afraid we've gotten off the subject. I don't know why you're so shocked by me wearing britches. What did your Mama wear when she went riding?"

Joe's smile turned to a look of horror. "My ma never set a horse a day in her life. Neither does Maria. In Texas, women are ladies. They ride in carriages. They certainly don't try to be like men."

Becky didn't comment further. If it hadn't been for the war, she would have never known the freedom of wearing britches. Her mother would have insisted she wear split riding skirts. Although they were practical, they certainly weren't as comfortable as the britches she now wore.

"You've mentioned Maria before. Who is she?" Becky asked, in an attempt to change the subject.

"Now you're the one who is forgetting. I told you that Maria is our housekeeper. If the truth be know, she was more of a mother to me than my own ma."

"How could you say such a thing?"

"Ma was sickly. She rarely left her room. Maria was the one who took care of us when we got sick or hurt. She made sure we ate our meals, washed or faces, and said our prayers. Ma died when I was ten. I hardly remember her. Of course, it seems to me you're just trying to change the subject. You certainly remember us having this conversation before."

Becky felt tears escape from the corners of her eyes. "Now that you mention it, I guess I do. I have so much on my mind these days I hardly know what I'm doing most of the time. I find the whole thing rather sad. I can't imagine growing up without my mama."

"Becky!" she heard her mother call, from the kitchen. "Do you have Joe's dishes?"

Joe watched Becky get up.

"I have to go. I should have been out helping Papa."

"I shouldn't have kept you so long."

"It's all right. I'll see you tomorrow."

Becky picked up the tray and left the room. Confined to the bed, Joe could only follow her with his eyes.

~ * ~

When the lock clicked into place, he allowed his body to relax. With the relaxation came the indulgence of self-pity he'd experienced so often since he'd been brought here.

Until he saw Becky's tears, he thought little of the circumstances of his home life. Maria's position in his household seemed as normal to him as Emma being in the Larson kitchen did to Becky.

What had he missed by not really knowing his mother? If Lydia Kemmerman's health had not been so fragile, would she have been the one to love him? Would it have been her voice he remembered repeating his prayers?

He closed his eyes and for the first time in longer than he cared to remember, could see her face. His vision showed her, not in bed, as he saw her so often, but standing on the porch of the ranch house which graced the Lazy K.

Her long honey colored hair hung around her shoulders and her blue eyes reminded him of the vast expanse of the Texas sky in summer.

The vision lulled him into a deep sleep. His slumber was soon interrupted by the dream filling his subconscious.

In the dream, he was back on the Lazy K. Instead of the Lazy K he remembered, it was the one he longed for. His mother tended the roses in the garden Maria referred to as Lydia's.

"Why aren't you in bed, Ma?" he asked.

"There is no need, Joseph. In this life, I am no longer in pain."

"What life, Ma?"

"The life that comes when one leaves their physical body."

"Is Luke with you?"

"He visits, but this is my world, not his."

"Where is his world?"

"It's on the open range. He's not interested in roses. You see, when I arrived here, I was given my choice of the world where I wanted to spend eternity. The place that brought me the most peace was my rose garden. Every so often, I have a chance to change my world, but I don't want to. My roses are beautiful. I could never be happy anywhere else. Of course, I do have visitors and I visit with others as well."

"Others, like who?"

"Your grandparents, my sister and brother, and now Luke. I never get lonely and have met some lovely people I never knew in life. There are many travelers who enter my world, while searching for their own. I feel sorry for many of them. The poor souls don't know where they want to spend eternity."

"How did you know when Luke..."

"When he died? It's all right to say the word, Joseph. Death is just an extension of life. My guardian angel came for me when the Angel of Death hovered close to Luke. I was with him when he took his last breath so I could help him make the transition between life and death."

The Joe in the dream could make no comment.

"My guardian angel came again when you were so ill. I pleaded with him to save your life. He took me to the high tribune to plead your case. I told them you were too young to die and they granted my request."

"What about Paul?"

"My poor lost child. When this war is over, your father's heart will soften and Paul will receive all that he deserves. He will be very successful, but his future will never be on the Lazy K."

Joe's body jerked, waking him. He was drenched in sweat. The dream seemed so real. Had he really had a glimpse of what happened once someone died, or did his conversation with Becky prompt his dream of his mother?

Seven

It had been a week since Joe dreamed of his mother. Although most dreams dissolved and could not be recalled after he woke, this one stayed with him. Had he been allowed to see a vision of heaven? He doubted it. He certainly didn't want to believe in God and the afterlife. What he experienced had been a dream and nothing more.

Although Dr. Morgan insisted he stay in bed, Joe found himself getting restless. As he had done before, he waited until the house slept then got out of bed and tested his strength. For the past three nights, he'd done so and was convinced he should be sent back to the Marrow Place.

He heard a noise from the kitchen and hurried to get back into bed. He knew he would have to tell the Larsons what he'd been doing soon, but he certainly didn't want them to find him up and about.

"Good morning," Becky greeted him as she entered the room. "How did you sleep last night?"

Joe thought up any number of believable lies, but decided the truth was what he needed to tell. "I haven't been to sleep."

"Why not? You need your rest."

"I need to get my strength back. It's not going to happen if I don't get back on my feet."

Becky's expression told him she didn't approve. "You know what Tom said."

"How could I forget it? Everyone keeps reminding me of it. I want to show you something."

He fixed his gaze on her eyes as he got out of bed and took the few steps it took to get to her side. The floor felt cold beneath his feet, but it was something he'd become used to. To his surprise, tears ran down Becky's cheeks.

"It's—it's too soon. Don't you realize what you're being out of bed means?"

"Of course I do. I'll have to go back to the prison. Face it, Becky it's where I belong. Paul and the others are there. They haven't left, while I've been warm and well cared for. It hasn't been easy, knowing what they're going through. I belong there."

"No! No one belongs in a place like that. It's not right. I can't stand the thought of..."

Joe took her in his arms. Over the past two weeks, while he lay in bed, he'd thought about what it would feel like to hold Becky in his arms.

"Don't argue with me, Becky. I'm going to tell the Doc to go out there and tell Courtney to come and get me. There's too little time left for us to use it arguing."

Her response was to press her face against his chest. Tears moistened the front of his nightshirt, promoting him to hold her tighter.

"Please, Becky, don't cry. I don't want to remember you in tears. Your smile is what I want to see in my mind."

She lifted her head and forced the smile he'd asked her to give him.

"That's better," he said, before bending slightly to capture her lips with his own.

The softness of her excited him, as he molded her lips to his. He felt her arms entwine themselves around his neck. Tentatively, he ran his tongue over her lips. He was pleasantly surprised, when she opened her lips slightly to allow him entry.

His tongue spared with hers, causing a pleasurable sensation to overtake his body. Instinctively, he pulled back. Certainly Becky had no concept of where this could lead. Under his nightshirt, he could feel the warning signals. If he hadn't pulled away he was afraid he would have done something he might regret later.

"Is something wrong?" she asked, her voice laced with innocence.

Her question prompted him to smile. "Nothing's wrong. In fact, it's too right. If we went much further, I don't think I'd be able to stop."

"Maybe I don't want to stop."

Her comment surprised him. "You say that now, but what could happen wouldn't be right. We both know it. You mean too much to me to tarnish you."

He wondered why he said such a thing. Was he professing his love? Did he know what love was or did he experience lust?

Follow your heart, Joe. This girl is special. Don't lose her.

As much as he wanted to believe the words Luke whispered in his ear, he realized Becky was talking to him.

"What did you say?"

"I said I don't want you to go back to that place. I want you to continue to hold me and kiss me and..."

He put his finger to her lips to silence her. "What you're suggesting is best left for marriage. When this war is over, if it's ever over, I'll come back for you. I promise I will."

"Won't you be going home?"

"Not without you."

Becky's smile faded. "Couldn't you stay here?"

"I don't belong here."

"You must know I don't belong in Texas. Where does that leave us?"

"I'm not certain, but somehow we'll work it out. It's nothing we have to decide now."

~ * ~

Becky sat the three-legged stool next to one of her father's prize Holsteins. Instead of talking to the animal to keep her calm, Becky remained silent. Her mind raced with thoughts of Joe.

How could he so easily walk away from the care they were providing for him? He said he'd come back for her after the war ended, but could she believe him? If he did come back, how could he expect her to return to Texas with him and leave her family behind?

"Are you having a problem, Bek?"

She looked up at the sound of her father's voice. "No, why do you ask?"

"You've been sitting by that cow for the past ten minutes. Isn't she letting down her milk?"

"I'm sorry, it's just—just..."

She stopped unable to say the words, unable to tell him Joe would be going back to the Marrow Place soon.

Tears stung her eyes as she got to her feet and bushed past her father then ran from the barn. The chill of the morning didn't phase her as she hurried across the dooryard. She had no idea where she was going, only that she wanted to put distance between herself and everyone in her life.

"Whoa!" Tom said, when she almost knocked him down. "Where are you going in such a hurry?"

Sobs wracked her body, making verbalization of her thoughts impossible.

"Let's go up to the house, where you can sit down and compose yourself."

Becky shook her head no and tried to wrench free of his grip. "I—I don't want to go in the house. I don't want to be near..."

"Is it Joe? Has something happened? Is he worse?"

She again shook her head. "He's been getting out of bed again. He says he wants to—to go back to that place. He can't, you can't let him. It's too soon."

Tom put his arms around Becky and allowed her to vent her anger, to cry until there were no more tears left.

"Joe's right," he finally commented. "It is time for him to go back. I've been trying to prolong it, but I've been aware of his restlessness. He's ashamed of the care he's been getting here, knowing his brother and the others are suffering. I can understand his reasoning."

"Well, I can't." A new onslaught of tears rolled down her cheeks. She wished she could stop them, but it seemed impossible.

"What's going on?" John demanded.

Becky turned to see her father. She knew leaving in the middle of chores was rash and uncalled for behavior. "It's nothing, Papa."

"Nothing?"

"You go on in the house, Becky," Tom recommended. "I'll help your father with the rest of the milking."

"I—I," she stammered.

"Do as Tom says," her father said, the sound of his voice denoted concern rather than the anger she heard just moments earlier.

Instead of going directly to the house, she made her way to the outhouse. No one would question her need to go to the small building. Her decision came not from physical discomfort, but from her need to be alone with her thoughts.

~ * ~

Tom watched as John seated himself on a three-legged stool and began to milk the black and white cow that stood patiently waiting.

"I can't understand Bek's outburst this morning."

"I can. Joe's been getting out of bed. Becky found him up and about this morning. When she questioned him, he insisted on being taken back to the Marrow Place."

"Thank God. It's about time, if you ask me. The sooner that boy is out of this house, the better."

"I know you're thinking about his effect on Becky, but are you considering the boy? Going back there could kill him."

"Sending him back there is no worse than sending our boys into battle. All he has to worry about is a little cold and the food. My son is dead because of the likes of him. I say good riddance."

"You don't mean it. I remember you telling Becky to look beyond the uniform. Why can't you do the same?"

"I try, Tom, really I do, but when I see the effect he has on Becky, my blood boils. I can't help but think about what the boys would say if she took up with a Reb."

"You may have to put the boys' feelings aside. I'm afraid you'll have to be strong for Becky. Once Joe leaves here, I doubt if she'll ever see him again."

"What are you saying? Do you really think he'll die out there?"

"It's a possibility. It's more likely, once the war is over, he'll go back to Texas and try to forget any of this ever happened. If I'm right, Becky will be the one to suffer."

~ * ~

For the first time since his arrival, Joe put on real clothes. The britches and shirt were almost identical to the ones he'd seen Becky wear. When he questioned where they came from, she told him they'd belonged to her brother, Teddy.

I'm wearing a dead man's clothes, he thought to himself.

Does it matter where they came from? Isn't it enough to know they'll keep you warm?

Before he could formulate an answer to Luke's question, the door opened and Becky entered the room.

"Papa says I should say my good-byes to you now, before Captain Courtney gets here."

"I don't want to say good-bye to you, Becky. When this war is over, I'll come back for you. When I do, I plan to work for your pa until I pay him back for all your family has done for me."

Becky's eyes mirrored surprise at his statement. "There's no need..."

"Of course, there's a need. My pa taught me to pay my debts. What I owe you and your family is more than I can ever hope to repay, but I can certainly try. Besides, if I didn't come back, how could I ever court you?"

"Court me? I thought..."

"I'd like to think what I'm feeling is love, but I can't be sure. Neither can you. We need to get to know each other, but not as patient and nurse."

"Bek, it's time for you to get out of there," John's voice sounded before Becky could say more. "The men from the prison are almost here."

Joe felt the bottom drop out of his stomach. When he first made the decision to leave the Larson household and return to the Marrow Place, he thought only of being reunited with Paul. Now, the thought of going back to the cold and discomfort frightened him.

On an impulse, he took Becky in his arms and kissed her with the urgency of despair. The feel of her lips surrendering to his made him never want to let her go.

"Do as your pa says," he whispered. "It wouldn't be proper for Courtney to find the two of us here. When this war is over, I promise, we'll be together."

Becky's tears hurt more than the thought of returning to the Marrow place. He wiped them away with his thumb, all the while wishing he could keep them from falling.

"I'm sorry," she said, choking back a sob. "I promised myself I wouldn't cry. The end of the war seems so far away. How can I stand to do my everyday chores knowing you aren't here?"

"You'll do them step by step, day by day. Who knows what will happen? Maybe the war will end tomorrow."

Becky nodded.

It nearly broke Joe's heart when she removed her arms from around his neck. "Until the end of the war," she whispered, as she left the room.

For one last time, Joe listened as the lock clicked into place. The sound that so dominated his dreams, now represented security. In less than an hour, the security would disappear.

~ * ~

John and Emma sat at the kitchen table. "This is a terrible day," she commented.

John couldn't help feeling his wife's pain. There were no words to express his emotions regarding today.

"I'll be glad when he's gone," Emma said. She cradled her head in her hands, not trying to stop her tears.

"I know what you mean."

"How could you? I honestly like the boy."

"I never said I didn't like him, but his being here is trying. I like the town drunk, the parson and the man who runs the livery stable, but I can honestly say I don't want them under my roof, filling my daughter's head with thoughts of the future. Becky's an impressionable child. Joe is the first person , her age, to pay serious attention to her. I know she thinks she's in love with him, but today he goes back to the prison and no one knows what tomorrow will bring. I tend to agree with Tom. It's entirely possible we'll see no more of Mr. Joe Kemmerman."

"I'm afraid you're right, dear. I do worry about Becky, though. She so wants to believe he loves her. As for Joe, I'm certain he's so homesick he has mistaken gratitude for love. I think his going back to the prison is for the best, but I worry about it being too soon. He's not strong enough."

The outside door opened and Tom joined them. He had, long ago, ceased knocking, as he often came late at night to check on his patients.

"I came to check Joe one last time before he goes back," Tom explained. "How is he doing this morning?"

"I took him some breakfast and clean clothes earlier." Emma replied. "Becky is in with him now, saying good-bye."

"It's best if she gets out of there. I saw a wagon heading this way when I came into the house."

John got up from the table and stood outside the door to the summer kitchen. "Bek, it's time for you to get out of there. The men are almost here from the prison."

Soft sobs and whispered words, were the only sounds to come from the room where Joe had fought his way back from the brink of death. Almost embarrassed to be standing close enough to hear such things, John returned to the table.

As much as he wanted to relieve the tension in the room, he couldn't find the words. Instead, they sat staring into the mugs of coffee in front of them.

They all turned when Becky came out of the summer kitchen. Once she slid the lock into place, she rushed past them and went into the parlor.

John heard horses and a wagon in the dooryard and went to the window. "The guards are here. Good lord, they've got four men with them. Who do they think they're coming for, General Lee and the entire Confederate Army? He's just one boy, for God's sake."

"We've come for the prisoner," Corporal Higgins, a burly guard said, as he and the three others entered the kitchen.

"You'll have to wait," John advised them. "Dr. Morgan just got here and needs to examine Joe. You're welcome to have some coffee while you wait."

"We'll wait outside, Sir," Sergeant Cook said. "Thank you anyway. The doc's got fifteen minutes then the prisoner is ours."

Tom got up from his chair and made a big production of unlocking the door to the summer kitchen. Once inside, he saw Joe sitting on the day bed, cradling his head in his hands.

"If you're having second thoughts, I'd say you're a bit late."

Joe looked up, his eyes mirroring his indecision. "It's my decision, Doc. You know I'm well enough to be up and about and my breathing is better. My being here is an imposition on the Larsons. I belong with Paul and the others,. I don't deserve the treatment I've gotten here."

"I wish I could make you see what I do. You're a confused young man. You think because you've been nursed through a very serious illness you've been pampered. You need more rest. I've tried my best, but I doubt if I could change your mind."

"No, Doc, you can't. The Larsons have been good to me, too good. When this war is over. I'm coming back here. Even if they ship us East, I'm planning to come back to pay them back for everything they've done for me. I'm going to court Becky, too. I love her. I hope she loves me."

Tom shook his head again. Joe's feelings for Becky were as obvious as those she harbored for him. He could have predicted Joe's desires to return to this farm, although he doubted the promise would be kept. Once Joe returned to Paul and the others, he would change his mind.

A sharp pounding on the door startled Tom. "You've had your time, Doc," Corporal Higgins called. "We ain't got all day. It's time for us to take the prisoner back."

Tom opened the door to allow the men to enter the summer kitchen. His heart sank when one of the four men placed shackles around Joe's wrists and ankles.

"Is that necessary?"

"It's the rules, Doc," Higgins replied. "We have to live by the rules."

"I suppose you do, I just can't understand why it takes four guards to take back one boy who has been sick."

"He's a dangerous man. We can't be too careful when dealing with Rebs. I'm surprised he didn't try to murder the Larson's in their sleep."

When they started to lead Joe away, Tom touched the boy's hand. "I'll be out to check on you and Paul."

~ * ~

Tom's gesture caused Joe to look into the older man's eyes. In them, he saw a sadness that made his stomach churn with uncertainty. If he hadn't insisted on going back, he could have stayed here indefinitely.

Hours earlier, his decision made all the sense in the world. Now he questioned his earlier reasoning.

A quick glance across the kitchen assured him Becky stood to the side of the doorway on the other side of the room. From this distance, he couldn't be certain, but he thought she was crying. More than the comfort of this house, he would miss seeing her on a daily basis. As soon as he made eye contact with her, she took a step sideways and disappeared from his sight.

Instead of searching the dark recesses of the adjoining room, he focused on the people in the kitchen. Mrs. Larson stood by the stove, her face mirroring her concern, while Mr. Larson remained by the door, his expression unreadable.

"I want to thank you for all you've done for me. When this war is over, I'll come back here. I owe you a debt. Somehow I'll find a way to repay you,"

From behind him, Joe heard Corporal Higgins grumble about the unnecessary exchange.

"It's not necessary, Joe," John said, ignoring the complaints of the Yankee soldiers.

"Yes it is. My pa taught me to always pay my debts."

"Enough talk, Reb," Higgins snapped, pushing Joe from behind.

He stumbled and would have fallen if it hadn't been for John Larson. His strong arm broke Joe's fall.

"Hands off, Larson," Higgins ordered. "This Reb has to get used to being on his own. Back at the camp, he won't have anyone to fight his battles for him."

"He's just a boy," Emma protested.

"He was man enough to go to war. That makes him man enough to suffer the consequences. Ain't that right, Reb?"

Joe didn't dignify Higgins' questions with an answer. Instead, he regained his balance and made his way out of the house.

The cold bit at his face and took his breath away. In front of him, he saw a wagon with the words U.S. ARMY stenciled on the side.

Joe's heart began to race and he felt the urge to beg John Larson to allow him to return to the summer kitchen. Instead, he climbed, with great difficulty, into the bed of the wagon. The chains around his ankles hampered him and caused him to trip.

As he stumbled and struggled to regain his balance, the jeers and laughter of the guards infuriated him. Never before had anyone dared to laugh at Joe Kemmerman.

The wagon pulled away from the dooryard with a jerk and Joe realized the consequences of his decision to leave the Larson household.

"What are you thinkin' about, Reb?" Higgins taunted. "Are you looking forward to goin' home? It ain't the same as you left it. Those do-gooders were out and fixed things up. They made things better for you Reb's, but not for Micha Tallons."

"What do you mean?" Joe asked, perplexed by the comment.

"Old Micha went a little crazy. Captain Courtney said he was bein' too rough on you boys. Put him to cleanin' barns. I was there when Doc Morgan came out to see to your brother. Old Micha snapped and come at the Doc with his pitchfork. If I live to be a hundred, I'll never forget Courtney shootin' Micha down like a mad dog. I had to bury him in back of the barn. Do you know what it's like to have to bury your best friend?"

Joe's mind filled with images of the men from his company whose bodies littered the battlefield where he'd been captured.

"Are you listening to me, Reb?" Higgins asked, bringing Joe back to full attention.

"I was thinking about what you said. I was remembering..."

"I don't care about what you were rememberin'. I was saying that everything that's happened has been because of you. We didn't have no trouble until you went and got yourself sick. While we was goin' through hell, you were up at that nice house, sleepin' in that warm bed, with that pretty little gal there to tuck you in. Did she warm your bed for you at night? Was she good?"

Joe knew Higgins was trying to provoke a fight. "Miss Becky treated me like she treated all the other patients."

"Come on, Boy, you've got more confidence in yourself than that. Weren't you special? Didn't they keep you away from the others? Didn't she kinda slip between the sheets at night and give you a good roll? You know what they say about farmer's daughters."

Joe's temper over road his logic. Without thinking, he lashed out, praying his shackled hands would do some permanent damage. Before he could connect with Higgins' face, the corporal landed his own punch and Joe found himself lying on the bed of the wagon. His face pounded and something warm ran down his lip, tasting salty in his mouth. *Blood,* he thought, *it has to be blood.*

"Don't ever touch your betters, Boy. You'd do well to remember that."

Joe closed his eyes. He saw no point in answering Higgins' statement. The man's earlier words about the time Joe spent at the Larson's home echoed in his mind. He was kept separate, but not because he was special. He'd been as much a prisoner in the warm summer kitchen as when he'd sat in the cold corncrib. As for Becky, the feel of her body, the taste of her lips, and the beauty of her face, would have to sustain him until this war ended.

When he again opened his eyes, he saw the Marrow Place looming ever closer. Although he hadn't seen it from this perspective since last fall when he'd been brought here, he would have recognized it. Several soldiers milled around the yard while others stood guard at the corncrib.

"Can't understand why you sent so many men after me. One or two would have been enough," Joe said, repeating the inquiry made, not only by Dr. Morgan, but by the Larsons.

"Didn't you hear what I told them folk who were lookin' after you? You're a dangerous prisoner."

"I'm about as dangerous at that cat walking up to the house."

"Oh no, Boy, you're a dangerous man. You need special handling. We left a few men here to guard the others. They can't get out, so there was no reason to have all of us here, when you were so dangerous."

The wagon stopped and Higgins pulled Joe to the ground. He again stumbled and fell to his knees. As if oblivious to Joe's discomfort, Higgins dragged him to the corncrib.

Once the door opened, Higgins removed the shackles and pushed Joe into the dimly lit enclosure.

"Brought your friend back. He's got to learn his place. He's been up at that big house, being cared for by a sweet little gal. Believe me she is somethin' special. She's too good for the likes of you. She didn't think I saw her, but I did. She was crying because we was takin' away her playmate. You won't have to worry about her bein' lonely, though. They bring lots of patients to that hospital. They're all good Union men. Any of them will make her a good playmate. By the time the week is out, she'll be warmin' the bed of another man."

The door slammed and the laughter of the guards sifted through where the sunlight could not penetrate. The only light came from a lantern hanging from the rafters.

Once his eyes became accustomed to the darkness of the enclosure, he recognized Bret Collier and Backwoods, as they approached him. While they helped him to his feet, he searched for Paul.

Seeing his brother struggling to get up from the thin mattress on the floor made him sick to his stomach. Once on his feet, Paul walked hunched over, his right arm placed protectively across his midsection. The gesture made Joe think of Dr. Morgan telling him about Paul's broken ribs.

"Joe, is it really you?" Paul questioned.

The words sounded strained, as though the pain penetrated even his voice.

"I didn't think I'd ever see you again."

Paul now stood in front of him and pulled him into his arms for a bear hug.

Joe couldn't stop his tears. "Didn't Dr. Morgan tell you I'd be coming back?"

"It's hard to believe anything you hear from a Yankee," Paul said, his voice laced with sarcasm.

"Dr. Morgan's more than a Yankee. He doesn't believe in this war. He's not like the guards they have here. He's different."

The men, who now seemed more like human skeletons than the friends he'd once known, crowded around him. He wanted the conversation to center on something other than himself, but he knew it wouldn't.

"They told me Micha Tallons is dead," he finally managed to say, once he seated himself on the thin mattress. Feeling the hard ground beneath him made him remember the soft day bed in the Larson's summer kitchen.

"The commanding officer shot him. It surprised me." Joe could tell Paul wanted to change the subject. "How did you get that bloody nose, Joe? Did it have anything to do with that gal they were talking about?"

Joe nodded, aware that the dim light would mask his affirmative gesture. "You heard the way they were talking about her. I was just defending her honor. Isn't that what Southern Gentlemen do, defend the honor of young ladies?"

"Ain't no Southern Gentleman," Backwoods said. "Don't think I'd know one if I met up with him. Tell us about the gal. Tell us all about her. We want to know how she looked, how she smelled, and how she talked. Tell us everything."

Backwoods and the others hunkered down around Joe. He could tell they were all hungry for fresh conversation, news of the opposite sex as well as the outside world.

"Up at the hospital, the Larson home, they put me in the summer kitchen, away from the others. They have four sons off fighting for the Yankees. The youngest son, Teddy, was killed in November. They have a daughter, too. Becky is just about my age. She's a remarkable girl. She nurses the patients and helps with the cooking and cleaning, as well as the barn chores. She's a wonderment. It's hard to believe it, but she says now that her brothers are gone, she even breaks the horses they raise. I can't imagine a woman breaking a horse, but she says she does it."

"She sounds like quite a woman," Backwoods commented.

"She is. When this war is over, I'm going back there."

"Why?" Paul questioned. "Why would you go back to that Yankee house when you could be going home?"

Joe could hardly believe his brother's question. "I owe them, Paul. Pa taught us to honor our debts. They saved my life. I owe them more than I can ever repay. Let's just leave it at that."

"You love her. At least you think you do," Paul accused. "You're too easy to read. You don't love her, Joe. You're grateful to her folks, but you don't love her. You can't love a Yankee, you just can't."

Joe turned away from his brother, unwilling to continue the argument.

Bret Collier started to say something, but Backwoods stopped him.

"Think about it, Joe," Backwoods said. "The two of you are as different as day and night. That's the last I'll say about it. This is between you and Paul. The rest of us ain't got no say in it. You'll have to work it out for yourselves."

Joe breathed a sigh of relief. For now, the subject of Becky Larson would be a closed one.

~ * ~

Becky watched as Joe went out the door. The sight of him in chains was more than she could stand. Her tears flowed uncontrolled down her cheeks and she thought her heart would break.

She ran into the parlor and sat on the divan, burying her face in one of the delicate needlepoint pillows.

How could they take Joe away in chains? Would she ever see him again? Could she possibly believe he would keep his promise to come back to the farm and court her?

She felt a hand on her shoulder and looked up to see her father. "Come with me, Bek, it's time for you to get some rest."

"I just got up, Papa. There's work to do."

"I'll help your mother," Tom said.

She looked up, surprised to see him standing next to her father.

"Your folks and I agree," he continued. "You need to rest. I'm certain you didn't sleep much last night, knowing what was coming this morning. I'm going to give you something to allow you to sleep."

"I—I..."

"Don't argue with me, Becky. You won't do anyone any good if you get sick."

Becky nodded her head. Tom made sense, even if she didn't want to agree with him. "I'll do whatever you want me to, but I won't be happy about it."

"That's my girl," her father said, taking her in his arms and giving her a loving hug.

Becky reluctantly went to her room, followed by Tom.

"Don't you want to get more comfortable? Perhaps you should put on some night clothes."

"No," she replied, giving into her fatigue. To her surprise, Tom did not comment on her answer.

"Take this," Tom ordered, as he gave her a small beaker of medication.

She obediently drank the sweet tasting liquid, aware it contained a sedative. Slowly she drifted off to sleep. Perhaps not as peaceful a sleep as she would have hoped for, but sleep none the less.

In her dreams, Joe kept coming out of the summer kitchen in shackles. His haunted eyes searched for her before he went out the door. Over and over she could hear his voice saying, "I'll come back and repay you, I promise."

~ * ~

"Becky will sleep for several hours," Tom announced, when he entered the kitchen. "She's exhausted. What can I do to help you, Emma?"

"You can sit down and have a cup of coffee. John and I will take breakfast up to the patients."

"Emma's right," John said. "When we're finished, I'll go over and see if Lucy Neisuis can come today."

"Lucy's a good woman. She won't mind helping, considering the circumstances," Tom commented. "As long as I'm sitting here, would you have a pencil and some paper I could use?"

Emma produced a stub of a pencil as well as several sheets of paper. Once they left the room, Tom began his letter.

TO WHOM IT MAY CONCERN:

> My name is Dr. Thomas Morgan. I practice medicine in a small farming community in West Central Illinois, not far from the Mississippi River.
>
> If you could check your records, I'm certain you will see that last summer a farm, called the Marrow Place, was used as a holding depot for Confederate prisoners heading East.

The letter continued, outlining the entire situation and pleading for someone to do something, anything to alleviate the situation.

John and Emma returned to the kitchen, and once they each had another cup of coffee, John left to get Lucy.

"Poor Becky," Emma said. "I realize Joe said he's coming back, but you know, as well as I, it could be an empty promise."

"Do you think she loves him?" Tom inquired.

"I don't know what to think. I've raised my boys to adulthood, but Becky has always been a child. She doesn't talk about it, but her eyes sparkle when we mention his name. I'm afraid he'll break her heart."

"I know it's cruel, but the young heal quickly. It's too bad the same isn't true for us old folks."

"Oh, Tom, you aren't old."

"I feel like I am when I see boys like Joe fighting. Speaking of boys, what do you hear from yours?"

"You're changing the subject."

"I know, but I feel I need to. If anything happens to that boy because I sent him back there, I'll have to live with the guilt for the rest of my life. Talking about someone else takes my mind off it."

"If you insist. I hear from Ralph regularly, but he's in one place, not fighting, since he's with the medical corps. The letters from Herman and Edmund are sporadic and I doubt if they receive many of mine. I pray they all come home safely."

"Do you think Ralph will be content to return here?"

Emma shook her head. "In his last letter, he asked if you'd mentioned any more about sponsoring him for medical school."

"You can tell him I've already made some inquiries on his behalf."

"Is that the letter you just wrote?"

"No," Tom said, fingering the folded sheets of paper. "This one is to the war department. I thought someone should know what's been going on out here."

"Do you think it will help?"

"I don't know, but I have to do something. The worst that will happen is nothing will be done."

Emma nodded and Tom knew she wondered if he was as pessimistic as she. He saw little chance of his letter doing any good, little chance the war would end soon, little chance Joe Kemmerman would ever return to the Larson farm.

Eight

It had been mid-February when Joe left the Larson farm. Now, almost two months later, there were times when Becky wondered if it had all been a dream. Only the lock on the door leading to the summer kitchen attested to her memories of Joe.

Surprisingly, April warmed quickly, in sharp contrast to the cold and snow of March. The warm Southerly breezes made Becky wonder if Joe was enjoying the change in the weather as much as she. Had the corn shocks and hay been removed to allow fresh air to penetrate the interior of the prison? From what Tom told her, even sunlight couldn't penetrate to the area where Joe and the others were being held.

Inhaling deeply, Becky tried to imagine having only stagnant air to breath. As she did, she couldn't help the tears that sprang to here eyes every time she thought of Joe.

She shook her head and tried to focus on her duties for the day. In the past two weeks, her obligations had switched from nursemaid to farmhand. She'd helped with the field work, but last night's rain made doing so today out of the question. "A penny for your thoughts, Bek," John said, as he came out of the barn.

Over the past months, she'd tried not to mention her thoughts of Joe. "I was wondering what we could do today.

There's so much more field work to be done, but I'm afraid it's too wet."

"I couldn't agree more. I think we should drive the horses to the pasture. With the weather warming, they need a chance to stretch their legs. It won't be long until we have to start breaking them."

Becky nodded. The thought of breaking the horses that had been stabled in the barn all winter excited her.

By the time they reached the upper pasture, the sun was almost overhead. The horses ran, kicking up their feet and acing around the open meadow.

"They're magnificent," she said, as soon as the gate was locked. "Especially the black stallion. I can hardly wait to ride him."

"You'll stay away from that one, Bek. He's too much horse for you. I'll hire someone to break him."

Becky didn't argue. Seeing the horses running free excited her. They looked so different in this meadow, so much bigger than when they were in their stalls.

She knew she would ride the stallion. She would show him who was boss. It might take time, though. She'd have to wait until her father was occupied elsewhere. There was no reason for him to know of her plans.

It broke her heart to have to leave the young stock in the pasture. She'd cared for them. so lovingly, over the winter, she felt like a mother sending her child to school for the first time. By the time they brought them back to the farm, in late May or early June, they would no longer be the horses she knew and loved. They would be property to be sold.

Becky turned her own horse, Sugar, toward the barn and kicked her heels into the horse's side. Sugar went from a trot to a gallop, giving Becky a feeling of exhilaration.

She arrived at the barn ahead of her father. Reining Sugar to a halt, she wished she could continue to ride for the rest of the day, but responsibilities overshadowed desire.

Her father rode into the yard and dismounted beside her. "I wish I had your energy. Guess you and Sugar and put me and Buck to shame."

"It must be the warm weather, Papa. Why don't you go up to the house and get ready for dinner. I'll rub down Buck and Sugar then I'll be in."

Becky watched as her father turned from her. She wondered if it was her imagination that her father looked older than he had before the beginning of the war.

She put her questions aside and led the horses out of the barn. Once the tack was removed and the horses brushed down and fed, she left the barn.

When she stepped outside, she took off her hat, allowing her hair to cascade past her shoulders. She hated putting it up. It was necessary when she worked with the patients, but she still rebelled when it came time for chores. She found it much easier and more comfortable to stick it up under a hat.

"Becky! Becky!"

She looked up to see who was calling her name. To her surprise, Cal Thompson rode into the dooryard.

"Becky," he called again. "The war is over. It just came across the wire. Miss Adams closed school. I'm out spreading the word."

"Exactly what came across the wire, Cal?" Becky inquired.

"Lee surrendered to Grant at a courthouse, some place called Appomattox."

"It's so hard to believe the war is finally over. You ride on. I'll spread the word here," Becky said, wiping the tears from her eyes with the back of her hand. For the first time in months, her tears were ones of joy, rather than despair.

Without giving a thought to the dust covering her face, or the tears making clean streaks down her cheeks, she hurried into the house.

"The war is over!" she shouted. "The boys will be coming home."

"What?" her father questioned. "What did you just say?"

"Cal Thompson just rode in and said Lee surrendered to Grant at someplace called Appomattox. Miss Adams closed the school and sent the boys out to spread the word."

"Can it be possible?" Do you really think it's over?" Emma asked, dabbing at her tears with her apron.

"Of course it is, Mama. It won't be long before the patients are gone. When they are, the boys will be home and Joe will come back."

As soon as she spoke the words, she knew she should have kept her own council. Her parents certainly didn't approve of Joe's promise. No matter how they felt, she knew they would be ten times more understanding than her brothers.

Ralph had voiced his opinions, firmly, in his letters. Knowing he would be the easiest to win over to her side in the war she knew would erupt once the others came home, she worried about Herman and Edmund's reaction.

"I think you should be prepared in case Joe doesn't come back, Honey," John said, coming to her side to put his arm around her shoulders. "The differences are too great. Not only do you have to consider the feelings of your bothers, but he has a family too. Do you think they'll accept you? This war has left a lot of hatred. Just as we've lost Teddy, they lost a son as well."

Becky knew her father was right, but she refused to let go of Joe's promise to return. Instead of answering, she went to the stove to get warm water to wash her face.

When she turned back to the table where her parents were already eating, she found she had lost her appetite. Too many questions crowded her mind for her to think about food.

"Sit down and eat before your dinner gets cold," her mother advised.

"Leave the girl alone, Emma."

"But she has to eat."

"No, she doesn't. If I'm not mistaken, she'd much rather be alone than eat."

"You're right, Papa. I'd like to take a ride. I need time to think."

"I don't think it's..." Emma began.

"Go ahead, Bek," John interrupted. "Just be careful."

Becky prepared to go out to the barn, while she listened to her parents arguing about her riding alone.

"There's no need to worry, Emma," her father said. "She's as good on a horse as Ralph and Herman, better than Edmund and Teddy. I know my daughter. She needs some thinking time."

Papa's right, she thought as she closed the door on the conversation. *I need a lot of thinking time. If Joe doesn't come back, what will I do? Am I in love with Joe? If this is love, will I ever feel the same way about anyone else?*

Once at the barn, she backed Sugar out of her stall. "You enjoyed our ride this morning, didn't you girl?"

As though the dapple-gray mare understood the words, she snorted and nodded her head.

"Good. We're going for another ride. This time, take me where you will. You need to run free and I need to make some decisions."

Spring was in full bloom, as she and Sugar rode west. The pastures she passed through were full of wild flowers. The fields, freshly plowed, stood either sown to oats or ready to be planted to corn. The whole world seemed to be reawakening.

It was the best spring Becky could ever remember. The war was over, the boys were coming home, and Joe would be... That was where her thoughts stopped. If she listened to her parents, her friends, even her brothers, she would believe Joe would go back to Texas, forgetting she ever existed. If she listened to her heart, she had to believe Joe would return and sweep her off her feet.

Before she had time to further ponder her thoughts, she was surprised to see two Yankee soldiers approaching her.

"Just where do you think you're going, boy," the soldier Becky recognized as Corporal Higgins asked.

"What do you mean?" she questioned, trying to make her voice deeper to sound more like a young boy.

"You know damn good and well what I mean, kid. Ever since that Doc and them do gooder farmers started comin' here, you brats from town have been comin' around tryin' to see what you can see. As far as I'm concerned, you're trespassin'. This time I'm not goin' to run you off. This time, you're goin' to see Captain Courtney."

Visions of Delos Courtney and the lecherous look in his eyes, made her stomach churn with fear. "But..." she protested.

"No buts, boy," Higgins said, as he ripped Sugar's reins from her hands.

"You don't understand? The war is over." She prayed the worlds would save her from having to face Delos again. When they made no apparent impression, she continued. "It came over the wire this morning. Miss Adams closed school and I'm out spreading the word."

"What's your name, boy?" the other man asked.

Becky hesitated for a moment then as convincingly as she could, said, "Cal Thompson."

"Well, Cal Thompson, you can tell your little story to Captain Courtney," Higgins sneered, spurring his horse to a full gallop.

Sugar's sudden lurch to keep pace caused Becky to clutch the saddle horn in an attempt to keep her balance.

The Marrow Place came into view and Becky's heart pounded so hard she was afraid Corporal Higgins could hear it, as he rode next to her. The barnyard was full of army horses, good stock from what she could see. To her right was the corncrib. The hay and corn shocks her father and Tom described, no longer protected the men inside from the weather. She realized the warm spring had, more than likely, prompted the soldiers to use them for bedding and fodder.

She knew if the two men had not flanked her, holding her prisoner, she would have run to the corncrib to touch Joe's hand and stare into his brown eyes.

"This ain't no Sunday School picnic, boy. There's no time for gawkin'," Higgins said, as he grabbed her wrist and roughly pulled her from the saddle.

The unexpected jerk hurt her arm and caused her hat to fall off. As it did, her blonde hair cascaded around her shoulders.

"Take your hands off me, you son of a..." she left the rest of the unladylike curse unspoken.

"Well, well, well, it if ain't Miss Larson. Did you miss your playmate? Did you think we'd let you see him? Of course, I'm sure he'd like a roll..."

She cut off his words as she slapped him. "How dare you? How dare you say such a thing?" His accusations made her sick to her stomach.

To her surprise, he caught her hand, twisting it until she screamed in pain. "So, the little lady is a wild cat," he said, rubbing his cheek with his free hand.

"What's all the commotion out here?" Captain Courtney asked, as he came out of the house. "Why, Miss Larson, to what do we owe the pleasure of a visit from you?"

"I'm here quite by accident, Captain Courtney."

"I thought we agreed you would call me Delos."

"I have no memory of such an agreement, Captain. Now, if you'll instruct this animal to unhand me, I'll explain exactly what happened."

"You may return to your duties, Corporal. You too, Private." The two men saluted, mounted their horses and rode toward the barn.

"Come in, Miss Larson. May I offer you some refreshment? Tea? Coffee?"

"No thank you, Captain. I'd just like to explain and be on my way."

Delos led her to the sitting room, it's furnishings depicting a bygone era. She couldn't help the feeling of uneasiness that encompassed her. While Higgins' physical abuse frightened her, Courtney's silent assessment of her body terrified her. Here, she was defenseless. Anything could happen to her and no one would come to her rescue.

He motioned for her to be seated. When she started to lower herself into one of the chairs, he put his hand on her elbow and guided her toward the divan.

"Now, Miss, Larson," he began, brushing his index finger along the side of her face. "You say your coming here was an accident. I'm not certain I believe you. Could your appearance here today have something to do with one of the men we have in custody?"

"Absolutely not! This morning, one of the neighbors brought the news the war is over."

"What are you saying, Miss Larson?"

"It's true. The news came over the wire this morning. They closed the school. Cal said Lee surrendered to Grant at a place called Appomattox."

"If what you say is true, why did you come here?"

"After I heard the news, I needed to be alone to think. I went for a ride. I was lost in my own thoughts and had no idea I'd come so close to this farm. If I had, I would have given it a wide birth."

Courtney began to smile, although she could see no mirth in his expression. "You tell a nice story, Rebecca, but I'm afraid it's just that, a story. If the war was over, don't you think we would know about it?"

"What makes you so certain you'd be informed? The war department doesn't even know you exist. If they did, you wouldn't have spent the winter here." The boldness of the words surprised her. By the look on Courtney's face, she knew they shocked him as well.

"Perhaps we should check out your story. I'll escort you home, them go into town to confirm what you've just told me."

"I think it's a good idea. I do need to get back home for chores, so if you don't mind, I'd like to leave right away."

Becky got to her feet, trembling. Her heart was beating so loudly, she was afraid it would pound out of her chest.

~ * ~

"There's three riders coming in at a gallop," Paul said.

Joe joined the others as they gathered around Paul to peer out through the slats of the corncrib.

"It looks like a kid," Backwoods observed. "Another kid from town. I heered them guards talkin' about how they've been a comin' out here to see the men in a cage. Looks like they brought this one in to see the captain."

Joe elbowed his way to the front and watched as Corporal Higgins jerked the boy from his horse. As he did, the boy's hat fell from his head. To Joe's surprise, he recognized Becky immediately. "Becky," he gasped. "My god, it's Becky."

"Becky?" Paul questioned. "Are you sure? What would she be doing here?"

"I don't know why, but I do know it's her."

Joe strained, hoping to hear the conversation, but instead he saw Becky slap Higgins then heard her scream in pain as he grabbed her.

Captain Courtney appeared on the porch and once the two guards were dismissed, escorted Becky into the house.

Questions flooded Joe's mind. It was apparent Becky was in Higgins' custody, but why?

The door opened and Joe turned. Higgins entered and with long strides made his way to stand in front of Joe.

"It seems your little friend wanted you to come out and play. When we told her she couldn't play with you, she went in the house with Captain Courtney. He knows how to play with little girls, how to treat them right."

Joe winced at the words that were as sour as Higgins' breath. The picture he painted made Joe want to retch. Instead, he held his tongue. It would do him no good to provoke a confrontation.

"Seems to me thet gal didn't come with you willingly," Backwoods observed. "We seed her slap ya, heerd her scream."

"I ought to..."

"You ought to what," Sergeant Cook said. "Private Pometere told me you came upon the young lady before she was even on the property. He also indicated you brought her here against her will. I'm certain the captain will agree with me for confining you to your quarters."

Higgins and Cook left them, closing the door. Joe felt relieved to know some sort of action would be taken. He wondered if Captain Courtney would allow Becky to see him.

He doubted it. Perhaps she hadn't even been headed here when Higgins made her come with him. It could be she was only out for a ride, enjoying the warmth and sunshine of spring when Higgins came upon her.

"Someone's comin' out," Backwoods said, drawing Joe's attention back to the house.

~ * ~

"I'll make certain you get home safely, Rebecca," Captain Courtney said, as he held the door open for her.

"I don't think such an imposition on your time will be necessary, Captain. I'm quite capable of getting home on my own."

"I must insist. Your parents should know you came here today."

"That I was forced to come here, you mean. I told you before, and I will tell you again, I had no intention of coming here. It was your men who forced me."

"Begging the Captain's pardon," Sergeant Cook said, as he walked up the house and sharply saluted. "The young lady is right. Private Pometere told me the girl wasn't even on the property when they met up with her. I've confined Higgins to his quarters, pending your action, Sir."

"I'll take care of things as soon as I return, Sergeant."

"Now do you believe me?" Becky questioned.

"Somewhat. Just because Higgins found you before you were on the property, doesn't mean you weren't headed here."

"I'm sorry you don't believe me. If you're any indication of the men who are in charge of the Union Army, I'm ashamed to admit my brothers are fighting."

Becky swung into the saddle and dug her heels into Sugar's sides. Sugar took off quickly, leaving the stunned captain still standing by his horse.

~ * ~

"I'm worried about Becky," Emma said. "It's almost chore time."

John looked up at his wife and listened as the clock struck four. He, too, had begun to worry, but he dared not allow Emma to see his concern. "Becky will be home soon. There is no need to worry."

"But I do," Emma Lamented. "Anything could have happened to her. I don't like the idea of her riding alone."

John wished he could calm Emma's fears as well as his own. "As I told you earlier, there is no danger in her riding on our property."

"I know you did, but it still scares me, scares the daylights out of me. I'd never consider riding alone, never in a hundred years."

"You're not Becky. She's grown up under different circumstances. She's more independent than you are, more independent that most girls."

Before Emma could respond, they heard horses in the dooryard. John looked out the window and was surprised to see Becky followed closely by Captain Courtney.

Becky reigned Sugar to a halt, dismounted and threw the reins over the porch railing, before she ran up the steps and into the kitchen with Delos Courtney close behind her.

"Miss Larson, Rebecca," Delos said. "I do wish you would hold up a bit."

"I can see no reason to wait for you."

"What happened, Bek?" John asked, able to hear the concern in his own voice.

"Ask him! Ask Captain Courtney what happened! Make him tell you what his men did! I've got chores to do."

Becky turned toward the parlor, leaving John to face Delos alone. "Just what is going on, Captain?"

"It seems your daughter was out riding. Although she wasn't actually on the Marrow property, she was very close. Two of my men, Corporal Higgins and Private Pometere saw her. They came up to her and thinking she was one of the boys from town, escorted her to my office. We've had a lot of trouble with these young boys, these curiosity seekers."

"I don't give a hang about what kind of trouble you've been having, Captain. What happened to my daughter at the hands of your men."

"I'm sorry to have rambled. It's just that we've had such trouble ever since that business with young Kemmerman. Of course, I'm getting away from the point. I'm afraid Corporal Higgins was a bit rough."

"A bit rough!" Becky echoed, causing John to turn to see her standing in the doorway, her hands on her hips. "Papa, he pulled Sugars reins right out of my hands. I wasn't even on their property. Then he took me back there at a full gallop. When I was dismounting, he grabbed my arm and jerked me from Sugar's back. Of course, my hat fell off and he saw I was a girl. The comments he made were—were…"

"What did the man say to my daughter, Captain?" John asked, interrupting Becky.

Courtney appeared to be flusters. "Well, I—I don't think it is something we should be discussing in front of your wife."

"By god, man, I think you'd better discuss it. This is my daughter we're talking about."

"He just made some comment about her coming to see the boy and how they could—could…"

"Could what?" John demanded.

"He called me Joe's playmate and wanted to know if I came to give Joe a good roll. He said Joe would enjoy it. I've never been talked to like that before. Not with all the men we've had in this house."

John fumed over Becky's description of the vulgar comments made to her. "Your man was out of line, Captain."

"Your daughter is the one who was out of line, Mr. Larson. She had no business riding so close to our encampment. Her actions were suspect, specially considering she was dressed like a boy to conceal her true identity."

"She wasn't dressed to deceive anyone. I'd like to see you follow her around for a week. She was dressed in britches because she'd been working in the barn doing chores then she helped me drive our herd of horses to the pasture. She dressed that way because it's more comfortable when she goes riding. As for tucking her hair under her hat, she's always done it. It's much easier to work without hair in her face."

"But the fact remains, she did not reveal her identity when my men came upon her."

"I don't blame her. She wasn't on your property. I knew she was going riding, to give herself time to think. I can imagine she was frightened. A seventeen-year old girl, alone, being accosted by two of your men, would have good reason to be afraid. I've met Corporal Higgins and even as a man I'd be apprehensive about revealing my true identity."

Captain Courtney knotted his brows as he contemplated John's statement. "Perhaps you're right, but then she had the nerve to make up some preposterous cock and bull story about the war being over."

John realized Courtney was grasping at straws, as his every argument met with a logical counter. The man was so mad, the veins in his neck were standing out.

"It's no story. Lee surrendered to Grant at a courthouse, a place called Appomattox. One of the neighbor boys stopped by here this morning. It came over the wire, when it did, the teacher closed the school."

"We should have..." Courtney began.

John smiled as he interrupted. "Yes, you should have known. I agree with you. None of you should be here at all, but you are. Your men should be fighting somewhere, not sitting on an Illinois farm guarding a handful of Confederate prisoners. I think you'd better go into town and see what your position is. You have prisoners who need to be released and men who need to go home."

"You're right, of course," Delos said, before turning to face Becky. "I'm afraid I owe you an apology, Rebecca."

"You owe me nothing."

"You can be assured, I will take action against Corporal Higgins and Private Pometere."

John studied Becky's face. He couldn't help but notice how her eyes flashed with angry sparks. How many times had he seen the same reaction where her brothers teased her?

"Private Pometere was only in the wrong place at the wrong time. What happened was of Corporal Higgins doing. Private Pometere was a perfect gentleman."

"Whatever you say. I would appreciate it if you would accept my apology."

"I don't see why I should, since I will probably never see you again."

"Of course you will, my dear Rebecca. I'd like to call on you. I thought I made myself clear on the subject when we first met."

"And I thought I made myself clear at the same time. I think it's time you left, Captain. As for me, I have chores to do and as you can see, we are very busy caring for the patients. Your men will survive quite well. They'll go home and tell brave war stories. I hope Corporal Higgins can go home and brag about how he pulled a seventeen-year old girl from her horse and how brave he was when he did it."

Captain Courtney looked at Becky with a new respect. "I don't know what to say."

"There is nothing to say, Captain, nothing at all. It's over, it happened, it's done with. I can assure you, I will work very hard to forget it."

Without further comment, Courtney turned and left the house.

"Is that really what happened, Bek?" John asked, as he put his arm around his daughter's shoulders.

Becky nodded. "Oh, Papa, I had no intention of going there. They wouldn't have let me see Joe. It would have made things worse for him, probably already has. I'm sure he saw me."

"I don't see how he could with the hay and corn shocks piled around the corncrib."

"It's all gone. I'm sure it's been used for bedding for their horses. I know he saw me and I'm sorry. Maybe he will make up his mind and never come back."

"Don't jump to conclusions, Honey."

"Why shouldn't I? I've done a lot of thinking. No matter what, I love Joe. I know everyone is against it. When the boys come back, they'll be unrelenting. If Joe comes back, I'll prove to them I love him. I won't wither up and die if he doesn't come back. I'll hurt, I'll grieve, but I won't die. If this war hasn't done me in, nothing will. My life will go on. I'll meet someone, but I promise you this, there will never be another Joe. As long as I live, I'll love him. So, don't tell me it's for the best if he doesn't come back. I don't want to hear how happy you are not to have to deal with a Reb."

"I understand your feelings, Bek, but what about the boys?"

"They'll have to understand. They weren't here, they didn't know. They couldn't know. They've led their lives and I'll not question them on it. I've led mine and I ask them not to question me."

Becky left the kitchen and headed for the barn.

John turned to see Emma staring after her daughter. At last she found her voice. "How could something like this happen? Why didn't Becky ride east?"

"There's no sense in asking such questions, Emma. Whatever the answers, they won't change the consequences of her actions. At least she's beginning to accept the fact Joe won't be coming back."

"If he doesn't. What will become of her? I remember what it's like to be young and in love. If you recall, my parents weren't exactly in favor of us getting married. If I'd listened to them, none of this would have happened."

John took her in his arms and kissed away her tears. He knew her heart ached for Becky, because he harbored the same feelings.

Would Becky withstand a broken heart if the man she loved returned to Texas rather than the farm in Illinois?

Nine

Days turned into weeks until the calendar read mid-May. Four weeks had passed since the announcement of the end of the war.

The only evidence of any truth to the announcement was that one by one the patients were released and not replaced. The bedrooms the Larson boys once occupied were stripped of their cots. Slowly they began to take on the personalities of their former occupants. Feather beds replaced cots, while patchwork quilts and feather pillows took the place of Government Issue. The Larson home was returning to normal.

In the pasture, the horses waited to be broken. Becky spent time with them each day. Her father called it gentling, getting them used to her voice as well as her touch. During this time she introduced them to the halter, bridle, bit and finally the saddle. The only thing left to do was to break them into fine saddle horses and Becky itched to begin.

"The boys will be home soon," her father assured her when she begged him to allow her to start. "There's no need for you to go out and break them."

She didn't argue. Like so many other things, this was something over which she had no control.

134

By now, she knew Joe had gone back to Texas. It had been a month since her encounter with Corporal Higgins and Captain Courtney. She'd seen neither since. Her escapade had been forgotten. She saw only the pity in her mother's eyes whenever she talked to her. She knew her mother was thinking, poor Becky, so in love with Joe and him not coming back.

Thankfully, no one voiced their opinion on the subject. Her request had been honored. No one said they were pleased Joe didn't come back or it was for the best.

Life went on. Becky found little to do now. Tomorrow, her father would start planting the last of the corn. Since there were no more patients to care for and no rush with the horses, her life fell into a quiet routine of housework and gardening, in addition to helping with the morning and evening chores. She was grateful her father allowed her to continue helping him, as it gave her relief from the boring tasks of womanhood.

She viewed her life as filled with small tasks, compared with the hectic schedule of the past four years. It gave her time, too much time, to think about Joe. Were her parents right? Had his profession of love merely been gratitude to her parents? It seemed the only logical explanation, considering his failure to return. Acceptance of the fact became her only recourse.

She often thought about crying herself to sleep at night, but knew it would do no good. No purpose would be served by crying over spilled milk, as her grandmother would have said. Was that what Joe had become, spilled milk?

Her eyes were constantly gazing to the East, constantly watching for her brothers. Days ago she'd stopped looking to the West, praying to see Joe coming toward her.

As she waited for her father to return from town, she passed the time by setting the table for supper. He'd gone to pick up the mail and attend to some business. She prayed for a letter from one of the boys. Even outdated news would be a welcome relief from the tedium.

"Looks like you're going to get to break the horses after all, Bek," he said, once they sat down to eat. "I'm real sorry about it."

Becky nodded, checking her enthusiasm when she saw her father's face. He wanted her to be a young lady, but needed her to be a farmhand.

"When I was in town, I got a letter from the War Department. It seems there's still a war going on in the West, an Indian War. They want at least twenty head. They'll be here by the end of the week. We can't wait for the boys. We have to get this done."

Becky was excited. *Tomorrow,* she thought, *tomorrow, I can begin to live again.*

~ * ~

Major Stone reread the letter he carried. It came from some small town doctor, named Morgan. The letter had, for some reason, not crossed his desk until two days before the end of the war, only to be lost in the shuffle of paperwork. He wondered if the same thing happened to the prisoners held at the Marrow Place. Had they been lost in a quagmire of paperwork?

Only last week, he came across it again when he finally got to the bottom of the stacks of paper on his desk. How many men were left out there guarding six prisoners? The letter didn't say, and no one took the time to investigate. How had they received rations for themselves and their prisoners? These questions were the reason for his stop in Illinois. Before he could join his troops in the Dakotas, he needed answers.

Perhaps, it would prove to be academic. If Courtney had any sense, he'd taken it upon himself to dismiss his men and release his prisoners. With luck, he'd find a deserted farm. If that were the case he would have nothing to investigate.

He laughed to himself at the thought. If Courtney had remained in a situation never meant to be permanent without contacting Washington, he doubted if the man would have done anything to change the situation now.

As soon as his horse was unloaded, he mounted and rode through the small town. It was easy to find the store front office with the sign that read DR. THOMAS J. MORGAN, MD.

"Dr. Morgan," he said, when he entered the office. "I'm Major Robert Stone. I'm sorry to say I received your letter just prior to the end of the war and have just now been sent out to investigate your charges."

"I wrote that letter over three months ago," the man he judged to be in his late fifties said. The statement reinforced Stone's bitter thoughts over the situation.

"I realize how late this action is in coming. As a matter of fact, I pray there will be no reason for my trip. With any luck, these men will have been released."

"As far as I know, they're still out there. Shortly after Joe, the young man who prompted my letter, returned to the prison, Captain Courtney forbid me to return to check on his progress."

"What can you tell me about Captain Courtney?"

"The man is an arrogant ass. His men are no better. There are two I do have respect for, though. One is a sergeant by the name of Cook and the other a private named Pometere. They both seem to be good men, not as abusive as some of the others, like Higgins and..."

Tom's words trailed off and Stone felt obliged to finish the statement. "And the one you wrote about."

"Yes, Micha Tallons."

"How did he die?"

"He took a powerful dislike to me. I interfered with the way he treated the prisoners. I think he wanted me dead. He came at me with a pitchfork. It was Captain Courtney who killed him, before he had a chance to kill me. I feel sorry for his family."

Stone noticed a sadness in Dr. Morgan's eyes. Here was a man who dedicated his life to saving lives and now he felt responsible for Micha Tallons' death. "I sensed as much from your letter. I checked his records. There is no family. He was an orphan and never married. He worked in a coal mine before the war."

The relief on Tom's face was evident, as Stone continued. "Can you give me directions?"

"I'll go with you."

"That won't be necessary. Just tell me where I'm going. I have my duty to perform and it's best there are no civilians with me when I do it."

Whether Dr. Morgan understood, Stone didn't know, but the man did provide adequate directions.

As he rode toward the Marrow Place, he reviewed everything he'd read concerning this case. When he began his investigation, he'd pulled the files on this particular holding depot. Courtney, it seemed, had been assigned as commander at the beginning of last summer. He and his men were sent rations only until September. How had they lived? Where had they gotten their rations? If no one in town knew they were there, how had they survived?

He remembered checking the ration cards and was surprised to learn Courtney was receiving rations for many more men than were actually there. Had he been stockpiling? If so, it would account for some of the food.

It had been too late to check the records of the men who were held there, to talk to them in an attempt to learn more about Courtney and the others.

Was it possible the man didn't care about being stuck in the middle of Illinois for an entire winter with his men, as well as his prisoners? What about their pay? The pay had been sent until September. They all had money coming to them. It was as though they'd been wiped off the books, like they never existed.

Could Courtney possibly be a sane man? Did his command of this obscure post mean so much to him he could not stand to give it up?

The Marrow Place came into view. It looked much like he expected it to, although someone had resurrected an overgrown flower garden. Purple and yellow iris stood tall, someone had carefully weeded around them and turned the earth to give the flowers easier access to the warm spring sunshine.

Was this how these men spent their time? They certainly weren't patrolling the perimeter of the farm. So far he'd ridden in, completely unnoticed.

When he rode up to the house and threw his reins over the porch railing, a sandy haired Sergeant who was exiting the building met him. Obviously surprised to see someone of such high rank standing in front of him, the man saluted smartly.

"Is Captain Courtney in?" Major Stone asked, returning the salute.

"Yes Sir," the man answered, standing at attention.

"I'll be going in to see him."

"I'll see to your horse, Sir."

"What is your name, Sergeant?"

"Cook, Sir, Sergeant Thaddeus Cook."

"I'd like to meet with you in about an hour in Captain Courtney's office."

"Yes Sir."

When the man was dismissed, Stone mounted the steps to the porch. Entering the house, he could hear voices engaged in a heated argument.

"Why are we still here? That Larson bitch told you the war was over. You found it out for yourself, in town. Why don't we set them free and get the hell out of here?"

"Look, Higgins, we can't just set them free, not without word from Washington."

"Then let us go home."

"Who would guard them, Corporal? I'm not about to tolerate any more of this. You've been after me for the past month about these men. You seem obsessed with the Larson girl. Leave her alone. She doesn't want anything to do with you. It's best if you forget what she told us. This war isn't over until I receive word from Washington. Do I make myself clear? You're dismissed."

Corporal Higgins turned and almost ran head first into Major Stone. When he regained his composure, he too saluted.

"There's no reason for you to stand there staring at me Corporal. Your commanding officer told you, you are dismissed and so you are."

Higgins left and Stone turned his attention to the man behind the desk. "Captain Courtney, I'm Major Stone. I've been sent here from Washington to investigate this post."

"It's about time someone came."

"Why didn't you ever report this last group of prisoners?

"The men who brought them here said they would send the report. I never made any of the reports to Washington. The men who brought the prisoners always sent them. They realized I had too much to do here to be running into to town all of the time."

"When winter set in, didn't you think it was necessary to report this?"

"I assumed the people in Washington knew what they were doing."

"Never assume anything Captain. It only makes an ass out of you and an ass out of me. From what I can see you've done a good job of making an ass out of yourself. I certainly don't intend to have you do the same thing to me. These prisoners were never reported. If it hadn't been for a letter from Dr. Morgan, we still wouldn't have known you were here. As it is, the letter became lost in the paperwork, delaying things even longer."

Courtney cursed under his breath.

"I've come to dismiss you and your men," Stone said, handing Courtney an envelope containing his orders.

When the man made no attempt to open the envelope, Stone couldn't help but question him. "Aren't you going to read your orders?"

Courtney opened the envelope and pulled out the sheets of paper. To Stone's horror, he noticed the man held the pages upside down.

"Aren't you upset by your orders?" he questioned

"I haven't had time to completely read them, Sir."

"Perhaps you'd like to have me read them for you, as it is obvious reading is not a skill which you possess. Your orders state that you are dismissed with a dishonorable discharge. As soon as I receive the answers to some questions, you will gather your things and leave this post."

"Leave? Where will I go? The Army is my life."

"I suggest you return to Ohio. Our records indicate you have family there. It is where you will be contacted by a board of inquiry."

The defiance seemed to drain from Courtney's face. "You said you had questions, Sir. What are they?"

"To begin with, how did you come to command this post when you can neither read nor write?"

~ * ~

With little else to occupy their time, Joe and Paul talked softly between themselves, while some of the others slept. As usual, Backwoods watched what went on outside their world.

"I wonder what's goin' on out thar," he observed. "Twern't too long ago an officer come in."

"You told us," Joe replied.

"I know, but one by one all them guards, even the good ones, are goin' up to thet house. I wonder what it means?"

"It means someone from Washington finally realized we're here. They'll probably be shipping us East soon," Paul said.

"Thet'll be good," Backwoods continued. "We can finally git out of this here hellhole."

Joe could feel his heart begin to beat faster. If they were to be sent east, how would he ever return to Becky?

"Maybe the war is over," he suggested.

"Ain't likely," Backwoods drawled. "Iffen the war was over, we'd have heered about it."

"Maybe that's what this officer is coming to tell them."

"You're a dreamer, Joe. This war ain't ever gonna be over. I ain't never gonna git to see my wife and younguns again. Seems like I've been fightin' this war all my life. My younguns was just babies when I went away. They won't even know me. I don't know how they've been livin'. I hope they're all right."

"Before we came here, hadn't you had any word from them?" Paul asked.

"Wouldn't do no good. They can't write and I can't read. Wouldn't have done no good at all."

Backwoods turned from them, signaling an end to the conversation. Each man seemed to turn his thoughts inward to the ones they left behind, and to home.

Joe tried not to dwell on the prospect of being sent east. Instead, he turned his thoughts to Becky. As he had every day since his return, he closed his eyes and summoned a vision of her to appear in his mind. Each time he remembered the way she looked, he realized he loved her more. *How could I live without you,* he silently questioned.

As always, the vision only smiled at him. The Becky in his mind trusted in his return. Did the Becky of reality harbor the same trust?

It grew later and later in the day. Just as the sun sank behind the barn, Higgins brought in their supper. Surprisingly, he said little. It was as though he'd ceased to care about his favorite pastime of verbal abuse.

"Well, look at thet," Backwoods said, when they finished eating.

Joe joined the others, as they gathered around Backwoods to peer through the slats. "The men are riding out," he gasped. "We're here alone."

"Sergeant Cook wasn't with them," Paul observed.

"He was with them all right," Backwoods replied, a note of panic in his voice. "Courtney, Higgins and the others all rode out, he must've been with them. They've left us here to die."

"What happened to the officer who rode in earlier?" Joe questioned. "I didn't see him."

"I don't know," Paul replied. "What I do know is for the first time I'm scared. If they're gone, what will happen to us?"

Joe knew Paul believed, as did the others, that their fate was sealed. With the guards gone, who would know they were still here? Since the weather had become warm enough for fieldwork, the neighbors were too busy to care. No one, not even the boys from town, had come to the Marrow Place since the day he saw Becky ride with in Higgins and Pometere.

As if marking time, Joe counted the days since he'd seen her abused by Higgins. It had been over a month ago. Now, he was certain, he would never see her again.

The opening of the door shattered his thoughts. To everyone's surprise, Sergeant Cook, Private Pometere, and the officer Backwoods saw earlier stood in the doorway, the dwindling light of evening at their backs.

"My name is Major Stone," the officer began. "I've been sent here to advise you the war is over. It has been for a month now. I've also been sent to investigate Captain Courtney and the others. As of this moment, you are free to go. Of course, I would not advise your leaving until morning. Unfortunately, I cannot give you horses, but I can divide the remainder of the provisions among you. Should you decide to remain here tonight, you are welcome to come up to the house to take breakfast with us before you leave."

They all stood, stunned by Major Stone's words. "What happened to the others, Sir?" Backwoods finally asked.

"They were dismissed, sent home. Some, like Captain Courtney, will await his imminent court marshal."

"You're usin' mighty big words. You got to remember, we ain't all educated like you is."

"I'm sorry, young man. Imminent means it will happen. Captain Courtney will be held responsible for what has gone on here. He will receive a dishonorable discharge from the service. The same is true for Corporal Higgins and several of the others. Sergeant Cook and Private Pometere will stay on with the Army. They have assured me they will go with me to fight Indians in the West. I leave you to whatever decision you must make. I trust we will see you in the morning."

Once he left, Joe looked from one of his friends to the next. "Free," he said, once he found his voice. "The war is over and we're free to leave. It's been over for a month. Becky was here a month ago. Do you think she knew?"

Paul scratched his head. "Anything's possible. Maybe she came here to tell you about it."

No matter what Paul said, Joe knew Becky would never come to the Marrow Place willingly. The danger to himself by her coming would have been enough to deter her.

Lost in his own thoughts, Joe wandered outside. Above him, stars studded the black sky complimenting the three quarter moon.

"Beautiful, ain't it?" Backwoods said from behind Joe. "It's one of the things I've missed the most. I've always looked forward to the quiet of night time."

"I never thought much about it," Joe replied. "It just never seemed special before. It will never be the same again."

One by one, the others joined them. Joe paid little attention. Awed by the beauty around him, he sought the solitude he'd so missed these past months.

"What will you do now, Joe?" Paul asked, intruding on Joe's private moment. "Are you ready to go home?"

"I thought I'd made myself quite clear. I'm going to Becky. I have to at least offer her my love."

"I must have been talking to the wall all these months. I thought we'd come to an understanding. What about our plans to go home?"

"Don't you mean your plans to go home? I don't recall agreeing with you. You can go home. I won't stop you. I just can't go back without Becky."

"This girl is a Yankee, Joe. How can you love a Yankee?"

"What you don't understand is love is blind. It doesn't see Becky as a Yankee, doesn't see me as a Reb. All it knows is I care for her."

In the moonlight, Joe saw something alien in Paul's eyes. Never before had he seen Paul angry. The unfamiliar emotion in his brother both frightened and saddened him. "Don't ever use that word again. Don't ever call us Rebs." Paul punctuated his words with a blow to Joe's chin.

Joe reeled backwards from the force of the blow. Once he regained his balance he came back at his brother, ready to defend himself. It was Backwoods who separated them.

"Calm down, both of you," Backwoods ordered. "We've been here for months now and this is just what Higgins and the others wanted to happen. They wanted to see us fightin' among ourselves. Joe's right, we are Rebs, Rebels against the Union. I know you're against Joe and Becky, Paul, but you ain't gonna change his mind by beatin' him. As for you, Joe, I'm sure you can see how Paul feels too. You're gonna find your Becky, but at what cost? Fightin' with your brother ain't gonna make it easy for you."

Backwoods' words weighed heavily on Joe's mind. So heavily, in fact, he fell to his knees in the dew soaked grass. "I don't want to fight with you, Paul," he admitted, unaware of the unmanly tears running down his cheeks. "I just want you to understand what I feel for Becky. I'd appreciate it if you'd come back to the Larson farm with me. Of course, I'll understand if you decide to go home."

"If I can't change your mind, little brother, I guess I have no choice but to come with you. Those Yankee brothers of hers will eat you alive and spit you out."

Joe accepted Paul's help to get to his feet. When he did, he embraced his brother. "Thank you. I know you'll never understand until you get to know the Larsons."

~ * ~

"I can finish here, Bek," John said. "Why don't you go on up to the house?"

Becky agreed. It had been a long day. After dinner, she'd helped her father bring the horses in from the pasture. In the morning she would begin breaking the string of saddle horses the Army requested.

Once outside, she took a deep breath of the sweet spring air. The last rays of sunlight cast long shadows across the dooryard.

In the distance, she saw a lone rider approaching the farm. Her heart skipped a beat. Could the rider be one of the boys? Was she one step closer to returning to a normal life?

The closer the rider got, the more excited she became. Even without recognizing the face, she knew the uniform he wore was blue.

Excitement turned to horror when Captain Courtney dismounted, and with a minimum of steps stood in front of her.

"I've come to ask you to return to Ohio with me. I want you to be my wife."

Courtney's proposition made her sick to her stomach. "I thought I made myself clear when you were last here. I want nothing to do with you."

"Oh, but at that time you thought your little playmate was coming back to you. I assure you, the boy left for Texas weeks ago."

"Then why are you still here?"

"There was a lot of paperwork to finish up. It took a long time. Now I'm going home. I'm certain my ma would be pleased to have you as a daughter-in-law."

"But I don't..."

Courtney pulled her into his arms and cut her words short by covering her mouth with his. She tried to shake her head to get away from his bruising kiss, to no avail. Instead of freeing herself, she only managed to excite him more. His grip tightened and he forced his tongue into her mouth. The taste of stale tobacco made her gag.

Unable to think of anything else to do, she bit down as hard as she possibly could. Her action caused Courtney to release her as he yelped in pain.

Becky seized the opportunity and started to run. She made it almost to the house when Courtney overtook her. Grabbing her arm, he jerked her around to face him.

"Don't ever try to run away from me, bitch. I've come for what is mine."

"I'm not yours. I'm not property. I don't belong to anyone."

"That's where you're wrong. You wanted me that day you came out to the camp. Now I'm gonna give you what you want."

Before she could scream, he doubled his fist. She steeled herself for the blow she knew would come.

"Get your hands off my daughter!"

Becky looked up to see her mother standing on the porch, a shotgun in her hands.

Courtney loosened his grip then put his hands in the air. "Now you wouldn't use that thing would you, Mrs. Larson?"

"Don't tempt me."

Turning back toward the barn, Emma shouted to John.

"What's going on here?" John questioned, as he came from the barn armed with a pitchfork.

Courtney began to back away. "What's all the fuss about? Miss Rebecca and I have been planning to get married. I'm going back to Ohio. I came to get her."

"You're lying..."

"Shut up!" Courtney shouted, silencing Becky's accusations.

"I think you're the one who should be quiet," John said. "If you and our daughter had some sort of an agreement, don't you think my wife and I would have known? Now, you'll leave my property. Should you come back, I will not be responsible for the actions of either my wife or myself."

Ten

"Hello the camp."

Ralph and Edmund Larson looked up from their supper. The voice sounded familiar, even if the man behind it remained hidden in the darkness.

"Herman! Is that you?" Ralph called back.

"Ralph?"

Ralph got to his feet, tears stinging his eyes. When he'd started this journey, he'd never expected to be reunited with his brothers before he got home.

He'd met Ed after less than a week on the road. They made this trip together. Now, with home less than a day's ride away, the family was complete.

"I can't believe the two of you are actually here," Herman said, once he embraced both of them.

In the firelight, Ralph assessed his middle brother. As he did, he couldn't help but compare Herman and Edmund. When they'd first met up, he found Ed knew about Teddy's death and the recovery hospital the folks ran in their childhood home. What he didn't know was about the young Reb who had stolen Becky's heart.

"Have either of you heard from home?" Herman asked.

Ralph exhaled slowly, realizing he'd been holding his breath in anticipation of the question.

"I've gotten letters on a regular basis," Ralph said. "Ed wasn't so lucky. He hasn't had one in five months. How about you?"

"Eddy's got me beat. I haven't heard from home in over a year. Is there something I should know?"

Ralph drew in a deep breath. "Teddy was killed in November." He watched as Herman's shoulders slumped and his smile faded.

"Where did it happen?"

"Someplace in Tennessee. The folks didn't get much information."

"Are they still running the hospital?"

"The last I heard, the patients were being sent home. I suppose, by now, they've gotten back to normal."

"Normal!" Ed shouted, getting to his feet. "How can you call what's going on there normal?"

"What are you talking about?" Herman inquired.

Ralph wished he could prolong the inevitable, but he knew he couldn't. "Last winter, Dr. Morgan brought a patient to the house."

"What's so strange about that?"

"This one was a Confederate prisoner."

"A Reb? He had the nerve to bring a Reb into Mama and Papa's house? What in the hell was he thinking of?"

"He was trying to save the boy's life," Ralph replied, as calmly as he could. "It seems the army turned the Marrow Place into a holding prison. I guess it wasn't bad in the summer, but somehow this last group of prisoners they brought there were forgotten. One of them, a boy of seventeen, contracted pneumonia. The folks nursed him back to health."

"I still don't understand what you're getting at. The war is over and he's gone back to whatever hole he crawled out of, end of story."

"Unfortunately," Ralph continued, "it's not the end for Becky."

"What's she got to do with it?"

"She's in love with the bastard, that's what," Ed spat. "Ralph would beat around the bush about this all night. That Reb of hers promised to come back and get her. No matter what, it's not right."

"How could the folks let something like this happen? Becky's just a baby for god's sake."

"She's a young woman," Ralph interjected. "If it wasn't for this war, she'd be married and have a baby of her own by now. We've all missed a big chunk of her life. In doing so, she's grown up without us."

"Since he probably ain't coming back, what's all the fuss about?"

"It seems Becky's broken hearted to think it might happen. The folks don't want us upsetting her."

"Then why tell us in the first place?"

"They wanted us to know, just in case the boy comes back. I don't think it's likely, but we do have to consider the possibility."

A rider approaching the camp, put an end to the discussion. Ralph breathed a sigh of relief. The appearance of a stranger would curtail the argument between himself and his brothers.

"I saw your fire," the man who rode up said. "I was hoping you might have a cup of coffee I could have."

"Of course, Sir," Ed replied, snapping to attention as soon as the light from the fire allowed him to recognize the man's rank as Captain. "You're welcome to join us for the night."

"That won't be necessary, Sergeant. I have a long way to go. Frankly, I want to put as much distance between this area and myself as I can."

"Where are you headed?" Ralph asked, handing the newcomer a cup of coffee.

"Ohio. It's a hell of a lot more civilized than here."

"What are you getting at, Captain?" Ralph pressed.

"I encountered a young lady and decided to take her as my wife. I thought we had an understanding, but when I went to claim her, she refused to accompany me. I pity the man who takes Rebecca Larson as his wife."

"Did I hear you right?" Herman asked. "Did you say Rebecca Larson?"

"Yes, do you know her?"

Ralph sent a look to each of his brothers he hoped said he didn't want them to let this man know who they were.

"By your silence, I assume you know the family. I'd steer clear of the whole lot, if I were you. The old lady pulled a shotgun on me and the old man came at me with a pitchfork. They're all crazy."

The man finished the last of his coffee then remounted his horse. "I need to be on my way. Remember what I said about those Larsons."

The three Larson men stood, mutely, watching the Captain ride away.

"Who the hell was that?" Herman asked. "He certainly didn't look like a seventeen year old Reb to me."

"Me, either," Ed commented. "Do you think Mama really came at him with a shotgun?"

Ralph couldn't help but smile at the verbal picture the man drew. "I don't know, but if she did, she must have had good reason. I sure would have liked to see it."

"Do you think he and Bek were, well, you know?" Ed questioned.

"I doubt it," Ralph replied. "That guy was old enough to be her father. If you ask me, he's the one who is crazy."

"I guess we won't get any answers until we get home," Herman said. "I'd like to get an early start, so I'm going to sleep."

Ralph watched as his brothers opened their bedrolls. Long after their even breathing became contented snores, he remained awake, staring into the fire.

What would they find when they returned home? How would he relate to his younger sister? Could he ever accept her love for the enemy?

By the time he settled into his own bedroll, a light rain began to fall. *Only one more night of sleeping in the out of doors,* he told himself.

Pulling the blanket snugly around him, Ralph drifted off to sleep and dreams of sleeping in his own bed, in his own room.

~ * ~

Becky stepped out onto the porch. Last night's rain left the air washed and the temperature a bit cooler. The grass glistened with the droplets still clinging to its blades and everything smelled fresh.

For the first time in weeks, Becky didn't scan the Western horizon. Joe wasn't coming back. She'd accepted his decision to return home. At least that was what she told her parents. In her heart, she knew she would never accept it. She would never forget the Reb who had spent so much time in the summer kitchen.

With work to be done, she shook her head to rid herself of such thoughts and made her way to the barn to saddle Sugar. Although they moved the horses to the pasture behind the barn, she would need her own horse to rope one of them.

As soon as she and Sugar rode into the pasture, she saw the horse she wanted. The little sorrel mare had been the calmest of all the horses. She would be easy to break. Her disposition was a plus, since it had been a year since Becky had been on an unbroken horse. She knew she should take the easy ones first.

In the field, the black eyed her, daring her to take him. As much as she ached to ride the big horse, she left him there. "Oh, no, big boy," she said to the stallion, once she'd roped the sorrel. "We'll get together, but not just yet."

With the rope secured around the saddle horn, she nudged Sugar into a trot and led the sorrel out of the pasture. After closing the gate, she directed both horses to the paddock.

The sorrel ran around the fenced in area, as though looking for a way out. Becky turned back to Sugar. "Are you remembering last year when I broke you? It wasn't so bad, was it? This time, you can stand here and watch the fun."

After tying Sugar's reins to the fence, Becky entered the paddock. "Are you ready girl?" she asked the sorrel. The horse shook her head from side to side, whinnying her protests.

Becky carried the bit and bridle over to the horse and slipped it over her head. Again, she protested. Becky smiled, thinking how useless the gesture seemed. Reaching into her pocket, she took out a lump of sugar and offered it to the horse.

Greedily, the mare accepted the sweet treat, nuzzling Becky's hand for more.

"You can have another, if you're a good girl. For now, we have work to do."

The mare began to fidget when Becky put the saddle on her back. It was as though she knew what was coming and understood the need for it. Becky continued to speak, never changing the tone of her voice, never ceasing to stroke the horse's neck.

At last, she swung, gracefully, into the saddle. The mare, surprised by the unaccustomed weight on her back, began to buck. Becky smiled, putting her full concentration, her full being, into the job. Much as the sorrel wanted her tormentor on the ground, Becky was determined to stay in the saddle, and stay she did.

Finally, the mare tired. Only then did Becky begin the work of training, getting her to respond to the necessary commands.

With the horse finally calm, Becky rode her around the paddock several more times. When at last she was satisfied with the morning's work, she dismounted.

A sadness overcame her. Why was she the one breaking these horses? The war had been over for a month. She knew Joe wasn't coming back, but what about her brothers? Why weren't they the ones doing the man's work she'd been forced to do?

Suddenly the war, the inequality of war, the fact she'd been left behind to take over, became too much for her. Burying her face against the horse's neck, she began to cry.

"Damn them!" she screamed. "Damn them all to hell!"

She couldn't believe it when she felt someone's hands on her shoulders. Who could it be? When she'd started breaking the mare, she'd been alone. Her father was finishing the last of the planting, her mother was in the house. Who could have invaded her privacy?

"Ladies in Texas don't break horses, and they don't damn anyone to hell," a man drawled.

Becky's head spun, her heart beat faster and the ground seemed to drop out from under her feet. She could hardly dare to believe the voice belonged to Joe. To confirm her hopes, to see the materialization of her prayers, she turned to face him.

"Joe, is it you? Is it really you? The war's been over for so long and..."

He cut her words short by covering her mouth with his. The kiss, which followed his brash actions, warmed her entire body, filling her with desire. His hands were in her hair, pulling her closer to him. She felt herself melting into his arms, praying it wasn't a dream.

They finally broke apart and she held his face in her hands. "I—I thought you'd gone back to Texas. It's been over a month. Captain Courtney..."

He put his finger to her lips in an attempt to silence her. "We were only told about it yesterday."

"I didn't think you were coming. The boys aren't home, there's so much work to do. I thought—I thought you didn't love me."

She saw him stiffen at her words. "I never stopped loving you. You'll never know how worried I was when I saw you at the prison. Why did you go there?"

Her heart ached. How could she explain what happened? "I didn't plan it. It wasn't supposed to happen."

"I don't understand. If you didn't plan it, why did you come?"

"The war was over. I needed to think, needed to be alone. I went for a ride and gave Sugar her head. I was lost in thought when Corporal Higgins rode up to me and made me go back with him. He thought I was one of the boys from town."

Joe's face radiated a look of concern. "I saw his surprise when your hat fell off and your hair came loose."

Becky cringed at the memory. If he'd seen what happened, he certainly saw her slap the man as well as his retaliation.

"I tried to tell them the war was over, but Captain Courtney wouldn't believe me. He thought I'd come to see you. I wouldn't have jeopardized your safety for a foolish whim."

"I know you wouldn't."

"As soon as I realized you'd seen me, I was certain you wouldn't come back. I was certain you'd think I came to see Captain Courtney and the guards."

Joe's eyes filled with what she could only call hatred. "That was what Higgins wanted me to think, but I knew better. I knew he only wanted to pick a fight."

Behind them, she heard a man clear his throat.

"I brought someone with me, Becky," Joe began. "I want you to meet my brother, Paul."

"Oh, Joe, I'm not fit to meet anyone. I smell of horse and sweat. I'm too dirty."

~ * ~

Joe couldn't help the smile tugging at the corners of his mouth. For the first time, he assessed Becky's appearance. Little spatters of mud clung to her pant legs and face. Tears had run down her cheeks, leaving tracks through the dirt and dust. It didn't matter to him she was still beautiful.

With a wink, he turned her to face Paul. As soon as Joe saw the look in his brother's eyes, he knew acceptance would surely come.

"It doesn't matter, Miss Becky," Paul said, as he took her hand in his. "We don't smell like roses ourselves."

"Where are my manners?" Becky remarked, once Paul released her hand. "You must be hungry, and of course, you want a bath. Let me finish with this horse. Then we'll go up to the house."

Joe and Paul watched while she unsaddled the sorrel, reattached the lead rope then mounted the dapple-gray mare that stood patiently at the fence.

Once she rode out of sight, Paul turned to Joe. "She is as beautiful as you said, but I still think you're making a mistake. What will happen when you need someone who is more than beautiful, someone who shares your background? What happens when you find you don't love her?"

Anger rekindled itself in Joe's mind. "I know what I'm doing. You don't have to stay here."

"I doubt it. What you keep forgetting is there are three Yankee soldiers on their way here. Are you going to face them by yourself? You against three Yankees doesn't make sense. You need me to stay here."

~ * ~

Emma watched Becky as she worked. From the kitchen window, she could see the paddock. The sorrel Becky worked, was a pretty little horse.

Watching the way her daughter handled the mare made Emma's heart swell with pride. Although she still worried each time Becky mounted an unbroken horse, she knew Becky was up to the challenge.

Her daughter had grown into a beautiful young woman. It broke Emma's heart to have to encourage her to do a man's work. What hurt even more was the knowledge the first man to capture Becky's heart had not returned after the war.

In the distance, she saw two men walking toward the house. At first she thought the men were her sons. As she watched, she realized they were coming from the West, not the East. These were not her sons. They could only be Joe and his brother.

Involuntarily, a shudder ran through her body. Less than twenty-four hours ago, Captain Courtney had assured them Joe returned to Texas weeks earlier. If that were the case, why was he walking toward the house, from the direction of the Marrow Place?

In the hopes of changing the inevitable, she stared at the two young men. Joe wore the same clothes he'd had on the day the guards took him away in chains. Although his brother wore gray pants, she recognized the shirt as one she sent out to be given to the prisoners.

Emma's emotions ran wild. Joe's return would boost Becky's spirits, but what would it do to the rest of the family? How would her sons react? What would they do when they returned home to find a Reb courting their sister? To her knowledge, only Ralph knew about Joe. The letters she'd received from Herman and Ed never mentioned the one thing she had specifically told them.

"Dear God," she whispered, "soften their hearts. Let them consider Becky's happiness rather than their own prejudices."

She again glanced toward the paddock. Becky was off the horse now, unaware of the men behind her. Emma watched her daughter rest her head against the mare and caught her words as she shouted them to the wind.

"Damn them, damn them all to hell!"

She couldn't condemn her daughter for the use of profanity. God only knew how much of it she had heard while working in the hospital. In Becky's place, she would have said the same things. Her poor daughter was so torn apart, so confused.

The thought no more than crossed her mind, when she saw Joe put his hand on Becky's shoulders. The look on Becky's face left nothing to the imagination. The love, the emotion, mirrored in Becky's eyes, forced Emma to turn from the window. To her, watching further would be improper.

With her back to the window and tears on her cheeks, she asked herself the question she prayed she would never have to ask. Could she condone this? Could she honestly be happy to see her daughter in love with a Reb? *Yes!* she shouted to herself. *Yes, I can!*

She remembered the opposition her parents voiced when she wanted to marry John and move west with him and his family.

"How can you even think of leaving Ohio, of going out to some god forsaken land on the edge of the frontier?" her father had bellowed. "And his parents, who are they anyway? They're immigrants that's what. They're foreigners, not even born here, not true Americans. They don't even speak good English. Their language is strange and their accent is different."

Her father's hateful words still rang in her ears, even after almost thirty years.

Was this how her sons would feel about Joe? He hadn't been born here, his accent was strange and she harbored no doubts, he would be taking their sister far away from home.

She again turned back to the widow and saw Becky ride out of the paddock, back to the field. The two young men were engaged in conversation. She strained to hear their words, but they were too far away. She couldn't help but wonder if Paul was as opposed to this as Becky's brothers would be.

Soon Becky returned from taking the sorrel to the pasture. After putting Sugar in the barn, she and the two young men headed toward the house.

"Mama," Becky said, as soon as she entered the kitchen. "Joe's back. He didn't go to Texas like Captain Courtney said. He's come back because he loves me."

Hearing Becky say the words, tugged at Emma's heart. She'd said the same thing about John to her own parents.

"So I see," she replied, as she gave Becky a hug.

Her daughter pulled away and took the hand of the other young man to bring him further into the room. "Mama, this is Paul, Joe's brother. They're both hungry and dirty. I know there's coffee on the stove and..."

"And some thick slices of bread or perhaps some coffee cake," Emma said, finishing Becky's sentence.

Once the two young men were seated at the table, Emma instructed Becky to get the copper tubs and take them to the summer kitchen.

"When you're finished with that, draw some water to replenish what I have on the stove. I was heating water to wash some linens, but dirty bodies are more important than seldom used bed clothes."

Joe stuffed the last of a piece of coffee cake in his mouth and washed it down with coffee. "I'll help you," he said, getting to his feet to join Becky.

Emma reached for the cup and plate he'd used, when Paul touched her hand.

"I'm sorry, ma'am."

"Sorry? Sorry for what?"

"For letting Joe come back here. The way I see it, Miss Becky was convinced he wasn't coming back. It would have been better if we'd just gone home. I worry about what this will do to the two of them."

"We all do," Emma sympathized.

"How can you be so accepting? She's your daughter. You have sons who fought for the Yankees. How will they accept it, when I can't?"

"Try, Paul. The only advice I can give you is to just try. I've accepted Joe, because I've come to know him, to like him. The man, not the uniform is what is important. I'm the first to admit, he frightened me. He and men like him fought against my sons. Then I realized this war had nothing to do with the men who fought it. There's good and bad on both sides. I'm certain it will take a while for my sons to realize it, but I've come to that conclusion and I'm content with it."

"That's all fine and good, Ma'am, but I don't know if I can come to the same conclusion."

"Think on it, Paul. Maybe you'll understand what I'm talking about. I know it won't be easy, but think about what's best for your brother and Becky."

"What about your sons? Will they be able to think about what's best for their sister?"

"I don't know. Ralph will be the most understanding. He's known about Joe since the beginning. I doubt if Herman and Ed even know. It will be hard for them. As a matter of fact, it will be hard for all of us."

"I still don't understand your acceptance."

Emma smiled. How could she expect any young man who had fought in this war to understand the feelings of a woman, especially one in love?

"This started as an act of Christian charity, helping a sick boy. I couldn't let a young boy die in that place. I couldn't be so cruel. I nursed him, gave him warm clothes, a bed, nourishing food and a safe place to stay. It didn't mean I had to like him, but when you're with someone for as many hours a day as we were with Joe, you can't help but come to like him."

"It's one thing to like him, but to allow him to care for your daughter is another."

"Perhaps it is, but I seem to remember another young girl who fell in love with a man her parents disapproved of. I married him, even though I lost my own family in the bargain. So you see, Paul, it will work out. If it doesn't it's something for those two children to come to grips with. It's nothing to us. We have no say in it, as much as my boys will think they do. They underestimate their sister."

"Joe said you were quite a lady and he's right. You're quite a lady indeed. You remind me of my mother. She was a well-bred lady from Virginia. She was beautiful and always knew the right things to say and do to make things easier for me. With you on his side, I know he'll be all right. You'll have to excuse me when I say I'm still skeptical. I'll still try and change his mind."

"I understand. You have to do what you have to do. Just think about what I've said."

The door to the kitchen opened and Emma turned to see Joe and Becky bringing in the copper tubs.

Once they were filled with the hot water from the stove, Emma left the summer kitchen, closing the door behind her.

In the privacy the closed off room afforded them, Paul and Joe stripped off their dirty clothes and eased themselves into the tubs of hot water.

After scrubbing with Emma's strong soap, the dirt was removed from their bodies. Once the long forgotten color of their skin returned, Paul confronted Joe.

"I'll never know why you feel this way Joe, but I respect those feelings. I won't stop trying to change your mind, but I will respect your choices."

Paul watched, as Joe began to smile broadly. "That's all I've ever wanted. You'll see, you'll come to love Becky as much as I do."

That's what I'm afraid of, Paul thought to himself. *It would be very easy to fall in love with Becky Larson. It's the reason I have to convince Joe to leave here and never come back.*

Eleven

Becky finished her coffee then reluctantly returned to the task of breaking the horses. It didn't matter that Joe came back to her. The chores wouldn't wait and there was no one but her to do them.

After getting Sugar from the barn, she returned to the pasture. Once there, the black raised his head, as if issuing a challenge.

"Do you want to be next?" she asked.

The black continued to stare at her for a few moments then shook his head and whinnied his reply. It took only one throw for her rope to land securely around his neck.

Once in the paddock, Becky repeated the steps she'd done earlier with the sorrel. The black allowed her to stroke him, to talk to him, as though he anticipated the sweet treat he would receive as a reward. She knew his calm demeanor was only a ploy. As soon as she was on his back, he would do his best to unseat her. It didn't matter. Joe was back and everything would turn out all right. She could do anything she put her mind to.

~ * ~

It had taken almost all morning for Ralph's clothes to dry from last night's rain. Beside him, his brothers rode in silence. He knew they were as lost in their thoughts as he was in his.

The subject of Becky's Reb had digressed from obscenities to a wall of silence.

Ralph secretly enjoyed the lack of conversation between himself and his brothers. It gave him time to think about the man who had stopped at their camp. What had he meant about marrying Becky? How did a Union Captain, especially one as demented as this one know his sister?

He searched his memory of the letters he'd received from home. The man had to be Delos Courtney, the commanding officer of the post at the Marrow Place. Becky's letter had described him as a foul man who made nasty comments about her and Joe. His father called the man an irresponsible bastard, who had no consideration for his prisoners. The man last night certainly fit both descriptions.

Landmarks became more familiar, denoting their closeness to home. "It won't be long now," Ed said, breaking the silence. "That's the Frederick's place. We should be on our own land soon."

"Soon," Herman teased. "You've been away from home too long, little brother. We crossed onto our land about three hundred yards back. It looks like Papa has the oats all planted. They're up and look good."

"I think we've got more to talk about than oats," Ralph commented. "What are we going to do if Becky's Reb is at the house?"

"That son of a bitch..."

"Stop it, Herman," Ralph warned.

"What do you want me to say?" Herman asked, as he reined his horse to a halt. "I've just spent a good chunk of my life fighting Reb bastards. Do you want me to forget everything I've been through?"

"I know you can't forget, but neither can Becky. Do you have any idea what her life has been like since we left?"

"What are you getting at, Ralph?" Ed questioned.

"Becky has had to take over everything we did. If the oats are planted, you can bet she had a hand in it. I happen to know she took over the breaking of the horses two years ago. Maybe you don't know it, but Papa fell on the ice that winter and broke his ankle. If Becky hadn't started breaking the horses, they would have had to stop breeding them. Don't you think she deserves some happiness in her life?"

"Of course she does," Herman retorted. "What I don't understand is why she can't be happy with one of the neighbors."

"I don't have the answers. Maybe Becky does. All I'm asking is for you to give her a chance to answer you."

"Ralph's right," Ed commented. "We won't get any answers sitting here. It's best we get home and see for ourselves what's been going on."

Ralph silently applauded his younger brother. Sinking his heels into the sides of his horse, he urged the stallion to a gallop. All that mattered was getting home.

The house came into view. To one side, Ralph saw the paddock. In it, he noticed a rider breaking a beautiful black stallion. It took little thought for him to be certain of the identity of the rider. Silently, he cursed his father for allowing Becky to become little more than a hired man. As soon as the thought entered his mind, he realized his father was not to blame. If blame belonged anywhere, it was with the heads of government who allowed this war to happen.

While lost in his own thoughts, he didn't realize Becky had seen them until he heard her scream. Refocusing on his sister, he saw her lying on the ground, the stallion rearing over her.

~ * ~

"I didn't know being clean could feel so good," Paul said, as he pulled on borrowed britches and shirt.

"I know what you mean," Joe agreed. "The smell of Mrs. Larson's soap was what got me through these past few months."

Joe picked up the bar of soap and held it to his nose. "Even though I know it contains a strong lye base, the scent of lavender certainly makes it more pleasing to the nose."

"Is this where they kept you?" Paul asked.

Joe turned to face his brother then put the soap down on the sink. "Sure is, only then the windows were shuttered and that door was locked. At first, it was terrifying, but it soon became comforting."

"You can't go back to that time, Joe."

"I don't want to. Why can't you understand I'm not interested in a future without Becky?"

"What about your education?"

"I don't want it, but you do. When we get home, I'm going to talk to Pa."

"Forget it. Pa's never going to send me to school. Once I see to it you're home safe, I'm striking out on my own. I figure I can get some kind of a job in Houston so I can go to school. You can't change Mark Kemmerman's mind about me, so don't try."

Paul watched as his brother's brows knotted. He knew Mark Kemmerman's attitude toward his middle son was puzzling to not only himself, but Joe and Luke as well. In all his life, he could never remember a kind word or loving gesture from his father. What had he done to warrant such scorn?

"Give me a hand with this tub," Joe said, breaking into Paul's thoughts.

Paul turned then bent to heft one side of the copper washtub. He saw Joe grimace at the weight of the tub full of water. It was evident last winter's illness had taken a terrible toll on his brother.

He was surprised to find the kitchen deserted. Without trying to find where Mrs. Larson had gone, they stepped out onto the porch. By the time they set the tub down, it was evident Joe's strength was drained.

A scream from the paddock drew Paul's attention away from Joe. He trained his gaze to where Becky was working a black stallion, in time to see her land on the ground.

"Becky!" Joe shouted, as he ran toward the paddock, where the big black horse was threatening Becky.

"You go for Becky," Paul suggested. "I'll distract the stallion."

~ * ~

Ralph spurred his horse to a gallop, only to arrive at the paddock after the two strangers who came out of the house.

The younger of the two men ran to Becky's side then put his arms around her to pull her to safety. By the time Ralph dismounted, Becky was lying on the grass outside the fenced in paddock.

The stallion had turned his rage from his victim on the ground to the man who had entered his line of vision. Ralph could hear the young man shouting at the horse, trying to catch the reins in his hands while the horse towered over him.

A gunshot frightened the horse away from his tormentor. "Get the hell out of there," Ed shouted.

Ralph watched until the young man was safe, before he turned his attention to Becky and the boy who lay on the grass beside her, gasping for breath.

"Herman, you and Ed get the boy into the house. I'll take Becky."

"Don't touch my brother!" the other young man shouted. His Texas drawl left no doubt, in Ralph's mind, as to his identity. "I'll take care of him."

"I doubt it," Ralph said. "It doesn't look like you've had enough to eat to have the strength to get him up to the house."

The man came at him, his fists balled. "Look," Ralph shouted, "there will be enough time to fight about this later. For now, these two need medical attention."

The man shrank away, allowing Herman and Ed to help the boy.

Ralph carried Becky into the kitchen, passed his speechless mother and into the parlor. Once he lay Becky on the sofa, he began to shout orders.

"Mama, bring me some water and a rag. Ed, ride into town and get Dr. Morgan. Herman, put that boy in the chair and prop his feet up on the footstool."

When Emma returned with the basin of warm water, Ralph took time to assess Becky's injury.

"What happened?" Emma asked, as though her boys had just come in from the field.

"Becky was trying to break a horse she had no business riding," Herman said. "She lost her concentration and he threw her."

"It looks like he clipped her forehead with his hoof," Ralph added. "I'll get it cleaned up, but I want Tom to check her over."

"Becky," the boy in the chair said, his voice hardly more than a whisper.

"She's going to be all right, Joe. Her family is with her," the young man who hovered around the chair said. "Just rest. They've sent for Dr. Morgan."

"Ed went into town to get Dr. Morgan for our sister, not for some Reb bastard like you," Herman growled.

"Stop it!" Emma commanded. "Joe is…"

"I know what he is, Mama." Herman commented. "He's the Reb scum Dr. Morgan brought here. Ralph told us all about his feelings for Becky. It's enough to make me sick. How could you and Papa allow such a thing to happen?"

"Don't talk to your ma that way!" Everyone turned to see Joe trying to get to his feet.

"Stay out of this, Joe," his brother warned.

"No," Ralph said. "Let him have his say. This has as much to do with him as it does with Becky."

Ralph watched as Joe allowed his brother to help him get back down into a chair. "Your folks had no say in my coming here. I didn't either, for that matter. If I'd had a say in it, I'd never agreed to come to a Yankee hospital. It was no one's fault I fell in love with your sister."

"How can you call it love, Reb?" Herman questioned. "Everyone knows animals don't love."

"I ought to..." Paul shouted.

"Not in my house," Emma warned, cutting him short. "Joe's right, he had no say in coming here. If you want to blame someone, blame me. I couldn't let a boy, yes, Herman, a boy, die because his uniform was gray rather than blue. Without that uniform, he's no different than the rest of you. I don't blame either of them for falling in love."

"Neither do I," Dr. Morgan commented, when he entered the room. "Now, I want all of you to clear out of here while Ralph and I take care of these two kids."

"I'm not leaving my brother," Paul declared.

"You are, and you will. I don't care where you go or what you do, but try not to kill each other. I don't have time to take care of any more patients."

Once the three men left the room, Dr. Morgan turned to face Ralph. "What happened?"

Ralph quickly filled him in on the events of the morning then stood by to be of assistance while Dr. Morgan took care of Becky.

"She'll need stitches in that cut on her head. Can you handle it?"

Ralph nodded.

"Ralph," Becky whispered, as her eyes fluttered open. "Joe's here. Please don't fight."

"Don't worry about it now, Bek. We just want to finish checking you over."

Dr. Morgan barely touched her midsection, when she groaned in pain. "Looks like you broke a rib, young lady. Once we get you to bed, your mother and I will get you bound up. Then, there will be no more breaking horses. Do I make myself clear? For now, Ralph is going to stitch you up while I check on Joe."

Ralph couldn't help but notice the look of concern, as his sister glanced toward the chair where Joe sat.

"Just lay still, Bek. We won't know anything about Joe until Tom finishes his examination. Now hold still while I stitch you up then I'm taking you to your room."

~ * ~

Paul ignored the older couple and the two Yankees in the kitchen. He didn't want to say anything to them and he certainly didn't want to take the food they offered. He wouldn't allow himself to be beholden to them.

Across the dooryard, he eyed the corral. What was it Becky called it? Oh, yes, the paddock. In it, the stallion pranced triumphantly.

"You think you won, don't you, Devil?" he asked as he climbed to the top board of the fence. "Come to think of it, Devil is a good name for you. If Becky hadn't lost her concentration, she would have broken you."

The horse shook his head, as if trying to disagree.

"Protest all you want, Devil. It's time someone taught you some manners."

Paul jumped down into the corral, making his way to where the horse stood. With the stallion calmer than he'd been earlier, Paul easily caught hold of the reins.

It took several minutes of gentle talking to get the horse to allow Paul to swing up on his back. Luckily, no one had taken the time to unsaddle the stallion.

"All right, Devil," Paul said. "Give me a good ride." Even struggling to stay in the saddle, Paul enjoyed the feel of sitting a horse. At last the stallion tired. It took little more for Paul to finish breaking the animal.

"Not bad, for a Reb."

Paul looked up to see one of the Larson boys standing by the fence. "It didn't take much, Becky had most of the fight out of him. He's quite a piece of horseflesh."

"I think so too, but Papa sent me out here to put a bullet in his head."

"Seems like a waste to me. He's worth good money. With lines like his, I know people who would pay two maybe three hundred dollars for him."

"Union money or Confederate script?"

"Gold. My pa says it's the only safe way to have money in a war. He figured no matter which side won, his money would be worth something."

"He sounds like a wise man. Why did he choose to back the Rebs in this fight?"

Paul's anger threatened to boil over. "My pa didn't choose either side. My brother, Luke, got all caught up in going to war right after it started. It only seemed logical for him to go with his friends and fight for the South. The only thing it got him was dead."

"If you feel that way, why did you join up?"

"It wasn't my idea, if that's what you're getting at. Joe got it in his craw to go. Pa and I both tried to talk him out of it, but he wouldn't listen. Pa finally said he could go then made me sign up to protect him. The way I see it, I did a damn poor job of it."

The man in front of him began to laugh, causing Paul to look up and study him more closely. This was one soldier who didn't miss many meals. In time, he would be called a heavyset man. For now, he was little more than a big boy.

"Just what's so damn funny out here?"

Paul turned his gaze toward the house. He recognized the voice as belonging to the belligerent brother. He watched as the man walked toward them.

"I thought Papa sent you out here to kill that son of a bitch, Ed."

"He did, but when I got out here..."

"You don't have to tell me. You went soft and couldn't do it. Well, I ain't no milk tit like you. I killed my share of horses and Rebs in the war. I must say I much preferred killin' Rebs, but I ain't got no qualms about puttin' down that killer."

"Can't say I'd be overly pleased to see you kill such a fine piece of horseflesh as this," Paul said, moving closer to the second man.

"Don't seem to remember asking for the opinion of a Reb."

"Don't reckon you did, but I'm giving it. I know we ain't welcome here, but I'm willing to make you a deal. I'll stay on here and help you break the rest of that string of horses, in exchange for you caring for my brother. As soon as I get hold of my pa, he'll wire me enough money to pay you back and buy Devil."

"Devil?" Herman questioned.

"That's what I've named the stallion. I know good horseflesh when I see it and he's as good as they come."

"How do I know you'll be able to keep up your end of the bargain?"

"He can do it, Herman," Ed answered, before Paul had a chance to say anything. "What I was trying to tell you when you came out, was how he broke the black. It was quite a sight to see. Had him actin' more like a puppy dog than the wild animal we saw when we fist rode in."

"Is that right?"

"Your brother is stretching the truth. I'm a bit rusty and your sister had most of the fight out of him. He just wanted to put up a little fuss before he finally gave in. If he's any indication of the kind of stock your pa breeds, I'm impressed."

"You should be," Herman said. "Just one question. Why in the hell did you come back here?"

"It wasn't my idea. My little brother is stubborn as a mule. He told me I could go back home without him. Since Pa sent me to take care of him, I couldn't let him come here alone."

Paul's statement met with silence. Through the conversation, he'd learned the names of the two brothers. At least they were easy to tell apart.

He, like them, carried a powerful hatred for the men he'd fought against. Even though he'd felt a bond start to grow between himself and Ed, Herman was another subject. The man would never change his mind about Rebs, especially the one who fell in love with his sister.

"Your mama says you're to get in here if you want your supper," John called.

Herman and Ed turned away from the corral, leaving Paul alone with Devil.

"It's time for you to go back to the pasture and get off this tack," he said, as he opened the gate.

Devil eyed him suspiciously. As though he knew what was coming he pranced away.

"Won't do you no good, Devil. Once Pa sends me some money, you're gonna be mine, so you'd just as soon get used to me now."

Paul swung into the saddle, allowing Devil his moment of independence, before he pulled on the bit to show him who was boss.

He was ready to set the horse to a full gallop when he noticed the older man still standing on the porch.

"Emma won't take kindly to you not eating with us, Paul. Joe should be awake soon. Dr. Morgan says he wants to check you over as well, before he goes."

"Can't see much need in it," Paul called back. "I don't want to insult Mrs. Larson, though. I'll take Devil into the pasture and be right in."

~ * ~

Joe stirred, the reason for him being in the soft bed raging in his mind.

When he opened his eyes, he saw the afternoon sun streaming through an open window. The trouble he had in breathing earlier seemed to have lessened. Each breath still came with difficulty, but the pain he'd felt in his chest was gone.

Slowly, he got up from the bed, wondering which brother this room belonged to. It didn't matter. He wouldn't be spending the night in this house, not with a pack of Yankees ready to slit his throat at a moment's notice. The barn would suit his needs a hell of a lot better than the corncrib where he'd been held for the past seven months.

Once he made his way downstairs, he heard voices coming from the kitchen.

"Is Paul coming in for supper?" Emma asked.

"I told him to. He's taking the black back to the pasture," John replied.

"I ain't never seen anything like the way he tamed that horse," Ed commented. "He says Becky had the fight out of the stallion, but that horse gave him one hell of a ride."

"Edmund Larson, watch your language," Emma scolded.

"Sorry, Mama."

"I thought I told you to put a bullet in that horse's head," John admonished.

"You did, Papa, but by the time I got out there, Paul was already on his back. When he got done, that stallion was acting like a puppy dog."

"He didn't look like a puppy dog to me, when Paul took him to the pasture. I do have to admit, the boy showed him who was in control."

Joe couldn't help but smile at the exchange. No one on the Lazy K could hold a candle to Paul when it came to breaking horses. He'd had only a minimum of training by an old Indian who worked for them one summer. The rest seemed to come naturally.

He remembered hearing Don and his pa talking about it. Don had said something puzzling. He'd made the comment about how Paul's horse sense was the one thing he got from his pa.

Now, as then, he realized Paul got his love of learning from their mother. The only aspect of ranch life Paul enjoyed was breaking the horses they brought in from the wild.

"Paul offered us a deal," Herman said.

The comment brought Joe to instant attention. He needed to know what was going on.

"What kind of a deal did my brother make?" Joe asked, as he entered the kitchen.

"It's none of your business, little brother," Paul commented.

Joe looked up to see Paul standing in the doorway, the afternoon sun to his back.

"I think it is. I can't imagine what kind of a deal you'd be interested in making, considering you aren't planning to stay."

"Whatever this is, it doesn't matter," Emma exclaimed. "I won't have this food getting cold."

Paul and Joe seated themselves beside Dr. Morgan, facing the Larson brothers. Joe had just reached for a bowl of potatoes, when Dr. Morgan took his hand.

"At this table," John explained, "we give thanks to the Lord, before we eat."

Following Dr. Morgan's lead, Joe clasped Paul's hand.

"Dear Lord," John began. "Thank you for bringing an end to this war and bringing ALL of our boys home. Bless this food and the hands that prepared it. And Lord, keep your hand on those who are still healing, both from the wounds we can see and those deeply buried in their hearts. A-Men."

Joe kept his head bowed, his eyes closed, for a moment longer than necessary. He could hardly believe John Larson had prayed for him. The man hadn't mentioned Joe by name, but his words still touched Joe's heart.

"Did you fall asleep, little brother?" Paul asked.

For a moment, Joe almost felt as though they were back in Texas. Upon opening his eyes, he looked not into Maria's warm brown eyes, but Herman Larson's cold blue stare. The smile, which had started to form faded.

"Not asleep," he replied. "Just thinking."

"Thinking about what, Reb?" Herman inquired.

He didn't answer. The sound of Herman's voice sent a cold chill through Joe's body. Of the three brothers, he realized Herman could be the most dangerous.

"I'm waitin' for an answer, Reb," Herman pressed.

"I was thinking about home. About Pa and Maria."

"Then why don't you go there? Ain't it obvious no one wants you here?"

"I'm not here to please you. I came back for Becky. The only way I intend to leave is if she tells me to go."

"Then I'll make certain she sees you for the animal you are," Herman shouted.

"Not at this table," John said, pounding his fist hard enough to make the silverware rattle. "This war is over. North or South, blue or gray, it doesn't make a difference. At this table, I see five young men. The future is in your hands. It's time to put the past behind you and work together to rebuild this country."

"It's easy for you to say those words, Papa," Herman argued. "You didn't fight them, didn't see your best friends killed by them. Some man signs a paper at a courthouse somewhere no one has ever heard of and we're supposed to forget what we've been doing all these months. It doesn't work that way. Not for me, at least."

Herman pushed his chair away from the table and started to get up.

"Sit back down, Herman," Tom commanded. "You've been fighting this war, but so have your folks. They've picked up the pieces of what both sides have done to each other. Your father was as against Joe being here as you are. He learned to look past the uniform to see the man. You have to do the same. It won't be easy, but you'll find it's worth the effort."

Twelve

Becky awoke, her head aching, each breath causing her great pain. From the shadows cast across the floor, she knew it was well past chore time. She tried to remember why she lay abed when there was work to be done.

The door opened a crack, causing her to move her head to see who could be entering the room.

"Are you awake, Bek?"

Tears rolled down her cheeks. Whether they were the product of the pain she'd experienced since opening her eyes, or the joy of seeing Herman enter the room, she didn't know.

"Don't cry, Bek."

"I—I thought I dreamed you came home."

Herman came closer then sat down on the side of the bed, taking her hand in his. "It's hard to believe, but I just met up with Ralph and Ed last night."

"What happened? Why am I in bed, when there's work to be done? Why does my head ache and breathing makes my chest hurt?"

"Don't you remember?"

"Would I ask if I did?"

"Guess not. You were breaking a black stallion when you saw us and lost your concentration. He threw you and clipped your forehead with his hoof."

Becky nodded. Herman's explanation brought bits and snatches of memory to the forefront. "If you, Ralph, and Ed weren't a dream then Joe and his brother must be here as well."

Herman's eyes mirrored the hatred she knew lay close to the surface. "That's what I came in to talk to you about. You can't have feelings for a Reb, not after what we've all been through."

The anger she'd sensed in Herman, exploded within her heart. "What right do you have to tell me how to live my life?"

"Months of fighting more Joe Kemmermans than I care to count. I've seen those stinkin' bastards up close."

"Are you telling me you smelled any better? It was a war, not a day in the country. Going was your decision. You couldn't wait to jump into the fighting. Don't you think they felt the same way about you?"

The exertion of such a long speech caused Becky to lie back, her eyes closed.

"I thought I saw you come in here, Herman," Dr. Morgan said, as he entered the room. "I figured you had more sense than to inflict your views on Becky when she was too weak to resist. Now, get out of here, so I can check on your sister."

Becky opened her eyes in time to see Herman storm from her room. "Has there been a fight?" she managed to ask.

"Only a fight of words," Tom replied. "Nothing for you to fret about. Between your folks and me, we've been keeping a lid on things."

"How badly am I hurt? Herman says the black threw me and clipped my forehead with his hoof."

"Sounds about right. Ralph put six stitches in your forehead. It's not a bad wound. What worries me more is your broken rib. I want you to stay in bed for at least a week."

"A week!" Becky echoed.

"That's right. After all the men you cared for, you must know rest is the most important thing. You will do as you're told. Now, how are you feeling?"

"My head hurts, and breathing, as well as moving, is uncomfortable."

"Maybe that's for the best. It will make it easier to keep you in bed."

"What about Joe?"

"He collapsed while trying to get you away from the stallion. After checking him over, I'm convinced he never fully recovered from the pneumonia. As impossible as it sounds, I've suggested he rest as well."

"And Paul?"

"He's silently seething. For the time being, he's made a deal with your brothers. Until his father can get some money to him, he's agreed to work for them in exchange for Joe's care."

"Doesn't he know it's not necessary?"

"It is for him. Now, I want you to take this medication. It will make you sleep."

"When can I see Joe?"

"If you're a good girl and do as I say, I think you can see him tomorrow. For now, both of you need to get some rest."

Feeling defeated, Becky took the beaker of medicine from Dr. Morgan. The bitter liquid burned its way to her stomach. Although more questions crowded her thoughts, she gave into the urge to slip into the bliss of a drugged sleep.

~ * ~

"We need to discuss sleeping arrangements" Emma said, as she entered the parlor.

Joe welcomed her intrusion, if for nothing more than a break in the tense silence. "There's nothing to discuss," he replied. "Paul and I will be quite comfortable in the hayloft."

"The hayloft?" John repeated the word as a question. "That's hardly a fit place for you, especially considering your condition."

"Because of MY condition, your family is in turmoil. Paul has consented to work for you in exchange for my care. I'll rest, like Dr. Morgan wants, but not in this house."

"Joe makes sense," Paul agreed. "As soon as Pa can send us some money, we'll repay you properly. Until then, it's best if we keep to ourselves. I'll do what I feel is best for my brother, and I trust you'll do the same for Becky."

Joe turned to leave, knowing Paul would be close behind him. Only the sound of Emma's voice stopped him.

"At least let me get you some bedding. Heaven knows we have enough to share."

Joe watched while Emma went to a closet and returned with blankets, sheets and pillows. "I'd be happier if you were sleeping in the house. You're welcome to Teddy's room, but I do understand your concerns."

Once they left the house, long shadows blanketed the dooryard, signaling the end of a long and trying day. Glancing to the west, Joe took a moment to enjoy the magnificent sunset. It seemed as though the entire horizon was on fire, setting off a red glow.

"Red skies at night, sailors' delight," Paul commented.

"I haven't heard that saying since Ma died."

"I know. Pa didn't want to be reminded of her, but I've never forgotten."

"Do you think he loved her?"

"I don't know. They had the three of us, but sex isn't love. I never could understand the two of them. I don't know why, but I'm positive I had something to do with the hostilities they harbored for each other."

"Don't know how you could."

"It doesn't matter. It's best if we get to sleep. Morning comes pretty early. I need to get some rest, if I plan to break horses tomorrow."

Joe climbed up to the loft then took the bedding from Paul. The weakness caused by the exertion left him gasping for breath.

Before Paul climbed the ladder, he lit the lantern hanging just inside the door of the barn, illuminating the entire lower level. After handing it up to Joe, he too came up to the loft.

"What did you mean in there?" Joe asked, once they lay on a bed of sweet hay.

"Don't know what you're talking about, little brother?"

"Of course, you do. You told the Larsons you'd do what was best for me. What do you think is best?"

"Do I have to spell it out for you? What's best is for you to go back to Texas and forget about Becky. Why is it everybody but you and her can see it?"

"Maybe it's because none of you know how we feel about each other."

Paul grunted his answer. After pulling the blanket over himself, he turned his back to Joe. It didn't take long for Paul's contented snores to tell Joe his brother had fallen asleep.

Wrapping himself in his own blanket, Joe lay staring into the darkness. He wished sleep would overtake him as easily as it had his brother.

Dr. Morgan's words about how he'd never made a complete recovery, echoed in Joe's mind. How could he rest when Becky remained in the house, just a matter of a few feet away? How could he allow Paul to work for the Larsons in exchange for their room and board?

Finally, he fell asleep, only to have his mind stay active with dreams. In them, he held Becky in his arms. The feel of her body pressed against his, filled him with contentment.

"Go slowly, little brother," Luke said, as he appeared behind the Becky in Joe's dream. "I cannot tell you what to do where Becky is concerned. The road to take is somewhere between Paul's opinion and your own. If you intend to take Becky to Texas, be prepared to have to fight for the privilege."

~ * ~

Ralph stepped out on the porch, his pipe in hand. The smoke curled heavenward in the light from the kitchen. How could so much have gone wrong?

He genuinely liked Joe and Paul. The two boys from Texas seemed to be well educated.

"Do I have to ask what's on your mind, Son?" John questioned.

"Probably not. How are we going to get Becky to understand what she's doing to this family is wrong?"

"We aren't. She loves him. I remember the same opposition in your mother's family. I've never forgiven myself for taking her from them. I was the outsider, the son of immigrants with strange ways. Your mama's parents disapproved and were very vocal about it. They vowed to disown her if we married. I never thought they would keep their vow, but in all the years we've been married, she's never heard from them."

Ralph sat down on the top step then took a long pull on his pipe. The aroma of the smoke filled his nostrils, giving him a sense of peace. Never before had he heard the story his father just told him.

"Didn't Mama write to them?"

"Of course, she did. She wrote every year on her parent's birthdays, as well as those of her brothers and sisters. She also writes at Christmas. Her letters are never answered. I've pleaded with her to stop sending them, but with each one she prays she will receive an answer.

"What does this have to do with Becky?"

"Can't you see, Becky is in love with Joe? Whether or not we give our approval, she will marry him. Do you want to see your sister living in Texas, with no contact from her family?"

"You know I don't. But a Reb, Papa, how can she love a Reb? I've tried to convince myself what she wants is the important thing. I've even tried to tell Herman and Ed they owe it to Becky to be understanding. I wish I believed it, but I don't."

"Then try. Maybe with him here as an equal, she will change her mind, but I doubt it."

"I'll think on it, Papa."

Ralph got up and walked out toward the paddock. In his mind's eye, he could see Becky on the back of the black. Until she'd seen them, he knew she'd been in complete control. The little girl he'd left behind when he went to war, had grown into a beautiful, confidant young woman and he'd missed it. The thought saddened him.

Could he ever look past Joe's uniform to see the man his sister professed to love? Presently, he doubted it, but he would never let Becky know his feelings. He would bury his emotions for Becky's sake. He couldn't do anything about Herman and Ed's prejudices, but he could deny his own.

~ * ~

Joe awoke with a start. Luke had come to him again. Was he going crazy, or did his older brother find a way to communicate with him from beyond the grave?

From the dooryard, he could hear muffled voices. After propping himself up on one elbow, he looked out the open loft door. In the light from the house, he could see John and one of his sons engaged in conversation. Were they talking about him?

Of course they are, Luke's voice sounded in his mind. *Why shouldn't they talk about you. If you had a sister, would you*

*want her falling in love with a Yankee? I wouldn't, but then I
fought more battles than you and Paul.*

What should I do? I can't go home without her.

Go slowly. Let her family get to know the boy I remember.

~ * ~

The bawling of cattle brought Joe to full awareness. It took
several moments for him to realize where he'd fallen asleep.
Although the sun hadn't penetrated the loft, he sensed he was
alone. He didn't hear Paul's even breathing last night's sleep
had produced.

"We don't need your help, Reb," he heard one of the Larson
boys say.

"There must be something I can do, Herman," Paul replied.

"I don't suppose you know the first thing about milking a
cow. I guess you could carry the milk." Joe recognized John's
voice. "I'll show you what to do with it."

He listened to the footsteps that indicated his brother left the
barn.

"What does Papa think he's doing?" Herman asked, his
voice loud enough for Joe to easily hear.

"The kid offered to work for us," Joe recognized another
voice, the one belonging to Ralph.

"He offered to break horses, not stick his nose in where it
doesn't' belong. If Papa is so set on having that Reb help with
the milking, he can do it without me."

"Calm down. Papa has been doing this alone for too long.
This situation is difficult enough without you putting more of
the load on Papa."

Joe ceased listening. *Why does love have to hurt so much,* he
silently asked.

He waited for a response from Luke, but none was
forthcoming. Instead, he closed his eyes and prayed for sleep to

block out the angry words coming from below. He'd just started to relax, when he heard someone climbing the ladder.

"Are you awake?" Ralph inquired, his voice hardly more than a whisper.

"Yes," Joe replied.

"Tom asked me to check on you. Did you sleep all right?"

"Do you care?"

"It doesn't matter. Tom does and that's enough for me. I spent the war working in a hospital. As a medic, I don't care about blue or gray. I've treated both."

"But you've never been asked to treat a Reb who's in love with your sister."

"Can't argue with you there, but you didn't answer my original question. How did you sleep?"

"Better than I have since I went back to the prison camp. This loft isn't the soft bed in the house, but it's not the rat infested conditions I'm used to sleeping in."

"Good. Mama wants you to come up to the house for breakfast."

"Will I get to see Becky?"

"I don't know. It's up to Tom. It's best if you don't insist on it in front of Herman and Ed, though. They're the ones who did the fighting."

"I understand. My brother feels the same way. He wants us to leave."

"Maybe you should listen to him."

"Everyone has an opinion about this, but what you all seem to forget is Becky and I are the ones who are in love. The only way I'm willing to leave is if she tells me to go."

~ * ~

Becky listened as the house came alive. She wondered if Joe heard the same morning noises when he slept in the summer kitchen.

Earlier, she'd heard her brother's voices. The realization they were home prompted memories of the tension she felt between them and Joe.

Tears formed in her eyes at the thought of the fight she knew she would eventually have with her brothers over the decision of her heart.

"Good morning." She looked up to see Ralph enter the room. "How did you sleep?"

"How do you think? The medicine Tom gave me made me sleep very soundly."

"Tom?" Ralph questioned. "When did you start calling him that?"

"I don't know. I asked myself the same thing several months ago. It seemed quite natural when he was coming out here on a daily basis."

Ralph nodded sagely then sat down on the side of the bed.

"Are you going to study to be a doctor?" she finally asked.

"I want to. I know Mama and Papa want me to take over the farm, but I do love medicine. How did you know?"

"Mama guessed as much from your letters. Tom did, too. Mama and Papa will never stand in your way. They're proud of you."

"I hope so. How did they take Teddy's death?"

"Hard, very hard. If it hadn't been for the hospital, I don't think they would have made it."

"I can understand. I dealt with death every day, but hearing about Teddy..." His voice drifted off, as if it were too painful to continue.

"You didn't come here to talk about Teddy, did you?"

"You know I didn't. I want to talk about this nonsense between you and Joe. Help me to understand. I thought you knew our position on this. Do you have any idea how we felt when we found him here?"

"There's nothing to talk about. I fell in love with Joe."

"In love, Bek? I doubt it. You were attracted to a very sick young man. I can understand how it happened. You were working long hours, you thought he needed you. At the time, maybe he did. The two of you are from different worlds. Do you think he'll be content to stay here? Do you think you'll be happy in Texas, away from us?"

Ralph's voice went from soft and caring to hard and angry. Becky wished she could cover her ears to keep from listening, but she knew it would do no good. Of the boys, Ralph would be the easiest to reason with.

"What do you want me to say? Do you expect me to deny my feelings, to tell Joe to leave me? Do you think I'd be content to marry one of the neighbor boys, when..."

She didn't finish her sentence. She'd already admitted her feelings for Joe and in doing so, angered Ralph.

"Breakfast is ready," her mother called from the kitchen.

"I'll be back after breakfast," Ralph assured her.

"If you think you'll change my mind, don't bother coming back."

Ralph didn't make any attempt to answer her taunt, as he left the room.

Becky buried her face in the pillow and began to sob. Why couldn't her brothers be more considerate of her feelings, of the love she had for Joe?

~ * ~

"Mrs. Larson wants us to come in for breakfast," Paul said, after climbing up to the loft.

"You go ahead. I can't face another meal with Becky's brothers."

"I thought you were ready to fight for her. If you aren't man enough to face her brothers, you're not man enough to ask her to spend the rest of her life with you. We might as well pack up and head for Texas."

Joe raised his head at his brother's words. "I'm not going back without Becky. If it means facing her brothers then so be it. No one's keeping you here, though. You're free to go whenever you want."

"I can go home and you'll starve yourself to death. I've committed myself because I thought you'd done the same. I certainly don't plan to break horses on an empty stomach."

Joe couldn't keep from smiling. "All right, you win. I'll go in for breakfast. When we're done, I'll enjoy watching you try to break those horses. I haven't seen you thrown on your ass in a long time."

~ * ~

Emma watched as one by one her boys came in from the barn. Platters of bacon and eggs sat on the table beside a plate of toast and fresh cinnamon rolls.

Two places remained empty and she saw her sons becoming silently angry. John was just about to bow his head when Joe and Paul entered the kitchen and took their places.

"It's about time," Herman grumbled. "You won't make any friends in this house if you're late for meals."

"We'll have no arguments at this table," John warned. "I never tolerated it when you were children and I refuse to start now."

"Your father is right," Emma commented. "No matter how you feel about each other, at this table everyone will be civil."

"Yes, Ma'am," Paul said.

Emma smiled to have Paul be the first to agree to her mandate.

"Now that we have this matter settled, John began, "Let's give thanks for this morning's meal."

Joe grasped Ralph's hand on one side and Paul's on the other. When John's prayer ended, Joe helped himself to a spoonful of scrambled eggs. He vowed to remain silent throughout the meal. If he didn't say anything, he could avoid an argument.

"I've looked over the horses," Herman said. "How many have you offered to the army?"

"They want twenty head," John replied.

"We only have thirty head all together," Herman continued. "I say we sell ten to the army. That will leave us with twenty we can sell to the private market."

"If that's the case, I'd like to buy the black. I know you said he was mine, but it wouldn't be right for me to take him. He's worth any price you want to put on him."

His brother's statement surprised Joe. He'd never heard Paul get so excited about a horse before.

"If you hadn't broken him," Ed added, "I would have put a bullet in his head. As far as I'm concerned, he's yours. A dead horse isn't worth a plug nickel."

"Maybe he isn't worth anything to you, but I'd be willing to give you two hundred for him."

"You've got to be out of your mind," Joe protested. "There's no horse in the world worth two hundred dollars."

"Devil is," Paul replied. "He has the best lines I've ever seen. I wouldn't mind breeding him to a few of the mares Pa brings in from the wild."

"Just what good would breeding stock do a lawyer?"

For a moment, Paul remained silent. "You know, as well as I do, Pa won't stand for me getting an education and he certainly won't pay for it. If I can breed some good stock from Devil, I can finance my own education."

"Finance your own education?" Emma echoed Paul's words. "Why wouldn't your father..."

"It's a long story, Ma'am," Paul interrupted. "I doubt it would make for interesting conversation at the breakfast table. Joe and I should have never brought it up."

~ * ~

Emma studied the young man who sat on her left. Although Joe and Paul carried many of the same characteristics, that was where the similarities ended. Joe's dark hair and eyes were in direct contrast to Paul's lighter coloring and green eyes.

She searched her memory for a clue to what Joe told them of his life in Texas when he'd been their patient. The only thing she remembered was Joe's love for his father and his longing to return home.

Emma made a mental note to ask Becky about what she might remember. Surely, Joe must have talked about what seemed to be such a troubling subject.

~ * ~

Becky slept until dreams disturbed her rest. In the dream, Joe and Herman faced each other in the dooryard. The sun flashed off the blades of the knives they held.

Herman jabbed at Joe. Although Joe dodged to the right, a smear of blood appeared on his left arm. In retaliation, he slashed Herman's face.

Anger radiated from Herman's eyes as he wrestled Joe to the ground and held the knife to his neck.

"NO!" she screamed, in an attempt to stop the inevitable.

"Becky, Becky, wake up. You're having a nightmare."

Relieved to have the dream interrupted, she opened her eyes to see Joe sitting by her bedside.

"You—You are here," she stammered.

"Yes, I'm here and it looks like we've changed places. As I sat here watching you sleep, I thought of how you did the same for me, not too long ago."

Becky smiled. "I remember wondering what color your eyes would be and what your voice sounded like. Should you be here? Tom said..."

"I know, he said he told you I haven't regained my strength."

"Then shouldn't you be in bed?"

"You Larsons have the strange idea that the only way I can rest is if I'm flat on my back. I'm resting very well by sitting in this chair, thank you."

"What about my brothers?"

"If you're wondering about them being happy, they aren't. Open hostilities haven't broken out, but only out of respect for your folks."

Becky nodded. She knew things would be different if her parents didn't like Joe.

A light rap at the door prevented any further conversation. It came as no surprise when Tom entered the room.

"I thought I'd find both of my patients in here. How are you feeling this morning, Becky?"

"Very foolish. The boys are here and so is Joe. I can't spend these glorious days in bed."

"You didn't answer my question."

"My head aches and sleep comes too easily."

Joe tightened his grip on her hand. "Sleep is what you need," he reassured her.

"You should listen to Joe," Tom agreed.

"But I don't want to sleep. When I do, I have terrible dreams."

She watched as Joe nodded. He'd seen the effect of one such dream. Even now, she shuddered in her remembrance of it.

"I agree with your logic about the boys being home. It certainly takes the burden from you," Tom mused. "I can see where you would want to be up and about, but I don't think it wise. You took a severe blow to your head. Rest is the best thing."

"Couldn't I rest on the porch in the sunlight? Surely the fresh air would be better for me than being confined to this bed."

"I will allow you to sit on the porch, but someone will have to carry you out there. When you tire, you must admit to your weakness and come back to bed."

Becky's mind shouted for joy at Tom's words. She knew being able to be outside would hasten her recovery.

Thirteen

Once her mother helped her dress, Becky waited excitedly for one of the boys to come and take her out onto the porch. She wished Joe could carry her outside, but she knew such wishes were foolish. It would take longer than two days of freedom to replenish his strength.

"At least my little sister still knows how to get her way," Herman said, when he entered the room.

Seeing Herman standing in front of her came as a surprise. She'd expected Ralph, not the brother she knew would be the most strongly opposed to her relationship with Joe.

"I don't know what you mean," she replied, trying to sound like the innocent child he remembered.

Herman's hearty laughter filled the room. "You know darn good and well what I mean. How did you talk Tom into letting you get out of bed?"

"I just reminded him what a wonderful cure fresh air and sunshine could be. Of course, Joe..."

"How can you speak that Reb's name in my presence?" he interrupted, all signs of laughter gone from his voice.

"How can you ask me to deny my love? Joe and Paul may have worn gray in the war, but they never fought you or Ed or Teddy. They were only in one battle then they were captured."

"One battle! Do you know what a battle is? Do you have any idea how many men can die in one battle? How many Union soldiers did Joe kill before he was taken prisoner?"

Becky's anger loosened her tongue, bringing forth the tart responses she promised herself not to speak. "How many Confederates did you kill, Herman? How many men died at your hand? What if the tables were turned? If you'd been the prisoner befriended by the enemy, how would you have felt?"

"I wouldn't have fallen in love with a Reb."

Becky took the opportunity to be the one to laugh. "Don't you understand? No one can control love. I didn't plan to love Joe, just as he didn't plan to love me. He's a good man, so is Paul. For my sake, please try to understand."

The fight seemed to go out of Herman, as he sat down on the bed beside her. "You must know I love you, Bek. More than anything in this world I want you to be happy. I just can't accept you loving the enemy."

"I love you too, but unless you come to grips with my feelings, you'll destroy my life."

"I can see how you talked Tom into letting you get up. You wore him down with your chatter. For your sake, I'll try, but I make no promises. Now that Reb of yours is waiting for us on the porch."

~ * ~

Joe sat on the porch railing. Across the yard, Paul and Ed worked at breaking the horses. Joe couldn't help but compare the scene before him to such an event at home.

Breaking horses always served to be a time of good-natured teasing. In his mind's eye, he could see his father and Don Parsons on the backs of the wild mustangs. How he wished they were here now. If they were, they could persuade these Yankees that he was a good man.

A man, Joe? Luke's voice questioned. *Are you a man? By experience, I guess you are, but in years, you're still only seventeen. You have a heavy burden on your shoulders, both here and at the Lazy K.*

"That brother of yours certainly has a way with horses," Ralph said, silencing Luke's voice.

"He always has," Joe agreed.

"Did you mean what you said about Paul wanting to be a lawyer?"

Joe nodded. "Paul has a head for learning, but it's me Pa wants to send to school."

"Why?"

"Be damned if I know. He's got this fool notion an education will make me a better rancher."

"Will it?"

"I wish I could give you an answer, but I don't know. The only thing I want is to run the Lazy K."

"What about what Becky wants? This is her home. Do you think she'll be content to leave?"

"You keep asking questions with no answers. I guess I hadn't given it much thought. Maybe that's why I came back. I have nothing to offer her in Illinois, but in Texas, I can give her a good life. As the wife of the owner of the Lazy K, she'll have a good social position. She won't ever have to work. My father has always had servants."

"What if I want to do my own work?"

Joe and Ralph turned to see Herman bring Becky out onto the porch.

"Do you think she should be out here, Ralph?" Herman questioned.

"I can see no harm in it. The fresh air should do her good."

In the distance, Joe saw two riders coming toward the farm. To his surprise, he recognized Major Stone and Sergeant Cook.

Fear clutched at his heart. Had they realized he and Paul came here rather than returned to Texas immediately? Were they coming to take them into custody?

The riders entered the yard and reined their horses to a halt at the corral.

"Kemmerman?" Joe heard Sergeant Cook question, when he recognized Paul. "What are you doing here?"

"What do you think?" Paul replied, when he dismounted the chestnut he had just finished breaking. "I couldn't let the kid come here alone."

"Makes sense," Major Stone observed. "We've come to see Mr. Larson about the horses you're breaking."

Joe turned to see Herman gently place Becky on the porch swing. "I think I can help you," he said, before walking toward the corral.

"Shouldn't your Pa be talking business with the army?" Joe inquired.

"Papa went into town with Tom to take care of some business. With me considering a career as a doctor, Herman will be the one taking over the farm. He'll make a good deal for the stock."

Joe ceased listening to the conversation between Herman and the Yankee officer. Instead, he focused on Becky. Even with the bandage on her head, she looked beautiful.

For a moment, he concentrated on the conversation he'd carried on with Ralph. He'd never asked Becky how she felt about leaving Illinois. They'd only talked about his plans, his future. He thought Becky wanted the same things he did, but how could she? Becky didn't know the Lazy K the way he did. How could she love it? Would Becky understand his desire to return to Texas?

~ * ~

Becky tried to hear the discussion between her brother and the officer. She wondered if he would be able to shed some light on why the prisoners were detained for over a month after the end of the war.

"We're looking to buy at least twenty head of your horses," the officer said.

"I'm willing to sell you ten," Herman replied. "With the war being over, the civilian market will be a profitable one."

"I'm prepared to offer you an additional five dollars a head. Will that change your mind?"

"I'll split the difference with you. We have thirty head to break. I'll agree to sell you fifteen of them."

The officer nodded. "Agreed. How long before you'll be done?"

"With Kemmerman helping, it should take at least until the end of the week. We've already broken six, two yesterday and four this morning. It's probably best if you check the herd. Then take your pick of the stock. We'll work on yours first. There's only one horse you can't have."

"Why is that?"

"The big black stallion is already promised."

Becky picked up on what Herman was saying. "The black is promised? Who is he promised to?"

"To Paul," Ralph replied.

"But why?"

Joe turned, his smile so broad it warmed her heart. "Your Pa hates that horse as much as your brothers do us. Guess he decided it was better to let Paul take him to Texas than to put a bullet in his head."

"A bullet in his head!" Becky exclaimed. "Why would he want to do such a terrible thing? The black is worth ten times what any of the others are."

"Calm down, Bek," Ralph said. "Papa was responding to what Devil did to you."

"Devil?"

"It's what Paul named him," Ralph continued.

"I see. Is he the second horse that was broken yesterday?"

Ralph nodded.

"If Papa wanted him put down, which one of you crossed him to break that son of Satan?"

"None of us. Ed went out to put him down and found Paul breaking him. Paul persuaded Ed and Herman to allow him to help break the horses in exchange for Joe's care."

"He must know that's not necessary."

"Yes, it is, Becky," Joe said. "Once we can contact our Pa, he'll send us enough money to make things right. Until that time, Paul's not going to be content to sit around when there's work to be done, especially when it's work he's good at doing."

Becky turned her attention to the paddock. Paul was mounting another horse. This one was a stallion she'd envisioned herself breaking. A twinge of jealousy tugged at her heart. She should be the one breaking these horses. They were hers, gentled by her own hand.

Paul made the work look easy. She'd never seen anyone as at home in the saddle as he appeared.

"I've never seen anyone break a horse the way Paul does. Is that how your father taught you to do it?"

For a moment, Joe hesitated. "Paul learned from a half breed we had on the ranch for a while. His name was Johnny Little Hawk. He saw Paul had a knack with horses and said he should know the proper way to break them."

"Did he teach you as well?"

"Pa wouldn't allow it. He insisted on teaching Luke and me himself."

Becky said no more. Instead, she turned her thoughts inward. During the time he'd been sick, Joe hinted at the rift between his father and Paul. Until now, she'd forgotten about what he'd said. Whatever the problem, she knew it troubled Joe. She wished she could understand and take away the pain she saw in his eyes.

"Ralph, go out and get your brothers and Paul. I made some lemonade. It's so warm, they should have something to drink."

Becky looked up to see her mother standing on the porch with a tray containing a pitcher and several glasses. Ralph took the tray and set it down on the small table next to the swing.

"I hope you have more of that lemonade in the house," he said. "We have company."

Becky watched as her mother scanned the dooryard. "Company? Who is it?"

"An officer from the army and his aide are here about the horses. They're out in the field with Herman."

"Then they'll join us, too."

Becky studied Joe's face, trying to decide how he felt, being surrounded by Union soldiers and officers. With no readable expression, he got up from the railing and headed toward the paddock, while Ralph went out to the pasture.

"Do you think you should be out of bed?" Emma inquired, as she handed Becky a glass of lemonade.

"Yes, Mama, I'm positive. If it weren't for the accident yesterday, I'd be out there helping them."

"Now you're being silly. Surely you've known your brothers would never allow you to continue doing their work."

"I thought if they could see what I can do, they'd understand. I enjoy breaking the horses and helping Papa."

"I was afraid that would be your answer. You've learned there is more to life than cooking and keeping house. With the war over, you must forget you've ever walked in a man's world. You're a woman, and unfortunately the roll you're destined to play in this life is one of wife and mother, not hired man."

Becky realized her mother made sense, even though she didn't want to admit it. "Why does it have to be that way? Why can't women do the same work as men?"

"We often do, but our men folk don't acknowledge it. Many times I've helped your father with the chores, even though he thinks I'm too frail to be considered a farmer. When I was a girl, many widows ran their husband's farms and made a good living by doing so."

"I still don't understand."

"You will. Men want to think they're protecting us. If the truth be known, women are the stronger of the sexes. There's not a man alive who could stand the pain of childbirth."

"What's all this talk about childbirth?" John questioned, as he walked up to the porch. "Don't tell me you want to start another family."

Becky smiled at the easy banter between her parents. They made no secret of their love for each other.

"I think we're too old to be parents," Emma replied. "Now is the time for our children to make us grandparents."

The remark brought laugher from Becky's brothers, who were now joining them on the porch.

~ * ~

Joe listened to the teasing between Becky's parents. Had his own mother and father ever been this comfortable together? He doubted it. His memory of the two of them consisted of an unbearable tension between the two of them.

"You have some beautiful horses, Mr. Larson," Major Stone remarked. "Your son has driven a hard bargain. As much as I'd like to buy the twenty head I wanted, I'll be content with fifteen."

Mr. Larson and his sons discussed the prudence of keeping half the herd for the private market, but Joe quit listening.

Instead, he tried to read the thoughts behind Paul's eyes. He'd always been able to expertly hide his feelings. After gulping the lemonade, Paul drifted back to the corral. Knowing he wouldn't be missed, Joe followed.

"Something on your mind, little brother?" Paul asked when he turned to face Joe.

"Guess I'm not entirely comfortable with that many Yankees."

"You'd better get used to it," Paul replied, punctuating his statement with laughter.

"It's good to hear you laugh, but this isn't funny. I have no doubt about my love for Becky, but her brothers complicate the matter."

"That's why it's best if we go back to Texas as soon as I finish breaking these horses."

"Not without Becky. You can leave whenever you want but..."

"I know what you're going to say and you're a fool for hanging on to such notions. Don't get me wrong. I honestly like all the Larsons. Ed is one hell of a worker and Herman has a good head for business. Can't comment on Ralph, though. He's not like the others."

"No, he's more like you. He wants more than this farm, more than digging in the dirt for the rest of his life."

"Well, that's where the similarities end," Paul observed. "He'll get his education. His family will see to it."

"You'll get an education, too."

"Sure I will, but not because Pa wants me to have it. Face it, Joe, if the old man has his way, I'll be your hired hand for the rest of my life."

Paul turned and went out to the corral to get the stallion's lead rope. Joe knew their conversation had officially ended. Over the years, he'd seen Paul turn away when a situation got out of his control. As Joe remembered the gesture always angered their father.

For the first time, Joe understood both his father and Paul. One side of him wanted to demand Paul stay and continue their conversation. The other side wished he had Paul's strength to walk away and cool down. Joe knew his own hot temper often got him into trouble.

He watched as Paul mounted Devil and led the stallion back to the pasture. Joe didn't have to be a genius to realize Paul wouldn't bring back another horse. When he was in a mood like this one, he would disappear for an hour or so. It they were at home, he would ride to the north pasture. Here, it was anyone's guess where he would go.

Instead of going back to the porch and be surrounded by Yankees, Joe made his way to the barn. With the Larsons engaged in conversation and Paul gone, Joe decided he could best use the time to take a nap. Dr. Morgan told him to rest. If he wanted to regain his strength, it was best he do as he was told.

~ * ~

Becky listened to the conversation of the men around her. She was painfully aware of Joe and Paul distancing themselves from her family.

It seemed good to hear her brothers' voices, to know they were home and finally safe. Yet, she prayed they would come to accept her decision concerning Joe.

Contentment mingled with exhaustion as she closed her eyes and drifted off to sleep. Her subconscious was filled with dreams of Joe and how good it was to have him back in her life.

~ * ~

"Becky's asleep," Emma observed. "I knew she should not have been out here."

"Of course she should, Mama," Herman assured her. "The fresh air is good for her, so is sleep."

"Herman's right," Ralph agreed. "I can understand her frustration at being confined to a bed."

"I think it's time Sergeant Cook and I got back to the post," Major Stone said. "We'll be back the first of the week to get the horses."

"Please stay and have dinner with us," Emma suggested. "I'm certain it's been a long time since either of you has had a good meal."

"I'm afraid you have your hands full already, Ma'am," Sergeant Cook replied. "Not only are your sons home, but you have the two Kemmerman boys. Add us to the group and we'd be too much of an imposition."

"Nonsense. For the past two years I've cared for sixteen patients. I don't think two extra for dinner is anything I can't handle."

"If you insist, Mrs. Larson," Major Stone agreed.

Emma smiled as she got to her feet. It wouldn't take her long to put a meal on the table. From the corner of her eyes, she saw Paul mount Devil and ride the stallion from the paddock. She paused to watch for a moment then saw Joe head for the barn. She doubted if either of them would come to the house for diner.

"Ralph," she heard John say. "You take your sister into the house and I'll give your mother a hand in the kitchen. Herman, you and Major Stone can finalize the deal for the horses. Ed, you and Sergeant Cook best get cleaned up. Your mama won't be happy if you come to the table smelling like a horse."

Emma experienced the warm feeling of family, as she listened to John giving orders to the boys. For a moment, they were all children again and she was their proud mother. A single tear slid from the corner of her eye, as she remembered the one child who wouldn't be sitting at her table today. Her poor Teddy lay in a grave far from home. Did anyone even say a prayer when they laid him to rest? Did they have any idea how many times she had comforted him when he had bad drams and awoke, afraid of the dark?

Are you afraid now? She silently asked.

Although she expected no reply, she could feel his presence and knew he was smiling.

~ * ~

When Joe awoke, he could hear muffled voices coming from the corral. Looking out the door, he saw the Larson boys and Paul standing together.

"We've done a good day's work," Joe heard Ed say. "With the three of us working this afternoon, I count nine horses broken. That makes a total of fifteen."

"But not the fifteen Stone wants," Herman observed. "We've still got another six to break tomorrow. I say we call it a day. We're all tired and we've got chores to do."

"You go ahead with the chores," Paul suggested. "You said it this morning, I'm not a good farmer. I could get another two or three horses broken before dark."

Joe quit listening. Paul made a good argument, but Joe prayed the Larson boys would discourage him. Even though Paul hadn't been sick, he had been injured. Rest was as important to him as it was to Joe.

"I thought I'd find you still sleeping," Paul said, as his head appeared at the top of the ladder.

"I've been awake for a while. Long enough to hear you make some dumb suggestion about breaking horses alone. You know how Pa feels about that."

"Pa's not here. Besides, since when have I given a rat's ass about what he thinks?"

"So, why are you up here and not down in the corral?"

"It seems Herman and Pa think alike. He sent me up here to get you for supper. Since you missed dinner, I agreed with him."

Joe hated to admit it, but he was hungry. He hadn't done anything to account for it, but the thought of one of Emma's meals sounded good.

He ran his fingers through his hair to rid it of any hay clinging to its strands. More than hunger, he longed to see Becky again. She'd looked so beautiful when Herman brought her out to the porch. Even the bandage on her head and the bruise surrounding it filled him with desire.

~ * ~

Becky woke, surprised to be in her own bed. She'd fallen asleep on the porch swing, so how did she get here?

"I see you're awake," her mother observed, when she entered the room. "I told Ralph I didn't think you should have been outside."

"What did Ralph say?"

"He assured me the fresh air would be good medicine. How are you feeling, honey?"

"My head doesn't ache as bad as it did this morning."

"Good. Now, if you're up to some company, I'll have Joe come in and take supper with you."

At the mention of Joe's name, she could feel her body begin to tingle. When she'd been on the porch, they'd talked, but only in polite conversation. She yearned to be alone with him, to talk about the future, their future.

Putting her hand to the bandage on her head, she wished she could get up to wash her face and brush her hair. What would Joe think when he saw her in such disarray?

~ * ~

Joe entered the kitchen, relieved to find only Ralph and his parents there.

"We met up with Captain Courtney on the way here," Ralph said.

Joe realized he'd walked in on an ongoing conversation.

"I've never met a more arrogant man. Did he really think Bek was in love with him?"

Joe stopped in his tracks. He knew Becky and Captain Courtney had met on more than one occasion. What had she done to make the man think she was in love with him?

"Joe," Emma said, "I didn't see you come in."

"What made Courtney think Becky was in love with him? Is there something I should know?" he asked, ignoring Emma's comment.

"I'm certain there's plenty you don't know," Ralph replied. "None of it has anything to do with Becky, though. You might as well sit down. I was just going to tell the folks what I learned from Stone."

Joe pulled out a chair and seated himself at the table. "Did that Yankee officer tell you why they kept us there so long after the war ended?"

"As a matter of fact, he did. It seems Courtney received his promotions in the field. When Stone finally learned the truth, he realized Courtney was illiterate. He depended on the soldiers who delivered the prisoners, to report them to Washington. When you and Paul arrived, he assumed the people who brought you would do as the others had done. Obviously, they were as illiterate as Courtney."

"Why didn't he have Cook or Pometere send the wire?" Joe inquired.

"He didn't want his men to know he couldn't read or write."

"If he couldn't read," John interrupted, "How did he know when to send the prisoners East?"

"That was easy," Ralph continued. "The Army sent out a patrol. There were never any written orders, or if there were, Courtney only pretended to read them."

"So, why did he think Becky would go with him?" Joe asked. "Did she give him any reason to believe she wanted him?"

"Of course not. Stone said Courtney was obsessed with her. Sergeant Cook confirmed it. From the first time Courtney saw Becky, he was certain she wanted him."

"Did she?" Joe asked, almost afraid of the answer.

"How can you ask such a thing?" Emma gasped. "Becky was terrified to be around him. He came here the night before you arrived and insisted he was taking her with him. I don't think I'll ever forget her scream. The only thing I could think to do was to grab John's gun."

To Joe's surprise, Ralph began to laugh. "No wonder he told us the Larsons were all crazy. Somehow, I can't imagine you holding anyone at gunpoint. If he was right about that, Papa must have come at him with a pitchfork."

"Sure did," John replied. "It actually made my stomach churn to see that scum with his hands on my little girl."

"Did he hurt her?" Joe questioned.

"Frightened, is more like it," John replied. "He told her you'd gone back to Texas, and wouldn't be coming back."

Joe ached at the thought of what must have been going through Becky's mind. He'd gone back to the Marrow Place and had, as far as she was concerned, disappeared. What must she have thought when she was told he had left for Texas and gone back on his word?

"Something smells good," Ed commented, causing Joe to abandon his thoughts.

"Supper is ready," Emma announced. "If you boys are cleaned up, just take your places at the table. Joe, I want you to take this tray in to Becky."

The silence following her instructions made Joe uneasy. He was certain she wanted him out of the kitchen and away from her sons who were less than comfortable in his presence.

Without question, he allowed Emma to lead the way through the parlor to the bedroom where Becky lay. Although he'd offered his help in carrying the tray, Emma declined it.

The door to Becky's room stood ajar. Joe expected to see her sleeping soundly. Instead, she sat propped up in bed, wearing the dress he'd seen her in earlier.

"It seems like we've done this before," she said, once her mother set the tray on the bedside table and left the room.

Joe couldn't suppress the smile that crossed his lips. "We have, only I was the one in bed and you were sitting on the chair."

"How did you stand it?"

"What are you talking about?"

"I'm restless and I've only been in bed for one day."

Joe began to laugh. "As I recall, I didn't stand it at all. I got up even when you hated it."

Becky giggled. "I didn't want you to get up because it meant you would have to go back to that place."

"I knew that was what you were thinking. I must admit, I questioned my decision as soon as they put me in that wagon. I knew I'd made a big mistake. I let my guilt over being warm and well cared for cloud my judgment."

"It doesn't matter. We can't change the past. What we need to focus on is the future."

Joe felt uncertainty wash over him, like the waves he'd seen when his father took him to the coast several years earlier.

"Do we have a future, Becky?"

"What do you mean? You came back here rather than go to Texas. Am I mistaken in thinking you came back because of me?"

"You know you're not. It's just..."

"Just what?"

"I can't promise you I'd be content to stay here. In time, I will be going back to Texas. I'm not a farmer."

"Did I ask you to stay?"

"No, but your brothers and parents might have other ideas."

Becky reached out to take his hand then pressed it to her lips. "Why don't you ask me what I want?"

"Because I don't want to pressure you into a decision you may come to regret."

"Are you saying you'll be going home soon?"

"I won't leave until I've had time to court you properly. We don't even know each other, not really. I can't leave without getting to know you better, without giving you the chance to make a decision we can both live with."

~ * ~

Paul stepped out onto the porch. For the first time, he could sympathize with the hands at the ranch when his pa decided to take meals with them.

The Larsons, at least the parents, seemed like logical people. They'd tried to make him comfortable.

"Care for a smoke?" Ed asked, just before the door leading to the kitchen slammed.

Paul turned then smiled as Ed offered him a cigar.

"I haven't had one of these since before I left for the war," Paul commented, inhaling the rich aroma of the tightly wrapped leaves.

Ed had already lit his cigar when Paul bit off one end then held a match to the other and took a deep drag until it ignited. He enjoyed the heady sensation now, as he had in the past.

"What's he like?" Ed asked.

"Who?"

"Your brother. What's he like?"

"I used to think he was a snot nosed kid. Now I think he's a hard headed fool."

"It sounds like you're talking about Becky. When I left, she was a little girl. Now that I'm back she's become a strong willed woman. I think Ralph and Herman had their hands full with her."

"Only Ralph and Herman, why not you?"

"I'm closer to her age. I saw enough during the war not to question what she'd become or why. Did you kill anyone?"

Paul shook his head. "Hell, I only saw one battle and then we were outnumbered. If I fired three times, I was lucky. What about you?"

"More than I care to count. I can still remember the first one, though. He was a kid, not much older than Teddy. He came at me with a bayonet. I didn't have a choice. I tried to tell him I was sorry, but he was talking. He said he didn't know it would hurt so bad then he died. I saw him die every time I fired my gun."

"I know what you mean. I might not have killed anyone, but I saw my friends die. I knew they had families. Until Joe got sick, I never thought Yankees had families like we did."

Ed took a long drag on his cigar. "How will your folks take to Becky?"

Paul ran his fingers through his hair. "Ma's been gone for seven years now. As for Pa, he'll love her. She's the kind of woman he'll take to."

"What about you? How will you feel with Becky sharing your home?"

"I have nothing to say about it. As soon as Joe is home, I'm striking out on my own. What I want, I can't find on the Lazy K. Let's just leave it at that."

Paul turned away from the porch. As he did, the kitchen door opened and Joe came out of the house.

"Becky's sleeping. I think it's time I did the same."

Paul turned to face his brother. The smile on Joe's face betrayed the emotions reeling in his mind. Any further attempt to change his decision about Becky would be fruitless. The fight, for Joe, would now be between himself and her brothers.

Fourteen

"What do you mean you're going home?" Joe asked Paul the day after the last of the horses were broken.

"Just that. You don't need me here. I've done what I could to help the Larsons out. As far as I'm concerned, the debt is paid. I'm hoping you'll come to your senses and come back with me."

Joe could hardly believe his ears. "How can you ask me to leave without Becky?"

"There's no use trying to talk sense to you. If you can't feel the hatred of the people here, I can't change your mind. God knows I've tried."

"If you're so damned worried about me, why leave? Do you think Pa is going to welcome you with open arms if you go home alone?"

As soon as he spoke the words, he wished he could take them back. The hurt he saw in his brother's eyes made him sick to his stomach. The words were unnecessary. There was no need to remind Paul of their father's contempt for him.

"I'm sorry. I didn't mean..."

"I know you didn't. Of course, we both know you only spoke the truth. Pa and I will never be the best of friends. I'll stay on the Lazy K until you get back then I plan to strike out on my own."

A call from below the loft interrupted their conversation. Joe could hardly believe his ears when he recognized Becky's voice.

Without further comment on Paul's statement, Joe hurried down the ladder from the loft to the main floor of the barn. Seeing her standing there caused a flood of worry to encompass his mind.

"What are you doing out here?" he questioned.

"Mama sent me out to call you in for breakfast."

"You know what I mean. Should you be out of bed?"

Becky laughed and he enjoyed the sound of it. "Tom came out early this morning and said there's no reason for me to stay in bed any longer."

"It's good to see you out of bed, Becky," Paul said, as he came down the ladder.

Once Paul left the barn, Joe took Becky in his arms. "I can't believe we're finally alone," he said, before kissing her tenderly.

"I'm afraid privacy is a luxury we won't be getting much of around here," Becky whispered, once they broke apart. "Mama wants you to..."

Joe silenced her with another kiss. Having her in his arms was a dream come true. He knew going to the house would put an end to this anticipated pleasure.

Without warning, someone clutched his shoulder and pulled him away from Becky. "Get your stinking hands off my sister, Reb," Herman shouted.

Startled, Joe opened his eyes to see the enraged man standing in front of him. He hardly saw the punch that landed him on his backside on the barn floor.

"Stop it, Herman!" Becky shouted, stepping between Joe and his tormentor.

"I can fight my own battles," Joe said, scrambling to his feet, his hands balled into tight fists.

"There are no battles here," John bellowed from the doorway. "I figured there would be trouble out here when I saw Herman leave the house. Now, all of you get up to the kitchen. Your mama has breakfast ready and it won't be good if it gets cold."

Joe watched as Becky skirted around Herman and her father then hurried toward the house. It came as no surprise when Herman stood his ground.

"I said get up to the house," John repeated.

"Stay out of this, Papa," Herman declared. "If this Reb thinks he's going to come in here and just walk off with Bek, he'd better be prepared to fight. I didn't spend all that time in the war to lose my sister to a stinking Reb scum like him."

The thought of physical combat with Herman, under normal circumstances, was ridiculous. The man had at least thirty pounds on him, to say nothing of three inches. considering his reduced stamina, he knew he could be seriously injured.

"I don't want to fight you with my fists," Joe declared, as he unclenched his hands. "I love Becky. I don't know how I'm going to prove it to you, but I will. I've verbally and physically fought my own brother over this. It was the hardest thing I've ever had to do, but Becky is worth any sacrifice I have to make."

"Listen to him, Son," John advised, walking further into the barn to stand between the two of them. "Joe damn near died in that camp. None of us knew if he would live or die for the first several days he was here. He says he loves your sister. I say they don't know each other enough to even recognize love. If I had my way, I would have moved heaven and earth to keep him from coming back here, but that would have been selfish."

Herman seemed to relax slightly. "What do you mean, selfish?"

"I think you know what I mean. Joe rubs you the wrong way because of what you've been through. He's special to Becky for the same reason. When you boys went off to war, she gave up her childhood. When she should have been courted, she was milking cows, planting crops, breaking horses and being a nursemaid. Don't you think she deserves happiness?"

"Happiness? With the likes of him? I'd rather see her dead."

Herman's statement made Joe's blood boil. "Do you think I would have ever come back here if I didn't think I could make her happy? I knew it wouldn't be easy. Paul told me as much every day since I left here. I've weighed every argument. No matter what it takes, I want Becky to be my wife."

"What you want and what will happen are two different things. There's more than one way to beat you. I plan to change my sister's mind before she makes the biggest mistake of her life."

Herman turned and stormed out of the barn, leaving Joe alone with John.

"You knew it wouldn't be easy," John commented. "I happen to agree with you. Becky is worth whatever it takes to win her over. I just hope you're up to it."

~ * ~

Becky glanced back toward the barn. The angry words drifting on the air disturbed her. Herman's ire frightened her.

"Hey, slow down, baby sister," Ralph said, when she almost bumped into him on the porch. "What's going on out there?"

"Herman's going to fight Joe. My god, Ralph, he'll kill him. Joe's never regained his strength. He's no match for Herman."

217

"Papa won't let it happen. You go on into the kitchen. I'll go out and see what I can do toward keeping the peace. If we leave Ed at the table too long, there won't be anything left for the rest of us."

Ralph gave her a quick hug and a peck on the cheek, before heading toward the barn.

Tears cascaded down Becky's cheeks as she went into the kitchen. Wiping them away with the back of her hand, she took her chair at the table.

"What's wrong, Sis?" Ed asked, putting his arm around her shoulders. "Did Joe hurt you?"

His question caught her off guard. Before she could answer, Paul got to his feet.

"It's not Joe, is it? It's Herman. What's he done to my brother?"

"They were going to fight," she sobbed. "Ralph says Papa won't let it happen, but..."

"Ralph's right, Sis," Ed interrupted. "Sit down, Paul. If Joe wants to be part of this family, he's going to have to learn how to deal with Herman. We've had all our lives to figure out how to deal with him. If this is meant to be, Joe will, too."

Listen to him, little sister, Teddy's voice sounded in her mind. *All of this has to happen. You need to see if Joe can stand up to the prejudices of this family.*

The door opened and Ralph entered, followed by Herman and her father. It wasn't until Joe came into the kitchen that she realized she'd been holding her breath.

"Are those tears in your eyes?" Joe asked.

Becky nodded.

"There's no need for you to cry, Bek," Herman said. "I didn't hurt your precious Reb. Papa made it seem as though it wasn't worth my time. I'm certain he'll come to see the logic of it by himself."

"I've heard enough of this argument," Emma declared. "We'll speak of this no more until the meal is finished, and not in my presence."

A strained tension settled over the table. To Becky's surprise, it was Joe who broke the silence.

"Paul says since all your horses are broken, he's leaving for Texas today."

"So soon?" Becky questioned.

"It's time," Paul said.

"Just how are you getting there?" John asked.

Becky watched as Paul's eyes filled with questions. "I'm going to ride Devil. I thought you said he was mine."

"Of course, he is. I know you have the means to go, but how do you plan to survive? It's a long trip. You'll need to eat."

"If we hadn't come here, I would have survived by scavenging, like the other Confederate prisoners of war we were with."

"I will not have one of MY boys scavenging," Emma declared. "We've talked it over and although we don't have much, we can offer to give you some money toward the trip."

"I couldn't take your money. We've taken too much already."

Becky again held her breath. She understood both sides of the argument. Her parents certainly couldn't afford to part with any of their money, while on the other hand, Paul couldn't make the trip without food. Her father's response caused her to exhale with relief at the prudence of his words.

"Emma's right. You've worked hard for us. Devil definitely belongs to you, since if you hadn't broken him, I'd have put him down. As for the tack, Ed told me he gave it to you, since he wanted to get a new saddle anyway. As far as I see it, we still owe you. If you want to call it a loan, so be it. I have no doubt about it being paid back."

Joe began to laugh. "It's good to see you finally out common sensed. You know I wrote to Pa asking him to send us some funds. That loan will be paid back before you ever get home. Don't get me wrong, I certainly can't say I want to see you go, but I'd be a lot happier seeing you make the trip with enough money to see you through."

Becky couldn't help but smile when Paul finally agreed. She could see the disapproval in Herman's eyes, but for once he was outnumbered.

~ * ~

Without further argument, Paul prepared to leave. Shortly after breakfast, he was on his way and Joe felt the emptiness of loss.

After his confrontation with Herman, he questioned his decision to stay and court Becky. As much as he loved her, he wondered how he could ever hope to fight Herman. Eventually, the two of them would be alone and open hostilities would break out.

"Mama wants us to go berry picking," Becky said, when she stepped out onto the porch, a basket in hand.

"Berry picking? Isn't it a little early for summer berries to be ripe?"

"I'm not talking about raspberries. There's a patch of wild strawberries down by the creek. They should be ripening about now. She also wants us to go asparagus hunting. We should find enough for supper in the same area."

Joe got to his feet, puzzled by the normalcy of Becky's suggestion. He had no idea what strawberries and asparagus were, but if Emma Larson insisted on having them, they must be good.

The creek was but a short walk from the house. Even so, it was the first time Joe had been there. He found the lazy flow of water, combined with the sweet song of the birds, to be relaxing. If the weather were warmer, he would have enjoyed a leisurely swim in the cold water.

"Do you swim?" Becky asked, as though reading his mind.

"Only when the river is high enough and the work is done."

"In the summer we come here after church on Sundays. Mama packs a picnic lunch and we all come here to go swimming. I was about five when Ralph and Herman taught me how to swim. As I recall, they carried me out to the middle and dropped me in."

Joe recalled Luke doing the same thing to him when he was about the same age. "Frightening wasn't it," he commented.

"It certainly was. Did the same thing happen to you?" Becky asked, as she set the basket on a rock and sank to the ground.

Joe quickly seated himself next to her. "I was about five when Luke decided it was time for me to learn to swim. I can remember thinking I was going to die."

"But you didn't," Becky commented. "I'm glad you survived the ordeal."

"Me too. I learned to swim, but I thought Pa was going to kill Luke. Ma wouldn't let me out of her sight for a week."

Becky began to laugh. "It sounds like she was very protective. At least Mama understood. She did ban Ralph and Herman from swimming for the rest of the day."

Joe took Becky in his arms and kissed her. Their shared experience gave them a surprising bond. As the youngest in their families, they had both been protected, sometimes with embarrassing outcomes.

At the height of their passion, Joe eased her back until they lay on the soft sweet grass. His hand caressed the swell of her breasts. Beneath the fabric of her dress, he could feel the taut nub of her nipple.

"This is wrong."

"How can something that feels so good be wrong?" he whispered in her ear.

"We aren't married. Things like this..."

He silenced her with another kiss. As much as he wanted to explore further, he moved his hands to Becky's back and pulled her into a tighter embrace. Instinctively, he opened his mouth slightly and ran his tongue over her lips. The sweetness of them made him yearn for more than she was ready to give.

When at last he broke the embrace, he rolled onto his back and stared up at the cloudless sky.

"I'm sorry," she said.

He didn't have to look at her to know she was crying. "You have nothing to be sorry about," he assured her. "You were right. Things like this are best reserved for marriage. I just don't know how we'll ever convince your family we should be together."

"We'll find a way," she assured him. "For now, we'd better do some berry picking before one of the boys comes looking for us."

Reluctantly, Joe got to his feet then he helped Becky get up. He didn't want the moment of closeness to end yet he knew it must. To continue would be like playing with fire. The taste of her lips made him want to claim every inch of her. He wanted to make Becky his own, for now and always.

"I knew they'd be ripe!"

Joe looked up and saw Becky kneeling beside a patch of green foliage. As he came closer, he saw red berries nestled in the green leaves with delicate white flowers standing in direct contrast to the fruit.

"So, those are strawberries," he commented, as he squatted next to her.

A look of amazement crossed her face. "You really haven't ever had strawberries before, have you?'

"Never."

"Well, there's no time like the present to find out what you've been missing."

He watched as she plucked one of the red berries from its nest among the green foliage. She nipped off the green cap then held it to his lips.

Like a bird waiting for its mother to feed it, he obediently opened his mouth. The rough texture of the fruit on his tongue was intriguing. Tentatively, he grazed his teeth across the surface, relishing the sweet juice. He wished he could hold the berry in his mouth forever, but the urge to chew and swallow overshadowed his desire.

Becky put her finger to his lips to wipe away the remaining juice then allowed him to lick it from her fingertip. "I must assume you liked it," she teased.

"Delicious doesn't seem to be enough to describe it. Do these grow wild, or did you plant them?"

"Mama keeps threatening to dig them up and replant them closer to the house, but never does. There are three patches all close to the creek. They're just starting to come on now. Once they start bearing at their peak, Mama and I will make strawberry jelly."

Becky's reference to doing daily chores with her mother sobered Joe. In Texas, there would be no jelly making with Emma. Was everyone right? Did he have the right to turn her life upside down because he loved her? Could she survive in Texas away from her family?

"Hello, are you with me?"

Becky's teasing tone cut into his thoughts. "I'm sorry. I was thinking about what you said. How would you feel about being away from your mother? Texas is a long way from Illinois."

"Is that why you got so quiet all of a sudden?"

"I guess so."

"Don't worry so much. I'm certain there are things I can do with Maria. Mama understands love."

Listen to Becky, Luke's voice of reason said. *She has given much thought to what will happen if she goes to the Lazy K with you. Her feelings are the least of your problems. Her Yankee brothers will be the ones you need to worry about.*

Fifteen

Becky watched as the return of her brothers changed the lives of everyone on the farm.

Although Ralph had voiced his opinion of her feelings for Joe in his letters, he seemed to have softened. With Joe's body obviously weakened by the pneumonia, Ralph became preoccupied with Joe's care. Since returning Ralph's actions showed his determination to become a doctor. Tom had been only too happy to use his influence with a medical school in Chicago to help Ralph get accepted.

To Becky's dismay, the war hardened Herman. It was evident he'd become obsessed with one day owning the farm. With Ralph more interested in medicine than farming, he posed no threat to Herman's ambitions. It pleased Becky to see him taking over the everyday business of running the farm and lessening the burden from her father.

Surprisingly, it was Ed who posed the biggest problem. He wanted to be a farmer just as badly as Herman. Had it not been for the situation with Joe, there might have been a confrontation. Even though the boys' opinion of Joe upset her, she knew it kept open hostilities from breaking out.

With the boys preoccupied with their own drives and ambitions, Becky found time to be alone with Joe. Their long walks down by the creek gave them the opportunity to get to know each other better. Each time he took her in his arms, she had trouble not allowing the liberties she knew were forbidden.

~ * ~

In the three weeks since Paul went back to Texas, Joe felt the loss of his brother's companionship. After so many months of being confined in such close quarters, the loft above the Larson's barn seemed very lonely.

He wished he knew what happened when Paul arrived at the Lazy K. He'd had plenty of time to get there. Joe couldn't help but wonder how his father had reacted to Paul arriving home alone.

Joe prayed the letter he'd written just after his release softened his father. He'd tried to explain Paul's hunger for an education, as well, as his own desire to run the Lazy K.

He finished dressing then climbed down the ladder to the main floor of the barn. As he turned toward the door, he saw the harnesses he'd been mending for the past two weeks. For an instant, Joe wanted to rip them from the wall. Although they needed minor repair, they could have waited. He knew Herman insisted they be mended to pacify Becky.

"It's certainly a beautiful morning," Ralph greeted Joe as he walked out into the bright sunlight.

"Sure is," Joe replied. "Guess I can plan on mending more harnesses." He knew his voice sounded sarcastic, but he didn't care.

"Not today. I'm going to town after breakfast. I thought you might like to ride along."

Ralph's offer puzzled Joe. "You go into town every day and you've never asked me to go with you before. What makes today so special?"

Ralph shrugged. "Nothing really. I just thought you'd like a change of pace. Besides, Tom said he'd like to see you."

"Why is it I don't believe that's the only reason?"

"I don't know why you would think such a thing," Ralph commented, with a shrug of his shoulders.

Joe watched as Ralph walked past him to enter the house. There was something more to Ralph's invitation than showed on the surface.

Inside, everyone was gathered around the table. No matter how many times Joe sat down to eat with them, he knew he would never feel either comfortable or accepted.

"What time will the Clarks be here?" Herman asked, once John finished grace.

The question caused Joe to look up from his breakfast. No wonder Ralph asked him to go into town. They were ashamed to have the neighbors see him.

"They said they'd be over about nine," Ed replied. "I certainly hope they haven't changed their minds."

Joe couldn't stand to listen to the conversation. Instead, he pushed back his chair, leaving his food untouched.

"If you're expecting company, I'd best go out and saddle up one of the horses. I certainly don't want to be an embarrassment to your friends."

"Whatever are you talking about?" Emma questioned.

"Ralph suggested I go into town with him today. I thought it was a bit strange, but now it all makes sense. I would have made myself scarce if you'd asked."

"It's not the way it looks," Becky assured him. "Please sit down and eat your breakfast while we explain."

"What's there to explain? I don't blame you for not wanting me to meet your friends. Feelings about Rebs must run pretty high around here."

"I know how this might look to you," John said. "Like Becky says, let us explain."

Joe sat back down, out of courtesy for John, and waited for him to make sense of the situation.

"Irv and Gertie Clark have been neighbors for years. Gertie was a Marrow, Bert and Amy's only child. When they died, she inherited the farm. It was assumed their youngest son, Merrill, was going to run it, but the war changed all that. He was killed at Gettysburg. During the war, Irv and Gertie let the land lay, since they couldn't run both places. When the Army wanted to use the buildings, they didn't object."

Joe shook his head in bewilderment. "I still don't understand," he interrupted.

"As it stands now, their son, Vince, will be running the home place," John continued. "That leaves them with two farms. Last week after church, they happened to mention they wanted to sell it. Since Ed has decided he wants his own place, we invited them over to talk about it. We thought you might be uncomfortable, considering what you went through out there."

Joe began to laugh. "Did you think I would hold the owners of the land to blame for what happened to me? The land had nothing to do with what the Yankee guards did. I thank you for your concern on my behalf, but it's unnecessary. As for Ralph's suggestion, I will be going with him. I think it's high time I went to see Dr. Morgan, instead of the other way around."

The tension seemed to drain from the table conversation. Although Joe appeared to accept the explanation of the situation, he harbored doubts about it. Instead of speaking out further, he kept quiet.

With breakfast finished, he went back to the barn. The sooner he saddled the horses, the sooner he could leave for town. He had no desire to meet the people who owned the Marrow place.

As soon as he stepped into the barn, he became aware of the heaviness of the air. Dust particles danced in the shaft of sunlight coming through the windows. Back home, where the air was drier, the dust would certainly settle more quickly.

In the back of his throat, a dry tickle grew more and more irritating. Unable to control it any longer, he began to cough. He hated the feeling over which he had no control. He knew before it was over, tears would form in his eyes and his chest would ache from the exertion.

~ * ~

Becky stepped out onto the porch. Joe's confrontation with the family at the breakfast table bothered her. Originally, she'd agreed it would be best if Joe were spared the meeting to discuss the Marrow Place. Now she questioned her decision.

The thought of Ed running the farm, living in the house upset her. How could she ever think of it as Ed's home, when she equated it with Delos Courtney?

In the distance, she saw a carriage as well as a rider approaching the house. The rider waved and spurred his horse to a fast trot.

Becky couldn't help the smile tugging at the corners of her mouth when she recognized Vince Clark. He had often come to the farm as a boy when he and Herman were growing up together. As a child, she fancied herself in love with both the Clark boys. The love of childhood had given way to the desire of maturity when she met Joe. Still, just seeing her lifelong friend made her heart pound faster.

"Becky, Becky Larson, when did you grow up?" Vince asked, as he dismounted.

It took only a few steps for him to join her on the porch. To her surprise, he swept her into his arms and kissed her on the lips.

"My memory of you kept me going all through the war," he said, once he released her.

"Now, how could that be, Vincent Clark?" Becky questioned as she removed his arms from around her waist. "As I recall, you used to find ways to avoid me. Why would a pesky child keep you going all the time you were gone?"

"Maybe it didn't, but seeing you now, it should have. You grew up in all the right places. I'll just have to ask your father if I can court you."

"Haven't you heard, Vince, I'm spoken for. As soon as Dr. Morgan says Joe is well enough to make the trip back to Texas, we're going to be married."

"I heard about you and that Reb. I didn't believe it, though, not with all your brothers off fighting and Teddy being…"

"Stop it, Vince! The war is over. Stop fighting it. Joe is no different than any of you."

"Isn't he?" Vince shouted back. "He's a Reb. I fought the likes of him. His kind killed Merrill and Teddy. He's probably waiting for the right time to sneak into the house and kill all of you in your sleep."

Becky became aware of not only the Clarks, but her own brothers listening to their conversation. "Joe is not a hardened killer. Maybe you'd be tempted to kill someone who befriended you because they had family fighting on the other side, but Joe isn't you."

Without waiting for anyone to answer her accusations, Becky brushed past Vince and ran toward the security of the creek. She didn't care what anyone thought of her. She was tired of defending her emotions. What these people thought was no longer important to her. When she and Joe could be alone, she would insist they leave as soon as their wedding could take place.

~ * ~

Joe led the chestnut mare from the barn. As he stepped into the sunlight, he saw a rider coming toward the house. A glance over his shoulder told Joe the man had seen Becky and was hurrying to get to her. As soon as he dismounted, he rushed up the steps to embrace and kiss her.

The alien feeling of jealousy nipped at his heart. Here was a man whom Becky had known all her life. Would his return from the war rekindle a spark of love in Becky's heart?

Whatever it meant, Joe certainly didn't want to stand here and witness Becky's pleasure at the man's attentions. He knew how she felt in his arms, how she would feel in this stranger's arms. He could almost taste the sweetness of her lips as he turned away from the scene unfolding before him.

Without waiting for Ralph, he mounted the mare and rode toward town.

"Hold up!" Joe heard Ralph shout from behind him.

Joe reined his horse to a halt and waited for Ralph to catch up.

"What spooked you? You took off like a bat out of hell."

"I saw those folks coming up to the house. I decided it was best if I made myself scarce and not embarrass Becky."

"I know what you saw and it wasn't Irv and Gertie. You taking off like that had nothing to do with Becky's feelings did it? I saw Vince kiss her. I also heard her tell him she was spoken for."

"I'm sure that didn't make your brother none to happy. It would please him to no end if I disappeared and left Becky forever."

"Don't be so hard on Herman. He's softening toward you. Just give him time. He did find something to keep you busy these past few weeks."

"Mending harnesses that don't need mending sure did keep me busy. The only reason he did it was to make Becky happy. It's all right though, I don't have the strength to do much more. You know about these things, Ralph, why do I get so tired?

Why does climbing up to the loft exhaust me? Why do I cough until my chest aches?"

"You're asking questions I have no answers for. Tom is the one who would know."

Joe noticed a tone of sadness in Ralph's voice. The man was hungry for the knowledge of healing and disappointed by the fact he couldn't answer Joe's questions.

The sleepy Mid-western town came into view. Joe found it a far cry from the bustling cow towns of Texas that he was used to.

Ever since Ralph first mentioned taking Joe with him, Joe had tried to imagine what it would be like to go into town again. He expected it to be like going home. The excitement of seeing cowhands on the streets and people milling around the railhead; was soon replaced by the peaceful scene before him.

Farm wagons lumbered down the main street that boasted a large meeting hall, bank, general store, feed mill, seamstress shop, haberdashery, small cafe and Dr. Morgan's office. Isolated at the far end of the street, Joe saw a saloon, only Ralph called it a tavern and referred to it with disgust.

After pointing to the sights, Ralph rode up to the general store and tied his horse to the railing in front. Joe followed his lead then stepped onto the wooden sidewalk.

"Jed and Effie Pratt own the store," Ralph told him. "They do just about everything from handing out the mail to tending the apothecary."

Joe looked around at the bins of flour and sugar, as well as the tables of yard goods. Tins of food lined the shelves behind the counter, while jars of penny candy stood to tempt even the oldest of children.

"Good morning," the woman behind the counter greeted them.

Joe assessed the woman. She was in her late fifties, with a face that would stop an eight-day clock, as his father would say. Her nose was too long and pointed, her eyes seemed to bulge from her head, but her outgoing personality made up for it.

"I bet you came for the mail," she continued. "Today, I think I've got what you've been waiting for. I got something for Becky's Reb, too."

"Becky's Reb, as you call him, is right here," Ralph said, pushing Joe toward the woman. "Effie Pratt, this is Joe Kemmerman. I thought he might like to come with me today. Guess the timing was right."

Joe chafed at being called Becky's Reb, all the while knowing that was exactly how these people saw him.

"Nice to meet you, Son," Effie said, her strained voice in direct contrast to the smile on her face.

"Jeb and Effie lost two sons in the war, Joe," Ralph explained.

"I'm sorry Ma'am," Joe replied, as he shook the woman's hand. "I lost a brother myself. Then I was fool enough to go to war. Guess we don't always learn from other's mistakes."

"No, Son, I guess we don't. I have a letter for you, all the way from Texas."

She turned from them to sort through the pile of envelopes on the back counter. "Here they are," Effie continued. "One from Texas for Joe Kemmerman, and one from Chicago for you, Ralph. It looks like it's from that medical school you wrote to. I hope it's good news."

"I do too, Effie," Ralph said, as he accepted the letter.

Joe watched as Ralph fingered the envelope. It was evident Effie wanted him to open it. Instead, he stuffed it into his shirt pocket.

"You tell your mama I miss seeing her," Effie commented, once she realized Ralph had no intention of revealing the contents of the letter to her.

"With everyone home, she's in seventh heaven," Ralph replied, with a laugh.

"And your father, how is he?"

"He's finally getting some time to relax, and grumbling about it. I do see him heading toward the river with his fishing pole, though."

When at last they said their good-byes, Ralph and Joe went out onto the sidewalk. Let's go to the cafe," Ralph suggested. "I could use some pie and coffee."

Joe didn't argue. He'd hardly touched his breakfast and the thought of getting something to eat sounded good.

"Morning, Ralph," the woman who ran the cafe called, as they entered. "Your usual this morning?"

"Sure, Lottie, and the same for my friend."

"You must come here a lot," Joe commented, once the woman gave Ralph a wink and a smile then went to what Joe assumed was the kitchen.

"I usually stop in the morning. I meet some friends, do some talking, and see Lottie."

"She must be special."

"She is. Her husband and I were best friends before the war. He wanted to go and fight, but he got sick before he could enlist. He died just after I left. There was nothing Tom could do. It all came on too fast. Guess it's one reason I want to be a doctor. With all the new advances, maybe I can help someone else."

"You said she's special. Is it just because she was married to your best friend?"

"At first it was. Now I'm not so sure. I'm trying to get up the nerve to ask her to marry me when I'm done with school. I don't know if I have the right to ask her to wait."

"Ask who to wait?" Lottie questioned as she sat the pie and coffee on the table.

"We'll talk about it later," Ralph replied.

"Just make certain you don't forget. You've got my curiosity up." Lottie winked broadly before she left their table.

Joe knew it would take little persuasion on Ralph's part to get Lottie to say yes to marriage.

"This town is so different from home," he commented, once he tasted his pie and coffee.

"How so?" Ralph questioned.

"Your streets are dirt, but they aren't dusty. You get enough rain to keep the dust down. You've got sidewalks, real wooden sidewalks. We had them, but they seemed to keep getting busted up. It's hard to keep them in good repair when some dimwitted cowboys insist on riding their horses across them. The biggest difference is, it's quiet."

"Isn't Texas quiet?"

"You ride into a town like this and there's usually some cowhand with money in his pocket and bullets in his gun. Saturday nights are the worst. Someone's always got hands in town with more money than brains. They get liquored up and decide to shoot daylight through anyone or anything that gets in the way."

"How good are you with a gun, Joe?"

"I'm not the best, not the worst either. I can hold my own in a fight. You have to know how to use a gun back home."

"Will you teach Becky how to use a gun?"

"I think so, if for no other reason than protection. Snakes are the worst, but unless their riled, they won't hurt you none. If she wants a weapon of her own, I'll get her one of those ladies guns."

"What about your mother? Could she shoot?"

"My ma wasn't Becky. She wouldn't set foot out of the house unless every hair was in place and her dress was perfect. She never rode a horse or drove her own carriage into town."

"And Maria?"

"She ain't quite like Ma. She's not above driving herself to town, but I've never seen her ride a horse. I doubt if she's ever touched a gun."

"What's she like?"

"Maria is Maria. It would be like asking you what your ma is like. I love her. She raised me. I was only ten when Ma died. Maria gives our family a bit of spice and a lot of heritage."

"What do you mean?"

"Ma was English. She had a certain air of dignity. I guess you'd call her regal. Pa is German, French and Indian. My great grandma was a Sioux princess and my great grandpa came from Paris, France, by way of Canada. It was an interesting mix. My grandma was their only child and Pa says she was a perfect mix of old world and new. Grandpa Kemmerman came from Germany. He ran away from home at the age of fourteen, to start a life in the new world. Maria made sure Pa told us about where they all came from. She says it's proper to know one's background."

Talking about home depressed Joe. He lapsed into silence as he drank his coffee. In his mind, he saw a far away scene from home. How would Becky fit in with her Scandinavian background? Would the Lazy K be enough for her? Did he have any right to take her away from her family, from the young man who was so excited to see her?

Drawing himself back to the present, he watched as Ralph opened and read the letter he'd received. As he did, a smile brightened his face.

"Good news?" Joe inquired.

"They've accepted me for the fall session. I have to go to Chicago a couple of weeks before it starts and take some tests. They're certain I can skip several of the courses because of my experience. I really am going to be a doctor."

"That's great news, Ralph. It's good to see someone get the education they deserve. Will you be able to afford it?"

"I think so, Tom's working on a scholarship for me. He's got some pull, since he went to school there. It's a good time for me. Because of the war, they didn't get many people to go on with their education. With the training I got in the Army, I shouldn't have any trouble getting help."

Joe nodded. He wished it would be as easy for Paul. Ralph would have his family to back him up, but what would Paul have? Whatever education he got would have to be on his own.

"What about your letter, Joe? Shouldn't you open it."

Ralph's questions caused Joe to reach for the envelope in his pocket. "I suppose so," he said, reaching for a knife from the table.

After slitting open the envelope. He began to read the letter out loud, as if by doing so, he could soften the harsh words he knew his father had written.

Dear Joe,

Your letter was so welcome. Paul hasn't returned home yet, but we expect him any day. As for the money he owes the Larson's consider it paid. I'm enclosing a draft and extra to help you pay your way as well.

Maria says we should thank God for the Larsons, but you know me and that Old Man ain't exactly on speaking terms. No matter what, we owe those folks more than we can ever begin to repay.

I look forward to when you and Becky return to the Lazy K. When you do, there will be some big changes. I'm already looking into sending Paul to school. I never realized how much he wanted an education. Just because Paul is going to school, doesn't mean the opportunity isn't still there for you. My offer still stands.

Your Loving Father

Joe put the letter down, momentarily stunned by its content.

"Draft?" Ralph questioned, returning Joe to his senses. "I thought everybody in the South..."

"Turned their money into Confederate script? Joe asked, finishing Ralph's sentence, as a question. "Not my Pa. He kept his money in Yankee gold. Texas is a funny place. Some fought for the North, others for the South. I guess we chose the South 'cause Ma came from Virginia. Pa never had any confidence in the Confederacy. He called it a flash in the pan. All through the war, both kinds of money were accepted, along with Mexican pesos. Texas is a strange land. The Comanche run free in the wilder sections, there are Mexicans but mostly they'r all Texicans from almost every country you can name. You must remember, Texas has been under many flags, Spain, Mexico, and the United States, not to mention being republic and ruling themselves. It's a strange mix, but one that works."

"Are you a Texican, Joe?"

"Guess I am. One of the originals you might say."

Ralph pushed back his chair then got to his feet. "I'm going over to the mill. Do you want to come with me?"

"I don't think so. I want to cash this draft at the bank then go to see Dr. Morgan. After that I'd like some time alone, to think. You go back to the farm. I'll come along when I'm ready. If I'm not there for supper, tell your ma not to worry."

"I don't like the thought of you riding home alone," Ralph said, concern sounding in his voice.

"I'm a big boy. I doubt if I'll have any problem finding my way back to the farm. I know what you're thinking. I promise I won't overdo."

Sixteen

Joe watched as Ralph headed toward the mill. As he did, he saw Ralph glance over his shoulder then turn and shake his head as if in dismay over Joe's decision to stay in town.

This morning's conversation with Ralph left Joe with more questions than answers. What right did he have to take Becky away from everything and everyone she loved? How could he hope to compete with the young men she'd known all her life?

I'm a damn poor substitute, he thought to himself. *I can hardly do a lick of work without feeling like I got a horse sitting on my chest.*

He looked down at the envelope in his hand then made his way toward the bank in order to cash the draft it contained.

The teller looked at him with distrust, but once assured the paper Joe handed him was good, counted out the money.

"Much obliged," Joe said, as he touched the brim of his hat.

The teller mumbled something about having to serve a no good Reb. The words hurt, but Joe didn't let it show.

With his business at the bank finished, Joe walked next door to Dr. Morgan's office. A little bell, fastened above the door, jingled merrily as he entered.

"I'll be right out," Dr. Morgan called.

Joe waited only a few minutes for Dr. Morgan to come from the back and meet him in the waiting room.

"It's good to see you, Joe," Tom said, breaking into a wide smile as he shook Joe's hand.

"It's good to see you, too," Joe agreed. "I've come to settle my account."

"Your what?"

"My account, Doc."

"You don't owe me anything. The Army paid me for the care you received while you were at the Larsons."

"That might be the case, Doc, but the way I see it, I owe you a lot. I just got a draft from my pa. I owe you much more than money. How much is a life worth?" Leaving his question hanging between them, he reached into his pocket and counted out fifty dollars. Laying it on the desk, he continued. "I hope this covers it."

"Of course it does, but..."

"No buts, Doc. Now we're square, even. From now on I'll pay as I go."

"I have no doubts you will. I just don't understand."

"There's no reason for you to understand, especially since I don't understand any of this myself. Now I want the truth. Fifty dollars ought to buy me the answers I want."

"I've never told you anything but the truth."

Tom's words sounded hollow. For weeks Joe had anticipated good health. Anticipation had turned to concern as the days passed with no improvement. "I'm not getting any better, am I Doc?"

Joe wouldn't have had to hear Tom's answer. The expression on the man's face said more than any words. "No, Joe, you aren't. For one thing you don't follow instructions. For another, you need to get back to Texas."

"What do you mean I don't follow instructions?"

"If I had my way, you would have been in bed for at least two solid weeks. Instead, you insisted on staying in the hayloft and being up and around after the first day, because you felt better. I know you've been mending harnesses. You may not think it's strenuous work, but it's more than you should be doing. You're not in bed and you're definitely not resting. That's what I meant when I said you don't follow instructions."

Joe opened his mouth to protest, but Tom held up his hand as a signal for silence.

"If you would have rested, you might have been well by now. You'll probably never be as strong as you once were. It won't be easy, but it's something you have to face up to. Unfortunately, no one can help you come to grips with this, but yourself."

Joe hung his head, shamed by the truth he'd asked for. "What do you think I should do?"

"You need to get back to Texas. I've done a lot of reading and I've learned Texas is much drier than Illinois. In order for you to heal, you need to get back to a drier climate. I only hoped you and Becky were getting married sooner than you planned."

Joe contemplated Tom's answer. He needed time to think, time to decide what to do. "I thank you, Doc, I really do. I'll be seeing you."

"Think about what I said, Joe. You don't have to prove anything to the Larons. They'll all come around. They only want what's best for Becky."

"Don't we all? I'd best be going."

Joe turned and walked to where he'd left his horse. As he swung into the saddle, Tom's voice echoed in his mind. *You'll probably never be as strong as you were.*

Can I accept the reality of Dr. Morgan's prediction, he silently questioned.

I doubt it, a voice from deep within his soul answered.

Rather than head toward the Larson farm, he guided the horse toward the opposite end of town. Ahead of him he saw the saloon. *No,* he corrected himself, *it's not a saloon. Here they call them taverns.* Saloon or tavern, it didn't matter. Here was where he could get a drink.

Inside the building set apart from the others, old men sat at a table playing cards. There were no pretty girls in fancy dresses waiting to share a drink and conversation with him. From what Joe could see, the place had only one employee. A man about his father's age stood behind the bar, drying glasses with a towel that was gray with age.

"Can I get you something?" the man asked, as soon as he noticed Joe.

"Whiskey," he answered, abruptly.

"Mighty early in the day for a whiskey, ain't it?"

"I don't give a damn about the time of day. I just want a whiskey." He reached in his pocket and pulled out two bits and laid it on the bar.

"Whatever you say, kid," the man said, as he poured the rich brown liquor into a shot glass.

Joe threw back his head and swallowed the bitter liquid. The taste brought back the memory of the night of his mother's funeral. Oblivious to the men around him, Joe allowed his mind to wander, to take him back seven years to the night he became a man.

"You boys are men now," his father's voice echoed in Joe's mind. Along with it, came a vision of his father pouring each of them a glass of whiskey. "Just remember, there's no mother here to coddle you any more."

Before his eyes, Joe saw himself as a boy of ten. Other voices invaded his mind. Eighteen-year-old Paul and nineteen year old Luke, argued with their father about the prudence of giving Joe whiskey. The sound of flesh hitting flesh silenced their voices, just as it had seven years earlier. Before his eyes, he could see his father handing him one of the glasses, insisting he drink its contents.

It wouldn't be the last time. Often, when no one was around, Joe would take a drink from his father's bottle. He enjoyed the taste, as well as the feeling it gave him.

"I'll have another," he said, placing the empty glass, along with more money on the bar. "I want a bottle to take with me, too."

The man pushed the glass he'd just filled with whiskey across the bar then reached for a dusty bottle.

"Not that stuff," Joe growled. "I don't want that crap. I'm paying with good Yankee money. I want the best."

"Big talk, Reb. Don't look so surprised. Everyone in town knows who you are. You want the best, I'll give it to you, even if you aren't old enough to be havin' it. Hell, you're still wet behind the ears. My boy was young, like you, when he went off to fight the war. He came back without his legs. He might as well have died. He ain't got nothin' left."

Joe swallowed hard. "Sorry," he replied, gulping the whiskey before taking the bottle and leaving the tavern. Before riding out of town, he stopped at the general store to purchase some peppermints. It was a trick he learned at home, when he dipped into his pa's whiskey bottle. To cover the smell of it on his breath, he would chew mint leaves from Maria's herb garden.

It had been a long time since he'd had a drink, too long. The warmth of the whiskey set his mind spinning. He knew what he had to do. He needed to go home. Paul was right. It wouldn't work with Becky. How could he saddle her with an invalid? There was no doubt the Lazy K could support them, but Becky deserved so much more.

Do you love her? Luke's voice sounded in his mind.

You know I do.

Than how can you leave her?

I'm leaving because I do love her. Why can't you understand? I love her too much to turn her life into a living hell. I'd rather she hate me now and get over it than for her to come to hate me and not be able to leave. It's better this way.

~ * ~

Becky sat at the kitchen table and listened as her parents and the Clarks talked about how good it was to have the war over and to have everyone who served home again. Next to her sat Vince, as the conversation weaved its way around them, he moved his hand to rest on her knee. As politely as she could, she brushed it aside.

"Becky," her mother said, as though she could sense the uneasiness Becky felt. "Would you get us all some more coffee?"

Becky nodded, relieved to have an excuse to push back her chair. To her dismay, Vince followed her to the stove.

"What's that Reb got that I ain't?" he whispered in her ear.

"Me," she hissed through clinched teeth.

She purposely pushed him aside, as she made her way to the table. Once the coffee cups were refilled, she went out to the porch. She knew Vince would follow, but she didn't care. She needed not only the fresh air but the chance to confront him, away from their parents.

Vince's hands on her upper arms startled her, even though his actions were not unexpected.

"Have you lost your senses?" he asked, as he turned her to face him. "How can you have feelings for a dirty, stinkin' Reb?"

"I love the man, not the uniform."

"Love? How can you love someone who might have killed Teddy or Merrill?"

"How could I love someone who might have killed Joe's older brother?" she retorted. "You, Herman, and Ed all killed Rebs in this war. Joe never fired a shot. He was captured during his first encounter. Does that make you better than him? I doubt it."

In retaliation for her biting words, Vince pulled Becky into his arms and kissed her brutally.

For an instant, it wasn't Vince Clark who held her, who kissed her. The man who's lips covered hers became Delos Courtney. Terrified, she wrenched her right hand free and slapped him with all her might.

Without loosening his grip on her waist, Vince moved quickly and grabbed her hand while it was still in mid-air. "Just what in the hell is the matter with you? I certainly didn't do anything your Reb hasn't done. If this is how you treat your lovers, it's a wonder he even came back."

The realization that it was Vince she slapped and not Delos, brought tears to her eyes. "I'm—I'm sorry, Vince. I didn't mean..."

"Get your hands off my sister," Herman demanded, cutting Becky's words short.

Vince loosened his grip enough for Becky to pull free and put some space between them.

"Now, just what's going on here? Herman questioned.

"All I did was kiss her. I didn't rape her. I never knew what a little wildcat she could be."

Becky watched as Vince rubbed his cheek for emphasis. Her heart ached, as the knowledge of the impact of her actions sank in. What if they refused to sell Ed the Marrow Place?

As the questions flooded her mind, the members of both families crowded onto the porch. Becky's tears fell freely as hysteria overcame reason. The only security she could see was her father's open arms.

"Did he hurt you, Bek?" Herman asked, while her tears drenched her father's shirt.

She shook her head no then looked into her father's face. "Oh, Papa, I don't know what happened. One minute Vince and I were arguing then he kissed me, only it wasn't Vince, it was Delos and he was going to take me away from here."

"Delos?" Herman asked, repeating the name as a question. "Delos Courtney?"

"How—how did you know about him?" Becky inquired, her voice shaking at the mere memory of the man.

"We met him on the way home." Everyone turned at the sound of Ralph's voice.

"Who are you talking about?" Vince demanded.

Becky listened as Ralph told the story of meeting Delos the night before them came home. Ralph's description of the officer they met brought back ugly memories of the animal that tried to take her from her family.

"How could the union Army put someone like that in command?" Vince questioned. "He sounds like an arrogant..."

"I know what you want to say," Herman countered. "We aren't with our regiments now. No matter what we think of the man, we must remember there are women present."

Herman's comment dissolved the vision of Delos and caused a smile to tug at Becky's lips. If the boys only knew the words she'd heard while caring for the patients, they wouldn't be so protective.

~ * ~

By the time Joe returned to the Larson farm, the house was completely dark. Even though he'd had nothing to eat since having pie and coffee with Ralph, he didn't go to the house. He needed no nourishment, other than the bottle he carried inside his shirt on the ride from town.

The lantern hung on a peg, just inside the barn door. Even without light, Joe knew where to find it. After striking a match and bringing the wick to life, he set it on the top of one of the stalls then unsaddled his horse.

"I know you ain't mine, not yet at least, but that's the first thing I'm gonna change."

The mare shook her head as if in agreement, causing Joe to smile. When Paul had offered two hundred dollars for the black, Joe considered him crazy. Now he understood. The Larson horses were some of the best he'd ever seen. He knew his pa would never agree to breeding horses like these. It really didn't matter. At least he and Paul would each have one of these magnificent mounts.

He hefted the saddle to the top of the stall then untied the package containing his purchases from the general store. After doing so, he took the package, along with the lantern to the loft.

Lowering himself to the floor, he untied the string from the brown paper holding his purchases. He took inventory of the contents, new clothes, paper, pencil and an envelope. He'd worn the new hat and boots.

He recalled his conversation with the storekeeper. "Are you plannin' to write a letter to your father?" Effie had asked.

He regretted the lie he told the woman. The writing supplies were not for a letter home, but his farewell note to Becky.

Before changing his clothes, he took another drink from the bottle. The whiskey bolstered his courage, made him certain he was doing the right thing.

After putting on his new shirt and britches, he carefully folded the borrowed clothes. He'd appreciated the loan, but with the money from his father he now had something of his own.

Taking the money from his borrowed pants, he counted to see how much he lad left. Of the original thousand dollars, there was over nine hundred left. Counting it a second time, he placed seven hundred in the envelope he'd purchased in town.

Finally he reached for the pencil and paper and began to write.

> My darling Becky,
>
> Can I ever put into words how I feel about you, how much I love you? I doubt it.
>
> I visited Dr. Morgan today and I now know I'm getting no better. I will never be a whole man, a strong man. It is so unfair of me to saddle you with that kind of responsibility.
>
> The draft my pa sent was considerable. I hope what I'm leaving with this letter is enough to cover my debt to you and your family.
>
> I never meant to hurt you. I pray it will be temporary. I know a life with such a man as I've become would mean a lifetime of hardship.
>
> I want you to find a good man and have a happy life.
>
> Don't cry, my love. Trust me, this is for the best.
>
> Joe

IIe hcld the paper close to the lantern and read the words he knew Becky would read in the morning. How would she feel? Would they be like a knife in her heart or a wave of relief? How long would it take her to marry one of the neighbor boys, like Vince Clark?

Joe knew he would never find another Becky. It didn't matter. In no way would he ever expect a woman to contend with an unhealthy man.

After reading the letter a second time, he folded the paper and put it in the envelope along with the money and a second sheet of paper, detailing the reasons he decided on the amount to enclose.

Once he again put the saddle on the mare's back, Joe secured the envelope to a nail about the peg that held the lantern. It took only a moment for him to turn down the wick and cast the barn into total darkness.

He led the horse outside and looked up at the night sky. The wind blew from the west sending clouds skittering across the heavens. The moon peaked in and out of the clouds. Even though he sensed the coming storm, he didn't consider turning back.

Before mounting the horse, he glanced at the two-story farmhouse where he'd spent so much time fighting to stay alive. Without shame, he wiped away the tears that escaped from the corners of his eyes. "Good-bye, Becky," he whispered, as he swung into the saddle.

With no idea of where he was going, he urged his horse West. He knew the river lay beyond the Marrow place. Once he was at the river, he would ride south until he came to a ferry. After crossing, he could rest. There would be enough distance between himself and Becky for him to rest.

He became so lost in his own thoughts the silhouette of the building surprised him. Why hadn't he realized how close to Becky he'd been while imprisoned here?

Joe took a moment to dismount and walk to the corncrib that had served as his prison. Here, ghosts of the past surrounded him.

"Tell us about the gal," Backwoods voice sounded in his mind. "Tell us about her, about how she looked, how she smelled, how she talked. Tell us everything."

Paul's voice drowned out Backwoods. "And you love her, at least you think you do. You're not that hard to read. You don't love her, Joe. You're grateful to her folks, you don't love her. You can't love a Yankee. You just can't."

"Yes, I can, Paul," Joe said aloud. "I will never stop loving Becky, but you were right. We're from two different worlds. I can't ask her to give up everything she loves to become my nursemaid."

Joe didn't know how long he stood outside the corncrib listening to the voices of the men who shared this prison with him for seven months. When he finally returned to where he'd left his horse, the storm he anticipated had begun. Although the rain fell lightly now, he knew it would become a full-fledged storm before morning.

"Rain or no rain," he said to the mare, "we're going to Texas. The sooner we cross that river and get out of Illinois, the better."

He pushed his heels into the sides of the mare and urged her to a gallop. Despite the familiar tightness in his chest, he pushed on.

Becky! Becky! Becky! his inner voice screamed.

Be quiet, he admonished his overactive imagination.

I can't be quiet, Joe, Luke's Voice overshadowed Joe's subconscious. *No matter how hard you try, you can't silence me. Someday you will realize what a mistake you've made tonight.*

Someday? Don't you think I already regret it? No matter how I feel, I won't, I can't destroy Becky.

Then you're a fool.

A fool? What does that make you? I remember when you dragged home that girl from the saloon. I thought Pa was going to explode when he saw her. I knew you loved her, but you did just what Pa wanted you to do. After you went to war, I heard she killed herself.

I know. God has done what I was too much of a coward to do. Sally and I are together the way we should have been all along. Don't make the mistake I did.

The sound of thunder drowned out Luke's voice. As the rumble subsided, Joe could hear water, hitting water. The river was close.

Dismounting, he gingerly walked in the direction of the sound. It took only a minimum of steps to reach the bank of the river.

"It's time to head south, girl," he said, as he seated himself in the saddle. Before he started to follow the river, he took another swig from the bottle. With luck, he would find a working ferry before daybreak.

Seventeen

A clap of thunder brought Herman to full awareness. Rain pelted against the windows, he fought the urge to go back to bed and be lulled to sleep by the sound of the rain hitting the roof. Instead, he lit the lamp on his bedside table then checked his pocket watch. It read four thirty, time to get up and head for the barn.

After pulling on his work clothes, he made his way to the kitchen, taking care to be quiet. It made no sense to awaken the rest of the household.

In the kitchen, he found Ed heating last night's coffee. "Where do you think Mama would keep a coffee cake?" he asked, when Herman entered the room.

"Your guess is as good as mine. Have you looked in the warming oven in the summer kitchen?"

Ed began to smile. "I'd forgotten about that. Remember how she used to hide stuff in there so we wouldn't find it?"

"Some things don't change," Herman commented, as he poured himself a cup of lukewarm coffee. "If you find some, bring me a piece. I'm going out to start chores."

He gulped the coffee then grabbed a rain slicker from the back porch. The rain came down so hard, he had problems even seeing the barn, but he went out into it anyway.

After running across the dooryard, he opened the barn door and reached for the lantern. As he lifted it off the peg, his hand brushed against a piece of paper.

When the lantern was lit, he examined the envelope he found secured to a nail. Turning it over, he found it wasn't sealed.

Inside, he saw two pieces of paper and a stack of bills. Ignoring the page with Becky's name on it, he opened the one marked The Larson Family.

> The enclosed money is for the horses and tack Paul and I have taken. For the first time, I've realized you are all right. I have no business taking Becky to Texas with me. After visiting Dr. Morgan, I know I will never be well. I can't sentence her to a life as a nursemaid to an invalid.
>
> If the $700 doesn't cover what I owe you, send a wire to my pa at the Lazy K and he will make things right with you.
>
> Don't let Becky grieve too long. Make sure she finds someone to love who will make her happy.
>
> I won't ever forget you or the kindness you've shown me.
>
> Joe

"What's that?" Ed inquired, as he entered the barn.

"That God-damned Reb," Herman responded. "He's up and run out on Bek."

The expression on Ed's face was one of bewilderment. "Are you sure?" he questioned, snatching the letter from Herman's hand. After reading it, he looked up at Herman. "Don't know why you're so worked up about this. You haven't kept your feelings about it a secret. God knows you've ridden him hard enough. Isn't this what you've wanted ever since you first heard about him?"

"I thought it was, but I know what it will do to Bek. It will destroy her. I'm going after him."

"I'll go with you," Ed offered.

"No, you stay here and start chores. I'll get Ralph to go with me."

"What about Bek?"

"I'll let her sleep. There's no use in upsetting her. By the time she gets up, we should have that bastard back here."

"But..."

Herman didn't wait to hear Ed's protests. Instead, he went out into the rain to return to the house.

Being careful not to awaken everyone, he tossed the money filled envelope on the table and went up to Ralph's room.

"Are you going to tell Becky?" Ralph asked, as he pulled on his britches and buttoned his shirt.

"Now you sound like Ed. If I woke her up, you know she'd insist on tagging along. I'm not ready to face her yet. You know she'll blame me."

Ralph didn't comment. Instead, he led the way down the stairs. By the time they reached the barn, Ed had the horses saddled.

"Which way do you think he went?" Ralph asked.

"If it were me, I'd go west to the river then turn south until I found a ferry. What he doesn't know is he should go north. There's a ferry about a mile up but nothing south for about twenty miles."

Ralph nodded. "He shouldn't be too hard to catch up with. No matter what time he left, I'm willing to bet he didn't get much sleep last night. His strength is bound to give out before he gets too far."

Herman mounted his horse, and then turned the mare to the West. The rain had let up as they rode out of the dooryard in silence. Herman's thoughts were mixed. Part of him questioned his motives. Was it only concern for Becky that motivated him? He doubted it. Guilt had to play a part in this.

In the weak sunlight now peaking through the clouds, Herman saw the outline of the buildings that would be Ed's farm. Seeing the corncrib sent an unnatural shiver up his spine.

"Do you think this is where they..." Herman's voice dropped before he could finish.

"I'm afraid it is. I wonder what thoughts went through Joe's mind when he rode past here."

"I don't even want to think about it. I heard about those Reb prison camps. I always thought ours were more humane."

"I can tell you, they weren't. There was one next to the hospital where I worked. Every time I had to go there, I got sick. They had men there who hadn't bathed in months and were infested with lice. There were hellholes on both sides."

Herman swallowed hard. All through the war, he'd thought of the Rebs as animals. Were the men on his side any better? Up until this moment, he would have denied such a notion. Now he wasn't so sure.

In the distance, he saw a horse standing next to a body, lying in the mud. He dug his heels into the sides of his horse. At the same time, Ralph imitated his actions.

As soon as they dismounted, Ralph hurried to Joe's side. Even before joining his brother, Herman could smell whiskey. Beside Joe lay a broken bottle. "Is he..." Herman began, unable to say the word.

"He's not dead, but I don't know why not. He's burning up, he's drunk, and he's soaked to the skin. We've got to get him back to the house, but if we throw him over the back of the horse, we'll kill him for sure."

"We'd best get him up on my horse and I'll ride behind him. Once we're both on the horse, tie this rope around the both of us then tie his feet together, under the horse."

"What ever made you think of something like that?"

"I saw it done during the war. If you've got a better suggestion, you'd best make it now."

~ * ~

Becky dragged herself out of bed. When Joe hadn't come back with Ralph, she'd worried. Even though Ralph assured her Joe would be all right, her fears were not eased. Apprehension followed her to bed. With each quarter hour, she listened to the mantle clock chime and strike. The last thing she remembered was the clock striking three. Now four hours later, the sleep she received did not give her the rest she needed.

Wearily, she finished dressing and made her way to the kitchen. She thought of a dozen excuses why she slept so late. How could she ever explain sleeping away the morning, while her mother did the work?

She turned her thoughts to her conversation with Ralph at supper last night. He'd said Joe received a letter and a draft from his father. She pondered the meaning of the money from Texas.

As soon as she stepped into the parlor, she could hear Ed's voice coming from the kitchen.

"How are we going to tell Bek?"

The question clutched at her heart, holding it in an icy grip.

"We'll find a way," her father answered, his voice sounding as weary as she felt.

"You'll find a way to tell me what?" she questioned, as she entered the kitchen."

Both her father and Ed looked at her, pity radiating from their eyes.

"It's Joe, isn't it? What's happened? Is he..."

"Joe left sometime in the night," her father explained, getting to his feet to embrace her.

"What?" she gasped, pulling away from her father's protective arms.

"We don't know when, but Herman thinks it must have been sometime after midnight. He took the mare and left for Texas. It's all in this letter."

Becky grabbed the paper from her brother and scanned it quickly. Tears brimmed in her eyes, as Ed handed her a second sheet, one addressed to her.

The words in the second letter were like a knife cutting into her heart. "He can't be gone, he just can't. This letter says he loves me. If he loves me, why did he leave?"

"You read it plain as us in the letter. He doesn't feel he'll ever be well. He doesn't want to be a burden," John explained, again pulling her into his arms.

"It isn't right," she said, between sobs. "I've got to go after him. It will only take me a minute to change my clothes then..."

"Ralph and Herman left two hours ago," Ed interrupted her.

Becky stiffened. "Ralph and Herman? How could you let Herman go after him? You know how he feels."

"Ssh," John whispered, stroking her hair. "Going after Joe was Herman's idea."

"Papa's right, Bek," Ed commented. "Herman knew you'd blame him. He's doing this for you. Now, you let Mama fix you some breakfast, while Papa and I go out and take care of the horses."

"Let me come with you," Becky pleaded.

"Not this time, Honey," John advised.

"I don't agree," Emma said. "Becky needs to keep her hands busy. If she stays in the house, she'll just fester on why Joe left."

Becky dried her tears then hugged her mother. No words were necessary. Woman to woman, they understood each other.

~ * ~

It was close to nine when Ralph and Herman rode into the yard, leading the mare Joe had taken. Becky was taken aback to see Joe riding in front of Herman.

"Joe!" she screamed, as she ran toward Herman's horse.

"He can't hear you. He's unconscious," Ralph told her, as he swung out of the saddle.

Becky watched Ralph untie the ropes securing Joe to Herman. With Ed's help, Ralph carried Joe into the house while Herman rode for town.

Once inside, Emma insisted Joe be taken to Becky's downstairs bedroom. Becky agreed then followed her brothers.

"I'll tell you when you can come in," Ralph said sternly, stopping her from entering the bedroom.

"But Ralph..."

"No buts, Bek. This time you do what I say."

Defeated, she paced nervously outside the door. At last Ralph appeared. The concern that showed on his face made her stomach churn with apprehension.

"Is he going to die?" she gasped.

Ralph led her to the divan and prompted her to sit. The look on his face frightened her. "I honestly don't know, Sis. We'll just have to wait for Tom to check him over."

"Can I go to him?"

As she tried to get to her feet, Ralph put his hand on her arm. "There is more you should know before you go in there. Joe's been drinking. There was whiskey on his breath and a broken bottle beside him."

"Whiskey?" Becky gasped. "How could he..."

"He had a hard decision to make. If you read the letters, you know how much being a burden to you tore him apart."

"I just don't understand. I've been taught that spirits don't solve anything. How can I ever forgive what he's put me through?"

"The same way you've forgiven him for being a Reb, for fighting against everything you believe in. I can't say I approve, but I figure you'll give him another chance."

~ * ~

Long after Tom left, Becky sat beside Joe's bed, holding his hand. Joe was so sick, she so concerned. Would it always be like this? Would she always be sitting and praying he would wake up?

Behind her, she heard the door open and turned to see Herman standing just inside the room. "Mama says you should eat something, Bek," he said, as he put his hand on her shoulder.

"I suppose," she replied, getting wearily to her feet. For the first time all day, she faced her older brother.

"Why did you go after him?" she asked, once they were out of the downstairs bedroom.

Herman stopped and put his arm around her shoulder. "When I read the note, I realized he was leaving because of me. I hurt you the most when all I wanted was to protect you. I only want your happiness and if Joe makes you happy, by god he won't leave you."

Becky's emotions were in knots. Herman's heart was in the right place. Somehow she would have to decide if she could ever forgive Joe for what he'd put her through. "Thank you," she said, as she hugged him tightly.

"After supper," Herman commented, as they walked toward the kitchen, "we'll have to get a wire ready to send to Texas. Joe's family should know about this setback, even if it was of his own making."

~ * ~

Paul rode into town for the first time since his return to the Lazy K. It felt good to ride into an area where he was familiar. Here he knew every store and shopkeeper. Here he could meet with friends he'd missed while away at war. There were men who fought for both sides, but they were still friends, no matter what uniform they chose to wear.

He stopped first at the sheriff's office. He'd been told Clay Peck was the deputy and Paul was anxious to see his old friend. As soon as he entered the office, Clay got to his feet.

"It's good to see you, Paul. I heard you were back. You look good."

"Thanks Clay. Just thought I'd stop in and see how you fared in the war."

"Not too bad. I heard you boys were captured."

"You heard right. We spent the war, what was left of it, in a prison camp up North,"

"The word is Joe didn't come back with you. Can I believe the story about him staying in Illinois for some gal?"

"Her name is Becky Larson." As soon as Paul said her name, he saw her face in his mind. Becky was too good for Joe, he knew it and so did her brothers, but none of them could persuade either of them getting together was a bad idea. As soon as the thought popped into his head, he realized just how much he cared for Becky. It would be hard seeing her with Joe, whenever since he first saw her he hungered for the taste of her lips.

"So how did Joe meet up with this gal?"

"He got real sick and the doc took him to her folks' farm. I have to say I like her, and her folks were real good to Joe. I just can't make myself be happy about the situation. It's the same for her Yankee brothers." Paul knew his words were as false as any he'd ever spoken. What started out to be his distrust of the enemy had turned into improper feelings for the girl Joe loved.

"Guess we can't control someone else's life. Did you hear about Jed Thomas fighting for the Yankees?"

"Pa told me he got killed. What's Alice doing now?"

"She went back to El Paso to be with her Ma."

"What about the Miller girl?"

"I heard she got married. Some traveling salesman who came through here on his way to California."

"I see," Paul commented. He'd planned to ask one of the two girls to the dance they were having in town tonight. He'd hoped their company would erase the memory of Becky Larson from his mind.

"Don't look so down. There will be plenty of girls at the dance tonight. It's best if you go stag and then take your pick. Some of those little girls grew up to be right pretty while we were gone."

"Sounds good. What about some of the others who fought?"

Clay remained silent for a long moment, as though pondering his answer. "Do you remember Billy Blue?" he finally asked. "He's running the telegraph office."

"Billy Blue stuck behind a desk? It can't be. He was one of the best wranglers Pa ever had on the ranch."

"I'd agree with you, but he got hurt in the war. He lost a leg. From what I heard, the tent he was working the wire in took a direct hit. He was in the hospital for quite a while. He got back about six months before the war ended."

"I'll have to go over and see him. It's not going to be easy, him being crippled and all."

"Don't pity him too much. As soon as he got back, he married Amy Collins. I heard they're gonna have a baby soon. Enough about Billy, what are your plans? Will you be taking over the ranch?"

"I'll leave that for Joe. I'm waiting for an answer to a letter I wrote to a school in Houston. I'm going to study law. Believe it or not, Pa is going to pay for it."

"What changed his mind?"

"Guess it was the war and loosing Luke. Of course, his marriage to Maria could have played a part as well. I have to admit, it's been a real surprise. It certainly wasn't what I expected."

They talked for about an hour before Paul went across the street to the telegraph office.

As much as he wanted to see Billy, he knew it would be hard. No matter what he'd endured at the hands of the Yankees, it couldn't compare to Billy's injuries. Life for his friend would never be the same. Paul's life would go on, his dreams would come true and the nightmare of the Marrow place would disappear. It didn't seem fair.

He walked the short distance to the telegraph office. Inside he could hear the tapping of a message. He saw Billy bent over the desk, intent on writing the letters as they came across the wire. When he finished, Billy looked up.

"Paul, Paul Kemmerman, what a coincidence. I just took two wires, one right after the other, for you."

"Two wires for me?" Paul questioned, his eyebrows raised.

"The first one came from Houston, the second from Illinois."

"I don't like the sound of your voice, Billy. What's in the one from Illinois?"

Billy handed Paul a paper with neatly printed letters on it. His hand shook has he focused on the words.

Paul

Joe very sick—Dr. Morgan insists on
complete bed rest—Wedding postponed until
he is well—Will wire planned arrival—Letter
to follow

Becky

"I'm sorry, Paul," Billy said. "I don't like bringing folks bad news."

"It's not your fault, Billy. Since you've been getting the wires, you must know what's going on. What's happened to our lives? What if Joe dies? What if..."

"There's no use in asking questions with no answers. From what I've heard, your pa welcomed you home with open arms. We're both alive. Not much else matters."

"How can you say such a thing? You've lost so much."

"Have I? There were five of us in the tent when the shell hit. Three of them died instantly. The fourth man lost both legs and his sight. I consider myself lucky. I got sent home and found Amy waiting for me. I may have lost a leg, but I can still work, love my wife and have a good life."

Paul couldn't help but smile. He had no right to complain. He'd come through the war with no physical injuries. Looking at Billy and listening to his positive outlook, shamed him.

"Aren't you gonna read the other wire?" Billy inquired.

Paul looked down at the papers in his hand. The wire from Becky had been devastating. The impact of it made him forget the second wire even existed. Compared to the first wire he'd read, this one was very short and to the point.

Mr. Kemmerman

Your recommendations excellent—You have
been accepted for the fall session.

"Better news?" Billy asked.

"You know it is. I'd best get back to the Lazy K. Pa will want to know about Joe."

Promising to come back for a better visit, Paul left the office. Once outside, he mounted Devil and headed out of town.

The dance, the women, even seeing old friends no longer seemed important. He had to let his father know what the wire said.

For a third time he'd failed to protect his brother. During the battle, he'd allowed Joe to be captured. Once they were prisoners, he'd been unable to keep Joe from becoming sick. Now, by leaving Joe alone with the Larson family, his life was in danger. Would his newfound relationship with his father suffer because of this?

The ride back to the Lazy K was filled with indecision. How could he tell his father about the wire from Illinois?

Upon his arrival, he found his father and Don Parsons at the corral. Fear clutched his heart. As much as he wanted to tell his father about Joe's illness, he hesitated. For the fist time in his life Mark Kemmerman accepted him, treating him like a beloved son, rather than an outcast.

"I thought you were going to the dance," Don greeted him.

"I was, but something came up."

"Can't imagine what could have kept your from all those pretty girls in town," his father commented.

Paul reached into his shirt pocket and pulled out the wire from Illinois. "It's Joe," he said, before Mark had a chance to read the words on the paper. "I've got to go back and be with him. I never should have left him there."

"Now you're talking nonsense," Mark admonished. "Your place is here, at home."

"But someone has to be with Joe."

"Someone does, but not you. You've done more than enough already. Maria and I have been talking about going to Illinois to bring Joe home. I want to meet the Larsons and so does Maria."

"But what about the Lazy K?"

"I think you and Don can handle things here. I promised Maria a wedding trip once you boys were safe. I guess this is as good a time as any."

Paul watched his father turn away from him and make his way to the ranch house. The few words he spoke would have been unimportant to most, but to Paul they were the acceptance he'd prayed for his entire life. Why had it taken a war for his father to show him the love previously reserved for Luke and Joe?

~ * ~

The next morning, Paul drove his father and Maria to the train station. Had it been only yesterday when he'd received the wire from Becky? He could hardly believe it. Still, the luggage was packed in the back of the carriage and his father had tickets to New Orleans in his breast pocket.

Once at the station, Mark went into the ticket office to check on the arrival time of the incoming train.

"Can I talk to you, Maria?" Paul inquired.

"Of course you can. What's on your mind?"

"You've always been a real mother to me. Sometimes I think you loved me more than my own folks. You've always been honest with me in the past. Now I need you to be honest with me again."

"Just what are you getting at?"

"I'm waiting for the other shoe to fall. I'm afraid Pa will wake up one morning and be like he was before I went away."

"I'm afraid you'll have a long wait. It's not going to happen. Through this war he's suffered a lot of heartache. In the midst

266

of it all, he realized what he put you through all these years. When things were the darkest and he was afraid he'd lost all three of you everything changed. I told you when you first came home to accept it and not to question the changes. I'll tell you the same thing now."

"The train is on time," Mark announced, ending Paul's conversation with Maria. "We have just enough time to go over to the hotel and get something to eat."

Paul nodded. Whatever questions crowded his mind, he knew the answers would have to wait until his father and Maria returned from Illinois.

~ * ~

Paul watched as the train pulled out of the station. He felt drained. It had been a trying morning, but he didn't want to go back home. They'd eaten dinner at the hotel and Don surely had things under control at the ranch. Going back there seemed futile. What was there to go home to? His pa and Maria wouldn't be there. The thought of returning to the now empty house defeated him.

Instead of riding out of town, he made his way to the saloon. Eli Benton stood at his customary place behind the bar. He acknowledged Paul, with a nod of his head, as soon as he came through the door.

To Paul's surprise, a girl he didn't recognize came up and put her hand on his shoulder. "My name is Sylvie. Would you like to buy me a drink, Cowboy?"

"Leave him alone, Sylvie," Eli advised, dismissing the girl. "Paul just got home from the war, he ain't interested in you."

"Thanks for the rescue," Paul said, taking a long drink from the beer Eli sat in front of him.

"Don't mention it. How are things out at the Lazy K?"

"Not so lazy."

At the end of the bar, an unkempt cowboy looked up at the mention of the name of the ranch. "Can't be two ranches with that name," the man commented. "Do you work for Mark Kemmerman?"

"Guess you could say that. Do you know the ranch?"

"I used to work for that bastard when he had a spread in Kansas. Didn't know he came down this way."

Paul knew better than to allow this man to know his true identity. "I heard Mark had a spread in Kansas, sometime back."

"It was a long time ago, must be twenty-five maybe twenty-six years ago. That bastard, he was younger than me, always given me orders, tellin' me what to do, like he owned me. He had everything, especially that pretty wife of his. Her, a new son and that big ranch, were more than he deserved. He thought he had the world by the tail. I hated the way he always was tellin' us what to do. Him and that son of a bitch, Don Parsons, made a good pair."

"So what happened?" Paul asked.

"They were gettin' ready to take a big herd to Wichita. I was itchin' to get out of that hellhole. They started pickin' hands to go and hands to stay. I said to Mark, what about me. He said you ain't goin' and you ain't stayin', your leavin' this ranch. I don't like you very much."

"Didn't he give you a reason?"

"Hell no! He just said he didn't like me very much. I got back at that bastard, though."

"How did you do that?"

"He'd been gone for about a day when I came back. I made sure no one was around and I got that little whore of a wife of his. She spread her legs real good for me. The way she kicked and screamed, you'd think she didn't like what I was doin' to her. I showed her who was the master. I rode her like I'd ride a buckin' bronco. Kept it up all afternoon. When I figured the men would be back, I left. I wonder if she would give me a good ride now?"

Paul's anger got the best of him. "My ma died seven years ago."

"I'm real sorry to hear that. Your ma, you say. You must be that little whelp who was in the next room, cryin' because you couldn't get at your ma's tit."

Paul didn't try to control his temper as he threw the first punch. The drifter landed on the floor then started to draw his gun, but Paul was faster.

"I wouldn't try it if I were you, mister. You do and you're a dead man."

"You're just like your old man. I hope to hell someone has the guts to shoot the both of you in the back. I can't think of anyone I'd rather see it happen to."

The man got up and dusted himself off before leaving the saloon.

Paul watched him go then turned back to the bar. The rest of his beer sat, unfinished. He had no stomach for it. The man's words echoed in Paul's mind.

He closed his eyes, but the vision of the man wouldn't go away. As he studied the memory, he realized the man's features reminded him of his own.

Had his conception been the product of rape? If it was, the knowledge certainly explained his father's treatment of him these past twenty-five years.

Eighteen

Becky sat beside Joe's bed, as she had six months earlier, watching him sleep, willing him to awaken. Tears streamed down her cheeks, her emotions fighting within her.

Joe's letter said he loved her. Earlier, he called her name in his delirium, but did he love her? He'd left, gone away, leaving her behind. The letter said he was going back to Texas. How could he go there without her? Texas was to have been theirs. They were to have gone there together, not Joe alone.

She shifted her thoughts to her brothers. Ralph, who had been the closest to Joe seemed to be rethinking his acceptance. Herman had gone after Joe and brought him back to her, even though his departure was what her brother wanted. What had happened to her world? Why was everything she accepted as normal being turned upside down?

Against the protests of her family, she'd hardly left Joe's bedside. Soon the first light of dawn would creep through the window and she could extinguish the lamp beside the bed. Although she'd dozed off and on during the hours of darkness, she'd remained attentive to Joe's breathing. During the night, the fever broke and now he slept peacefully, breathing evenly.

She tried to concentrate on the book she'd picked up, but was unable to focus on the words before her. Her mind was too cluttered with other matters, her heart too full of pain to enjoy even her favorite pastime. Frustrated, she buried her face in her hands and cried silently.

~ * ~

Joe was vaguely aware of being awake. He could hear the soft breathing of someone in the room with him. He wondered who it could be and where he slept.

Slowly, he opened his eyes. the room was the one he remembered Becky occupying at the Larson home. Beside him sat Becky, her face hidden by her hands. Regardless, he could tell she was crying.

He watched her, silently, for a moment. How could he ever make up for what he'd done to her? How would he ever say, I really do love you?

I only wanted the hurt to be temporary, he told himself. *I was afraid if I didn't get well, it would be permanent.*

"Joe! You're awake!" Becky exclaimed, as she looked at him and their eyes met.

"Yes, Becky, I..."

"Don't try to talk," she said, her voice sounding cold and flat. "I'll get you some broth."

Before he could stop her, she got up and hurried out of the room. Did she really feel the need to get him broth, or was she anxious to get away?

He was astounded by how tired she looked. He tried to remember if she looked so drawn six months earlier when she was nursing men and doing chores.

He heard someone enter the room and looked up, expecting to see Becky. Instead, Ralph moved closer to the bed.

"Becky said you were awake," Ralph observed, as he picked up Joe's wrist to check his pulse.

Joe couldn't help but notice the strain in Ralph's voice. Rather than answer, Joe merely nodded his head. He didn't try to talk. Instead, Luke's voice sounded in his mind. *Yes, you're awake, but you're not strong. If you ask me you're a damn fool. Can't you see what you've done to these people?*

"You pulled a damn fool trick," Ralph admonished, silencing Luke's persistent voice. "You broke Becky's heart, just like Herman said you would."

"I guess I wasn't thinking straight," he managed to say, each word draining what little strength he had left.

"Don't see how you could, with all that whiskey in you," Ralph accused.

Panic gripped Joe's mind. "Does Becky know?" he asked, not really wanting to hear the answer.

"Did you think we wouldn't tell her? Of course she knows."

Joe closed his eyes and willed Ralph to go away and leave him alone. ·

"You might as well know, it was Herman and me who brought you back."

Joe opened his eyes wide. "Herman!"

"He figured you left because of him. Maybe you did. He loves Becky very much. He never meant to hurt her. All he ever wanted to do was make her see you for what you are. Unfortunately, she's so much in love with you she can't see it. I wish there was something I could to do make her see the light, but I can't, none of us can. By God, Joe, you'd better be good to her. If you aren't..."

The door opened, cutting Ralph's threat short. As Becky entered the room, Joe could feel a tension between brother and sister and it bothered him.

"I have some broth," she said, ignoring Ralph to sit next to Joe's bed. "Since you're awake, you need to take it."

As it had earlier, Becky's voice sounded cold and strained. *I've caused her so much pain,* Joe thought to himself, *I need to make things right.*

Once Ralph left the room, Joe allowed her to give him several spoonfuls of the hearty broth. "Enough," he finally said, as she put the spoon back into the bowl for more. He reached out and touched her arm, praying she would look into his eyes.

"I'm sorry, Becky. I wasn't thinking. I never expected to wake up here. I thought it would be for the best if I left you alone, went home, let you find someone else."

"Well, it wasn't," she interrupted. "Don't try to talk. Let me have my say. You have no idea what you've done to me. When I saw the note saying you were leaving because you loved me, I was devastated. How could you leave me if you love me? I've asked that question over and over again. It's been three days since the boys brought you back. At times, while you were unconscious, you would thrash around and call my name. You say you love me, but I don't know for certain." Becky paused for a moment, as though carefully weighing her words.

"What about you, Becky?" Joe asked, holding her hand. "Do you love me?"

"How can you ask such a question? I've fought my entire family to prove my feelings for you are true. You've tested my love and you've hurt me. I'm beginning to wonder if everyone is right. Maybe I don't love you. I don't know anymore."

"I understand and I am sorry. I only wanted your happiness. I didn't know if you could ever be happy with someone like me. Does any of this make any sense to you?"

"I'm trying to, but it isn't easy. I asked Tom about your health. He told me he'd advised you to marry me and leave for Texas as soon as possible. He also said he felt you would regain your strength in a drier climate. He didn't tell you to run away."

"What if he was wrong? Could you live with a sick man?"

"I—I don't know. What I do know is you didn't give me the choice. How could you be so inconsiderate?"

Joe lowered his eyes. Becky's accusations were right. He had been selfish. He tried to remember what he was feeling when he wrote the letter and rode away from the woman he loved.

Memories of self-doubt and pity crowded his mind. He'd taken the coward's way out and now he was paying the price. Instead of continuing to avoid Becky's eyes, he stared into them, trying to see all the way to her soul. In them, he saw hurt and betrayal, overshadowing both emotions, was exhaustion.

"Have you had any sleep?" he finally asked.

"A little," she replied, her voice hardly louder than a whisper.

"I doubt it. I can see how tried you are."

"I'll be all right. You need to sleep now. Tom will be in soon. I promise, I'll try to rest."

~ * ~

Becky waited until Joe fell asleep, before leaving the room. She pulled the door shut behind her, taking care to do so without making a sound. Once it was closed, she leaned against it, allowing her body to absorb the tension building in her mind. Joe had tried to explain his actions, but she still had questions that weren't answered.

Defeated, she sank to her knees and buried her face in her hands. Was her love enough to sustain her? Could she ever forgive Joe for what he'd done?

"Becky."

She looked up to see Herman standing in front of her.

"Are you all right?"

"I—I don't know," she stammered, as Herman helped her get up."

"Ralph said HE was awake."

"He has a name," Becky retorted, in an attempt to defend Joe. She wondered why she did so when she was so uncertain of her feelings. Was it merely instinct, or did she really love him?

"I know he does. If you recall, I'm the one who went after Joe. What did he say to you?"

Joe's words echoed in her mind. "Nothing he didn't say in the letter," she confessed.

"Look at me, Bek," Herman said, putting his finger under her chin. "Do you love him?"

"I think so, but the trust I had before has been strained. I'm so uncertain about—about everything."

Exhaustion seemed to consume her entire being. Just as her knees buckled, Herman scooped her into his arms.

"It's time you went to bed."

"But what if..." A yawn cut her words short.

"Don't worry about Joe. One of us will be with him. I'm taking you up to bed. Don't get any ideas about getting up once I leave. I'm planning to set by your bedside until you fall asleep."

"You should be out helping Papa with the field work."

"Not today. Don't you hear the rain? We're having a real Illinois summer storm."

Becky closed her eyes and laid her head against Herman's chest. Sleep came almost instantly.

~ * ~

A clap of thunder jolted Joe out of his sleep. Rain splattered against the window, driven by a strong wind.

Without opening his eyes, he knew someone sat next to the bed, watching him sleep.

"Are you awake?"

The sound of Herman's voice shocked him enough that he opened his eyes. "Why did you bring me back here?"

"I didn't do it for you. Becky needs to see you for what you are."

"I love her."

"Then act like you do. Show her you're the man she thinks you are."

"Where is she?"

"I made her go to bed. She's exhausted. She hasn't slept since we brought you here. Was it like this when the folks ran the hospital?"

Joe nodded, recalling the look of exhaustion he'd seen on Becky's face, as well as those of her parents.

"It was a bad time," he finally managed to say.

"So I've gathered. How much time did they spend with you?"

"No more than necessary. I was a complication to their lives. They had a lot of patients upstairs to care for as well as the chores."

"Then how did you and Bek..."

"How did we fall in love? I don't know. It just happened."

Herman continued to bombard Joe with questions. Most of them had no answers. The ones that did were ones Joe considered too personal or probing to promote a response. As Joe slipped into a restful sleep, Herman's voice droned on.

Throughout the day, Joe alternated between periods of awareness and sleep. Each time he awoke a different member of the Larson family sat at his bedside.

Ed spoke of his plans for the Marrow place. His description of what he would do made Joe think of his own plans for the future of the Lazy K.

Listening to Ed, he knew why Paul had so easily formed a friendship with this particular Larson brother. Ed's outlook paralleled his own. They were more alike than Joe and Paul ever would be.

After another period of sleep, Joe awoke to find Emma bent over her needlework. It was Emma who told him of Becky's collapse.

"It would have been best if you'd let me die in that camp," Joe said.

"Don't ever say such a thing again," Emma scolded. "A life, no matter how terrible it seems at the time is worth saving. The Lord brought you to us for a reason. I believe that reason was to make Becky happy."

"Then why did I hurt her so badly? Why?"

"Because no matter what you've been through, you and Becky are still children. Children do things without thinking. In your mind, you were saving Becky from what you saw as a painful life."

"None of this would have happened if..."

"One thing we learn when we become adults is dwelling of what if is a good way to ruin your life. Whatever happens from this point on is between you and Becky. The best advice I can give you is to be honest with each other. If this is meant to be, it will happen."

Emma's words echoed in Joe's mind as he drifted back to the oblivion of sleep.

The next time he awoke, it was Ralph who sat at his bedside. The memory of his last encounter with the one Larson brother he once considered his friend filled his mind. The unspoken threat hung like a storm cloud between them.

"Just one question," Ralph began, not bothering with the normal pleasantries. "Why did you feel you had to drown yourself in a whiskey bottle?"

A myriad of emotions crowded Joe's mind. How could he ever begin to explain what it was like to be Mark Kemmerman's youngest son? His memories of home centered on his father's treatment of all three of his sons.

All Joe's life he had known Luke was the favorite. Luke would inherit the Lazy K. He'd heard his father say it enough times. He'd also heard how Luke had the business sense and love of the land to make it prosper.

His father's treatment of Paul had always been a mystery. Why had the invisible wall of hatred stood between them?

As for himself, he never felt part of his father's world. The first time his father took notice of him had been on the night of his mother's funeral. By drinking the whiskey like his brothers, he'd become a man in his father's eyes. Although Luke was still the favorite, Joe had found a place in Mark Kemmerman's heart.

Joe soon learned his father wanted him to be a man. The only way it could happen was for him to fortify himself with whiskey. He'd thought things would change with Luke's death. He prayed his father would change his attitude toward Paul, but it never happened.

Suddenly Joe was the favorite son, the one who would eventually inherit the Lazy K. The prospect weighed heavily on his mind, so heavily he'd become more and more dependent on the whiskey to accept what he couldn't change. Over the next few months, the whiskey helped him adapt to his new roll on the Lazy K.

"Did you hear me?" Ralph asked.

Joe nodded. "My world is different from yours. In mine, a man..."

"A man? Whoever said you were a man? You're a boy, with no business drinking himself silly. I can't even say you have cause because of the war. You didn't fight, you don't know what it was like."

"And you do?" Joe countered. "The way I heard it, you spent the war in a hospital. Your life wasn't in danger you didn't watch your friends die on the battlefield, with their bodies blown away."

The veins in Ralph's neck stood out and his face became red. "Don't tell me about the war. Who do you think put those men back together? I saw the same things as you, only I saw them on the operating table. You're right, I wasn't in danger, but I saw the damage both sides did to each other."

"The war!" Joe shouted. "It always comes down to the war. All that crap you gave me about how you accepted me didn't mean a thing. I'm still a Reb and you're still a Yankee, You're no different than Herman. You're fighting a war that is over. Why aren't you more like Ed? He treats me like a man. Even if he hates me, he tries to understand. Why don't you just get out of here and leave me alone?"

~ * ~

Becky's dreams were troubled. Joe stood before her, a bottle of whiskey in his hand. "NO!" she screamed waking herself up.

"Bad dreams, Baby?" her father asked.

She looked across the room to where her father sat in an overstuffed chair. As she did, she realized she was in Teddy's room.

"What happened, Papa? Why did Joe run away from me? What did I do wrong?"

"You didn't do anything wrong. It's the war and Joe's illness. From what I gathered in his letter, he didn't want to turn you into his nursemaid."

Becky's tears rolled down her cheeks. "I love him, Papa. Why didn't he ask me what I wanted?"

"I think he didn't ask, because he knew the answer. No matter what sacrifices he asked you to make, he knew you would accept them. He loves you, I know he does, but he was afraid what that love would do to you. Now, your mama has sent me up to get you for supper."

"Who's been with Joe?"

"The boys and your mama have been taking turns."

"*The boys!* How could you let them sit with him? You know they..."

"Ssh, Baby," her father said, moving from the chair to the bed to embrace her, "What we have here is an uncomfortable situation. Your brothers don't want to see you hurt. They won't do anything to harm him. They may make things miserable for him. He did leave without telling you. He needs to think about what he did and decide what to do next."

Becky agreed. No matter how much she loved Joe, she wondered if she could ever put the hurt behind her and learn to trust him.

~ * ~

Paul stepped onto the porch of the ranch house. At the corral, Don worked alone.

Ever since his return from taking his father and Maria to the train, Paul had not had a chance to talk to Don alone.

"Can I talk to you?" Paul asked, as he approached the older man.'

"Been wonderin'' when you'd be out to talk. You've been avoidin' me ever since Mark left. What's eatin' at you?"

Paul licked his lips. "After the train left the other day, I stopped at the saloon for a beer. While Eli and I were talking, he mentioned the Lazy K. From the other end of the bar, a drifter seemed real interested. He was older than Pa and said he worked on the Lazy K when Pa had the ranch in Kansas."

The expression on Don's face was one of concern. "Was he sort of an unkempt man, tall and lean?"

"Sounds like him.

"What else did he tell you?"

"He said Pa took a herd to Wichita. He also told me Pa fired him before he left. He bragged about how he came back to the ranch and raped Ma. I want to know if there's any truth in it."

Don ran his fingers through his shaggy brown hair. The action accented the gray Paul noticed when he first came home.

"There's truth in it," Don finally replied. "His name is Rusty Paxton. Your pa fired him for drinkin'. I'm not talking about a Saturday night drunk. He was drunk every day. Mark put up with it for a while, but when he damn near burned down the bunkhouse, he had to go."

"He told me there was no reason, other than Pa didn't like him."

"I suppose that's what he's been tellin' himself all these years. No matter what, he promised to get revenge. Mark took the threat with a grain of salt. It was the biggest mistake your pa ever made. Rusty waited until Lydia was alone..." Don's voice trailed off, as though he couldn't say the words.

"He raped her, didn't he?"

"That and more. He beat her so badly the doctor said it was a miracle she survived. After that, she couldn't stand to be alone in the house. Mark was heartsick, so he sold the ranch in Kansas and bought this one."

"There's more, isn't there? Ma couldn't forget, because I was always there to remind her. Rusty Paxton is my pa, isn't he?"

"I'm afraid so."

Paul slumped against the corral fence. "That scum, that drunken scum is my father. My God Don, it all makes sense. That's why I've never been good enough for Pa."

"That's right. Don't be too hard on him though. When he finally got the sense to ask Maria to marry him, she wouldn't say yes until he came face to face with what he'd done to you. He's tryin' real hard. You were never to know any of this."

"I wish I still didn't, but I do. It would have been better if I'd gone on thinking that he finally decided to love me."

"You don't have to doubt Mark's love. He's always been proud of you, even if you didn't know it."

"You aren't making any sense."

"I guess I'm not. Mark is my best friend. Over the years, I've watched the both of you. The first time you broke a horse I could see the pride in his eyes. It takes more than the physical act to make a father. He sees it now, even if he couldn't when you were a kid. He raised you in the same way he did Luke and Joe. It might not have seemed like it, but he did."

"Then why didn't he treat me like he did Luke or even Joe after Luke got killed?"

"If you remember, until Luke died, Joe was destined to be a hired hand on this ranch. As for why he didn't suggest you inherit this spread, he knew you would never be content to stay here. You've got a hunger, boy. He just didn't know what you were hungry for. Joe's letter spelled it out. You'll make a good lawyer and Mark knows it."

Paul hung his head. Looking back on his life, he realized he had been raised in the same way as his brothers. It wasn't the treatment that had been different, but his interests. Mark had been more generous than most would have been. Since he'd returned home, his father treated him the way he only dreamed of being treated as a child. The stigma of being the product of rape seemed to have disappeared. For that one small change, Paul knew he would be eternally grateful.

Nineteen

Mark Kemmerman stood on the deck of the paddle wheeler, Maria at his side. Before them, men worked to guide the boat to the dock at Hamilton. From Paul's description, Mark knew this was the closest port to the Larson farm.

The dampness of the air that hadn't seemed so bad with the breeze generated by the movement of the boat, seemed to slap them in the face. He could tell, by Maria's expression, that she suffered from the oppressive heat.

"It isn't Texas, is it?" Mark asked, trying to make a joke. "I'd forgotten what it's like in the summer up here."

"I never thought anything could be so terrible. I'm having trouble breathing and I'm healthy. It's no wonder Joe is sick. I will be glad to leave this country behind and return to the Lazy K."

Mark took Maria's hand and guided her down the gangplank to dry land.

Across from the dock, they saw a lean to with the words HORSES FOR HIRE crudely printed on the side. "I'll rent a horse and carriage and we can leave immediately for the town Paul talked about. With luck, we should be there by evening."

"Town?" Maria echoed. "Aren't we going directly to the Larson farm?"

"I think it's best if we wait to go out there until morning. We both need to rest and be at our best when we see Joe."

"Rest! That's all we've done on this trip."

"I know, but I'm selfish enough to want you all to myself for one night. I'm tired of sharing you at supper with the other passengers and having to make polite conversation with strangers. We are on our honeymoon you know. It's strange, we've known each other for longer than most folks are married, and yet I learn more about you every day. I was a fool not to have married you long ago."

"I wouldn't call you a fool. It just took you a long time to find out what I always knew, that we were meant to be together."

After getting off the boat they walked the short distance to the stable. Once there, a disheveled looking young man met them.

"Your sign says you have horses to rent," Mark said, as he approached the man.

"Yup," the man replied, eyeing him strangely, after hearing Mark's drawl.

"I'll be needing a rig for a week, maybe two," Mark continued.

The man spat a stream of tobacco juice onto the ground. "I git my money in advance."

"That sounds fair. How much do you get for a horse and a rig for a week."

"Twenty-five dollars a week, for YOU."

"That's a lot of money," Mark observed.

"Mister, I got the only livery stable in town. Do you wanna walk to where you're goin' or do you want to ride? It's as easy at that. I get twenty-five dollars for a horse and rig, you want it for two weeks, you pay me fifty dollars."

"It looks as though I don't have much choice. I'll pay you the fifty dollars now."

Mark watched the man's eyes widen as he pulled the money clip from his pocket. As the man reached out a dirty hand to take the money, Mark put the money back into his pocket.

"What kind of game are you playin', Mister?"

"No game at all. When I get a receipt, you get your money."

"A what?"

"I want a paper saying I gave you fifty dollars for the rent of a horse and rig for two weeks."

"You want a lot, being a Reb and all. Don't see what good a paper would be. I can't read or write. Guess you ain't gonna get no paper."

"Then I guess you ain't gonna get no money," Mark replied, mocking the man's manner.

"Suppose we could go over to the store. Someone over thar can write."

Mark smiled at the man's distress. "Good then let's go to the store."

"Do you want to go to the store with me?" Mark asked, Maria.

"I don't think so. As warm as it is here, I shudder to think of what it would be like confined inside a building."

"I won't be long," he replied, as he turned to follow the man.

Unlike the stable, the store seemed to be well maintained. Inside a man, not much older than the one Mark followed, stood behind the counter.

"Is there something I can help you with?" he asked.

"I am planning to give this young man fifty dollars for the rent of a horse and rig," Mark replied. "I'd like a receipt for my money."

"You renting those rigs by the year now, Pete?" the man behind the counter commented.

"Ain't none of yer business Clem. Just write out that paper, so I can git my money."

"This man says he can neither read or write," Mark continued, purposely ignoring Pete. "Is he telling me the truth?"

"Oh, he's truthful all right. Pete ain't got no folks. He grew up in that stable with his grandpa. When the old man died, Pete inherited the business. It's a shame old Jake never thought it necessary to get Pete an education."

"Don't talk about me like I ain't here," Pete growled. "I know enough to git myself a fair price for my horses."

"I don't call fifty dollars a fair price," Clem snapped. "Guess it's your business what you charge, but it ain't right."

Mark listened to the exchange with mixed emotions. He was the one being cheated and yet he couldn't help but feel sorry for Pete. How could anyone deny an education to their own kin?

The question no more than crossed Mark's mind than he thought of Paul. Before the war, he would have never consented to paying for Paul's education. If the truth be known, he was no better than Pete's grandfather. Mark thanked God Maria had made him see what his hatred for what happened to Lydia had done to Paul.

~ * ~

Maria fanned herself with the lace handkerchief she carried in her bag. From the corner of her eye, she saw two men approaching her.

"You one of them slaves?" the first man asked.

She realized her darker skin color had prompted the man's question. "I am Mrs. Mark Kemmerman," she replied.

"I didn't know them Reb's married their slaves," the second man observed. "I thought they just bedded them. Ain't that what you heard, Zeek?"

"I am not a slave, nor am I a Negro," Maria declared.

"Well, you certainly ain't white," Zeek continued, crossing the short distance that separated them, to put his hand on her arm.

"Take your hands off my wife," Mark shouted, coming to her rescue.

"Then she was tellin' us the truth. I never thought I'd see the day when a white man would stoop to marry someone like her."

"I'll thank you to keep your crude comments to yourself," Mark threatened.

Maria felt an overwhelming desire to find comfort in his arms, but she restrained herself. Surely these men had fought for the Union and thought they were not out of line.

Mark put his arm around her waist and guided her to the carriage the man from the stable brought out for them.

"I expect this rig back in two weeks," he growled.

"If I bring it back sooner, I expect to get a refund of part of the money."

The man looked shocked, as though he didn't think anyone would ever ask for such a thing.

"Did you get everything taken care of?" Maria asked, once they drove out of the make shift town.

"Of course I did. You didn't think I'd leave without a receipt did you?"

"I didn't think you would ever pay such a terrible price for the rent of a shabby rig and a horse that looks like he could lay down and die at any moment."

Maria's outspoken comment brought a smile to her husband's lips. "I'm sorry I snapped at you. This trip certainly isn't the wedding trip you deserve. I knew the man was cheating me, but I really had no choice."

Maria put her hand over his then leaned her head against his shoulder. "I couldn't have asked for a better wedding trip or a wiser husband. Once we see Joe, things will be less tense. We're both on edge not knowing what we will find when we get to the Larson farm."

Mark put his arm around her shoulders then leaned down to kiss her.

As they drove toward their destination, she marveled at the neat white farmhouses with their red barns and out buildings. They were so unlike the sprawling ranch houses of Texas, she suddenly became homesick. These houses reminded her of white boxes which stood tall and stately. Many of them, she felt certain, had recently received fresh coats of paint, along with new ideas as their young men returned from the war.

Cattle grazed, but they were not the fat Herefords or the rangy longhorns Maria loved. "What do you think of this farm land?" Mark asked.

"It certainly is different from home. Even the cattle are different."

"As I recall, the black and white ones are Holsteins and the brown ones are either Jerseys or Guernsey's. They're raised for their milk, rather than meat."

She nodded then returned her attention to the countryside. To her surprise, pigs and sheep grazed in the same fields with the cows. In Texas no one would think of allowing such animals to compete for the precious grazing land.

~ * ~

The town Paul told them was close to the Larson farm came into view and Mark breathed a sigh of relief to see a building with a sign that read HOTEL. He had been afraid they would have to find a boarding house and such a place would have afforded them little privacy.

After tying the horse to the hitching rail, he assisted Maria to step from the carriage. Together they entered the building.

"We'd like a room for the night," he said, not wanting to be taken as an easy mark by this man.

"That will be two bits," the clerk said, turning the register toward Mark.

Surprised by the man's easy manner, Mark signed the book. He put the pen back into the inkwell before turning the book back to the clerk.

"Mr. and Mrs. Mark Kemmerman," the man read aloud. "You wouldn't be related to that boy out at the Larson place, would you?"

"I'm his father," Mark replied.

"Thought as much. You folks can have number fifteen. It has a nice view."

"We'd like to stay a week, maybe two," Mark said. "Depending on what we find when we see our son, we might be needing a room for him as well."

"I have no problem with that."

The man's statement surprised Mark. "I thought you might want some money down, maybe even payment in full."

"Don't see why. I trust you."

"Thank you," Mark said, extending his hand.

"From the look on your face, I'll wager you met up with Pete Burke over in Hamilton."

"We certainly did. He charged me fifty dollars for a horse and rig for two weeks."

"I don't suppose he gave you any paper saying how much you paid."

"He didn't want to, but I forced the issue. He told me he couldn't read or write, but as soon as he realized he wouldn't get the money until I got a receipt, he found someone who could."

"Let me guess, he took you over to see Clem at the store. Clem's a good man. I'm surprised he let Pete get away with charging you so much."

Mark couldn't help but smile. If he'd been a bit more forceful in front of the shopkeeper, things might have been different.

"Be assured," the clerk continued, "you aren't the first person Pete's cheated and you certainly won't be the last. If you've got that paper handy, my boy will get your money back, right after he takes your bags up to your room. Most folks don't get a paper. When they don't there's nothing we can do for them. My brother runs the livery here. He'd like to see Pete run out of business, but there's not much he can do. He will get you a rig at a fair rate."

Mark hadn't quite known what to expect. It certainly wasn't any kind of acceptance in this world called the North. "Thank you," he managed to say, as he shook the man's hand.

After shaking hands, the man turned toward the back room. "Willard, these folks need their bags taken up to number fifteen," he called.

A boy, not much younger than Joe, appeared. Mark listened while the clerk recounted the story of what happened with Pete.

"You folks follow me," Willard said. "Once you're settled my Uncle Dan and I will take care of everything for you."

Once Willard left the room, Mark took Maria in his arms. "Alone at last," he said, before he kissed her. He could almost feel her melt into his arms and he wondered if it were because of his kiss or the heat.

"If it wasn't for the fact I want to see Dr. Morgan, I'd make love to you here and now Mrs. Kemmerman."

"Let me freshen up a bit and I'll go with you," Maria suggested.

"No, I want you to stay here and get some rest. When I get back we'll go out and have supper."

"But I want to come too. Joe is as much my son and he is yours. I've raised him ever since he was born and Lydia was too weak to do so herself. I want to hear what this doctor has to say."

"I don't think..."

"You don't have to think. I'm going with you and that is that."

Mark smiled at Maria's forceful tone. Lydia would have abided by his wishes, not wanting to put up a fuss. Maria was a very independent woman and used to getting her own way. She'd bossed him and the boys around for more years than he cared to remember. He knew any argument about her not going with him would be fruitless.

When they had both freshened up, they returned to the lobby to ask directions to the doctor's office.

"Just go across the tracks to the main street," the man told them. "Tom's office is right next to the bank. You shouldn't have any trouble finding it. If he's not in, just holler. He lives in the back. I haven't seen him leave town recently."

After leaving the hotel, they crossed the tracks to the main business district. As the man had told them, Dr. Morgan's office was tucked away between the bank and the general store.

When they entered the bell above the door jingled merrily. "I'll be right out," someone called from the back room.

Mark silently assessed the man who entered the waiting area. He was in his late forties maybe even early fifties, tall, slender and gray at the temples.

"I'm Dr. Morgan. What can I do for you?" he asked, extending his hand.

"I'm Mark Kemmerman and this is my wife, Maria. We've been told you're the man who has been caring for our son."

"I'm pleased to meet both of you. I must admit I am a bit surprised to hear you are married. Joe never..."

"Joe doesn't know," Maria said. "We were married while the boys were away."

"Does he know you're here?" Tom asked.

"We weren't certain how long the trip would take," Mark explained. "We didn't want to get his hopes up. We've come to you first because we want to know the truth. How is he?"

Mark listened while Tom related the story of how he'd come to meet both Joe and Paul. Most of it he knew, but when Tom told him of Paul's injuries, he was astounded. Paul had never mentioned being hurt.

"The truth is," Tom concluded, "your son has been more dead than alive twice in the past six months. This last time has been almost as bad as the first. He came to see me the day before he left and I knew he was planning to do something drastic. I never expected him to get drunk and leave without Becky."

"Drunk!" Mark exclaimed, hardly able to believe what this man was telling him. "Do you want me to believe my son was drunk?"

"Believe what you want, but when Ralph and Herman found him he was unconscious. He'd drank almost a full bottle of whiskey and coupled with his weakened condition the pneumonia returned."

"Why would he leave Becky?" Maria asked. "Weren't they planning to get married?"

"They were and they are. As I say Joe came to see me that day and we talked about him returning to Texas. I told him the drier air would be better for him. I never told him he wouldn't get well again. He thought of that all by himself. He figured he'd eventually become a burden on Becky and he couldn't stand to see it happen. Instead he ran away. I know his actions hurt Becky, but she can overlook them, or so she says. If she can it will be good."

"I don't see how she can ever forgive him for something like that," Maria declared.

"I don't either, but she says she can. She loves him, I've known it ever since the first time they looked at each other, but love can only go so far. They've taken the two weeks he's been in bed to do a lot of talking. Hopefully they can work things out."

"I hope so, too," Mark replied. "How have you been able to keep him in bed for two solid weeks."

"It hasn't been easy, but he's had some good watch dogs. Ralph and Becky haven't let him up and I'm sure Herman and Edmund have been just as adamant about him staying in bed. He won't ever be strong, but the body is a wonderful thing. He has healed much faster than I expected him to this time. It will be interesting to see how he does once he's up and around."

"Then there will still be a wedding?" Maria inquired.

"I certainly hope so."

"How much do I owe you, Dr. Morgan?"

"Joe has more than paid me."

Mark shook Dr. Morgan's hand then left the office with Maria. Together they walked slowly back toward the hotel. As they did he thought about Paul's father. He'd been a drunk whom Mark couldn't stand. He didn't tolerate drinking. Paul may have a beer, but he didn't drink heavily. Why had Joe felt the need for a whiskey bottle? Why had he allowed himself to get drunk? Why Joe? Why not Paul?

"Don't torture yourself," Maria said, putting her hand on his arm. "I can read your thoughts in your eyes. Whatever has prompted Joe to turn to the bottle is something we will have to come to grips with. It is nothing we can find the answer to tonight."

Mark took her in his arms and kissed her lovingly. He didn't care that they stood on the main street of the strange Northern town. She was his wife, his soul mate. Together they could face anything.

~ * ~

Joe took his time eating supper, if for no other reason than to prolong the time Becky sat at his bedside.

"Tom says you'll be able to get up tomorrow," she said.

Joe hated the sound of the tension in her voice. Would she ever find it in her heart to forgive him for his foolish actions?

"It will be good to get out of this bed," he replied, knowing he was telling her a lie. For the past week he'd been getting up when he knew no one would discover him. Day be day, he'd become stronger. Now he anticipated being able to walk freely wherever he pleased rather than pacing the width of this room.

"Promise me you won't overdo," she implored, putting her hand on his arm.

"Would it matter?" He watched her reaction to his question. If he was getting out of this bed in the morning, Joe had to know where he stood with her.

"How can you ask such a question? I've fought my brothers for you. I've prayed for you. I've..."

"Have you forgiven me for how badly I hurt you?"

Tears formed in her eyes. Without so much as one word passing between them, he knew the answer.

"What do you want me to say, Joe? Do you expect me to forget you were ready to leave me behind, to say nothing of being drunk?"

Joe wanted to smile at her honesty, but refrained. He knew for the healing to begin, Becky needed to put voice to her pain.

"I don't want either of us to forget. I've tried to explain my reasoning. I promise you, once I'm out of this bed, I will show you how much I love you."

"You must know I love you, but..."

"But you don't trust me. I can understand your mistrust. For now, let's try to put it behind us. Let tomorrow be a new beginning for us."

"Oh, Joe, I want to believe you. I want to trust you, but I'm afraid."

Her words made his heart ache. Of all the emotions she could have for him, the one he didn't want her to experience was fear.

~ * ~

The slamming of the kitchen door told Joe Ralph and Ed had gone out to do the milking. Joe knew he would have at least an hour before Becky and Emma came down to start breakfast.

In the parlor, the clock struck the half hour as Joe got out of bed. The first rays of the morning sun came through the window, giving him the light he needed to find his clothes.

Once he finished dressing, Joe made his way to the kitchen. With his long hours in bed, he'd had plenty of time to devise a plan to start paying the Larsons back.

As a child, he pestered Maria until she taught him how to make an egg bake. At the time it had been important to him. He'd wanted to do something special for his mother and to his childish mind, preparing her favorite breakfast suited his purposes well.

A pot of coffee simmered on the stove, inviting him to pour a cup to fortify himself for the day.

Depending on his memory alone, he deftly combined the ingredients to make the special dish. After placing it in the oven, he sat down at the table, surprised at how much strength this simple act took.

~ * ~

As soon as Becky opened the door separating her bedroom from the hall, a delicious aroma greeted her. Had she overslept? Had her mother fixed breakfast by herself?

When she reached the bottom of the stairs, she saw her mother coming from the bedroom she and John shared.

"I thought you were already up," Emma greeted her.

"I just got up myself. I thought I'd overslept. If you didn't start breakfast, who did?"

Together they went into the kitchen. To their surprise, Joe sat at the table, his head pillowed on his crossed arms.

"Do you think..." Becky whispered.

Joe stirred, making her wish she hadn't disturbed him.

"What do you think you're doing out of bed, young man?" Emma demanded, when he raised his head.

"Dr. Morgan said I could get up this morning. I thought it was time I did something to help you out, rather than make more work for you."

"Are you responsible for the delicious aroma coming from my oven?"

Joe nodded his head. "My ma always liked Maria's egg bake. It was the only thing I ever did just for her. I made Maria teach me how to make it. Pa and my brothers thought I'd lost my mind for learning how to cook. Especially for learning how to make something like this. At least they did until they tasted it. After Ma died, they asked me to make it at least once a week. I guess it reminded them of her."

Becky opened the oven door and checked on the pan of egg mixture that had not only started to set but had turned a perfect golden brown.

"How much longer does this have to bake?" she asked, after gently closing the oven door.

"It will be done by the time Herman and Ed get in from milking. If I hadn't fallen asleep, I would have set the table for you."

"I think you've done quite enough," Emma scolded. "I want you to go back to bed, but since you've fixed our breakfast, you deserve to sit at the table and eat with us."

Becky realized she was smiling when she saw Joe begin to grin. In the fight to regain his strength, he had won this battle.

By six, the rest of the Larson family had assembled in the kitchen and were sitting at the table.

"I don't remember you ever making anything like this before, Mama," Herman said, after tasting the egg bake. "Is this some new recipe you picked up at the church social last week?"

"Do you like it?" Emma asked.

"It's different," Ed commented, "but it sure is good."

"Joe made it," Becky advised them.

Herman's fork clattered against his plate, as he choked on the food he'd just swallowed. "You made this?" he questioned, when he regained his composure. "What kind of a man cooks breakfast?"

"I don't care who made it," Ed remarked, before Joe could answer. "This is good. I hope there's enough left for seconds. You know, Joe, if you didn't have your heart set on going back to Texas, you'd be welcome to come over to my place and do the cooking."

Becky hadn't taken her eyes from Joe's face. She relaxed only when she saw him smile.

"I'm, afraid you'd get mighty sick of egg bake. It's the only think I know how to make. You can't count beans over an open fire."

Joe's comment brought laughter from everyone but Herman. "Seems to me a real man wouldn't be so handy in the kitchen."

"Seems to me," Ralph interrupted, "if it hadn't been for a man doing the cooking, most of the troops would have starved. From what I hear, the cooks in those fancy hotels in the East are men. What about at the Lazy K, Joe? Who does the cooking for the men?"

"Pa hires a cook, but I certainly wouldn't call Red a woman. He's as crusty as they come. The way he tells it he learned to cook on the same trail drive where he almost lost his hair to a Comanche warrior. I wouldn't ever tell Maria, but his cooking is every bit as good as hers."

Becky glanced at Herman. He seemed to be half listening to Joe as he played with his breakfast with his fork.

"If you're not going to eat that," Ed suggested, "I'll finish it for you."

"I don't plan to go hungry so you can feed your face," Herman snapped. "I've got hay to cut today. I don't plan to do it on an empty stomach."

~ * ~

Becky squatted beside a row of peas in the garden and began to pick the ripe pods. It took little time for the dishpan to be filled to overflowing.

The mundane chore gave her time to think. The two weeks Joe had been confined to bed, they spent many hours trying to heal the rift caused by Joe's brash actions.

Her brother's protests had given way to their own pursuits. Ralph spent every waking moment with his nose stuck in the books Tom brought out to the farm. Other than a casual remark about the mistake he thought she was making, they rarely spoke.

Her father and Ed spent their days at the Marrow place, getting the buildings repaired and ready to be used. Although there would be no crops this year, the land promised to be fertile. By the time they returned at night, Ed was always too tired to do much more than eat supper and go to bed.

Herman gladly took over the daily running of the farm. It seemed as though he was everywhere doing everything at once and thoroughly enjoying it.

She was thankful for the things keeping her brothers too busy to interfere between her and Joe. Yet she couldn't help but wonder if following her heart would make her happy. Could she leave her family to go to Texas and a life she neither knew nor was prepared to live?

By the time she reached the end of the row, the second pan was full. She sat it aside then got up to go back to the beginning of the next row, where she left the third pan.

As she did, she saw a carriage drive into the dooryard. *Horse buyers,* she thought, as she assessed the rig. It certainly didn't belong to any of the neighbors.

She wiped her hands on her apron then made her way toward the strangers. The man pulled on the reins to bring the horse to a halt. Once the horse and carriage stopped, the man got down before assisting the woman with him. The man was tall, with wide shoulders. Although he wore a dark suit, she instinctively knew he would be more comfortable in work clothes.

The woman looked small in comparison. Her dark hair was perfectly styled in an upsweep tucked into a neat bun at the top of her head. Her dark complexion made Becky wonder what connection the woman and man shared.

"Morning, Ma'am," the man drawled.

To Becky's surprise, his voice sounded vaguely familiar. "Good morning," she replied, extending her hand. "I'm Becky Larson. If you're here to look at horses, I'll gladly take you out to the pasture."

"We haven't come to see horses, Miss Larson," he said, holding her hand a bit longer than necessary.

Becky studied the man's face. In it, she saw an older version of Joe. "Are you..." her voice trailed off. If she was wrong, she certainly didn't want to make a fool of herself.

"I'm Joe's father and this is my wife, Maria."

"W—Wife?" Becky stammered, turning the one word into a question. As soon as she spoke the word, Becky realized the couple must have heard the surprise in her voice. Nothing either Joe or Paul told her led her to believe Maria was anything more than their father's housekeeper.

"Mark and I were married while the boys were away," Maria explained. "When we received Joe's letter, we decided to make the trip North as soon as we knew when you planned to be married."

"You wanted to come to our wedding?"

"Joe is our son," Mark replied, putting his arm around Maria's waist.

"We had to come," Maria agreed. "We've been so concerned. Joe's letters and the stories Paul told were so terrible we had trouble believing any of it. When your wire arrived, we had to come and see Joe for ourselves. It's hard with him being so far away."

"I can understand," Becky said, remembering the letters they'd received from the families of their patients. "I'd feel the same if it were one of my bothers. I'm sorry, where are my manners? Do come up to the house for something cool to drink."

~ * ~

Joe stared at the ceiling. The dream that woke him seemed so real, he could swear he heard his father's voice coming from the Larson kitchen.

He closed his eyes and tried to regain his interrupted sleep. The events of the morning surprisingly drained his strength.

Before drifting off, he heard the bedroom door open. Undoubtedly, it would be Becky coming to tell him dinner was ready. He wished he could turn back the clock and take away the hurt he'd caused her by trying to return to Texas. He loved her so much he wished he could just make it go away.

Her lips said it didn't matter, she still loved him, but he knew better. His foolish actions would always be there, silently sitting between them. Even if she could forgive him, how could he forgive himself?

Slowly, he opened his eyes. To his shock, he found himself looking into his father's face. To his right, stood Maria. Unable to believe what he saw, he blinked several times. "Pa?" he finally managed to ask.

"Yes, son."

The sound of his father's deep voice and pronounced drawl, raised his hopes. At the same time, he felt a shudder of terror encompass his body. If they were here, they had to know why he lay in this bed, what method he'd used to bolster his courage to make the decision to leave.

"You are here. I thought it was a dream when I heard your voice."

"When we received Becky's wire, we had to come," Maria said. "We were so concerned, we couldn't stay away."

The tears that spilled down her cheeks caused Joe's heart to ache as much as the hurt he saw in Becky's eyes. "Coming here was a long and foolish trip. You must have known the Larsons would take good care of me."

"Of course we knew the Larsons would do their best for you," Mark said. "As for this trip being foolish, I disagree. This was a very necessary trip. We needed to see you for ourselves."

"What about Paul?" Joe asked, still unable to believe he was actually talking with his father and Maria. "Did he get home?"

"He arrived just days before we received Becky's wire," Maria said. "I can't believe he hasn't written you."

Joe searched his memory. Had there been a letter during the time he'd been in bed? "I got your letter the day I..." he left the rest of the sentence unsaid. "I'm a bit fuzzy on what's happened the past few days. If I got a letter, I don't remember."

"It's all right. We have something we must tell you."

His father's statement was puzzling. Before he could react, Mark continued. "Maria is no longer our housekeeper."

Joe's eyes opened wide with shock. "But why, Maria? You're part of our family. You can't leave us. I lost one mother, I don't think I can stand to lose another."

"I have no intention of leaving either you or the Lazy K. I really am a part of your family now. While you and Paul were gone, your father and I were married."

Joe enjoyed the smile spreading, uncontrollably across his face.

"I'm pleased you approve," Maria commented. "I think you and your father have a lot to talk about."

"Why Joe?" Mark asked, once Maria left the room. "Why a whiskey bottle?"

The smile that felt so good only moments earlier faded from Joe's lips. "Why not?" he countered. "You're the one who told me to be a man when I was ten. You're the one who introduced me to a whiskey bottle."

Joe watched as the impact of his words struck his father like a slap to his face.

"I didn't realize," Mark finally said, once Joe related the entire story.

"You weren't supposed to. I never thought my weakness would deprive me of the one thing I wanted even more than your acceptance. I'm afraid things will never be the same between Becky and me."

"Perhaps it's best if you and Becky put some distance between yourselves."

"Do you want me to go back to Texas without her just because you came for me."

"That's not what I said. I think it's best if you join Maria and me in town. You and Becky need to get to know each other as a young man and a young woman, rather than a nurse and a patient."

Twenty

Becky's dreams became nightmares, as she relived Joe's departure from the farm. For the third time, he'd turned his back on her and walked away. Even though he proclaimed his love and promised to come back to court her, she knew her heart had been broken beyond repair.

The clock in the parlor finally struck six and Becky gratefully got out of bed. She needed to keep busy. With Joe gone for a week, sleep had become so riddled by bad dreams, she dreaded the hours of darkness.

After dressing, she went to help her mother prepare breakfast.

"I hope you've got breakfast ready," Ed called, before entering the kitchen.

"Is food the only thing you think about?" Herman teased.

Becky listened to the good-natured banter between her brothers. She hadn't heard such lightness in their voices since before the war. Without Joe at the farm, her brothers had become the boys she'd grown up with and loved.

"Hey, Bek, do you want to come over to the farm with Papa and me?" Ed asked. "We're to the point where we need a woman's touch."

"That's a wonderful idea," her mother said. "You need to get away from here for a while."

Although Becky agreed, she fought to keep from saying she wanted no part of the Marrow Place.

~ * ~

Joe paced the hotel room his father rented for him. The week he'd been in town seemed even longer than his months of imprisonment.

When the guards took him away, no one cared if he rested or did the things he'd done before becoming sick. Under Maria's watchful eye, he hardly dared to get out of bed. The only reason he felt safe in moving around now was his father and Maria had gone to the cafe for breakfast.

"Joseph Kemmerman!" Maria exclaimed, at the same moment he heard the door to his room open. "What are you doing out of bed?"

"Let the boy be," his father said, when he entered the room. "I've allowed you to pamper him for the past week. He's never going to regain his strength staying in this bed. It's high time he got some fresh air."

"So what brought about this reprieve?" Joe asked.

"We saw Dr. Morgan at the cafe and he asked if you'd been out of bed," Mark replied. "Maria had to admit, she's been a bit overprotective. I rented you a horse at the livery. I thought you might like to ride out to the Larson farm."

Joe could hardly believe his ears. "I suppose you want to go out with me."

His father laughed heartily. "As much as I would like to, I think you and Becky need some time alone. It's hard enough to court a woman with her family hovering over her. You certainly don't need Maria and me watching your every move."

"If I had my way, you wouldn't be out of bed," Maria declared. "I do not agree with your father. What if something were to happen? What if..."

Joe crossed the expanse separating him and Maria then took her in his arms. "I love you for your concern. No mother could ever be more caring. I'm stronger than you think. I promise, I will go directly to the Larson farm. Once there, neither Becky nor Emma will allow me to do more than sit on the porch. I'll be back by suppertime."

Maria ceased her protests and smiled as she put her hand to his cheek. "You are like my own son. I was so very worried about both you and Paul, especially considering Luke's death. I was afraid we'd lost you two as well. Forgive me for treating you like the child I so vividly remember."

Her words touched him deeply. "There's nothing to forgive. Emma was just as protective, in her own way. It has something to do with being a mother."

Maria began to smile when he called her mother for the second time sine her arrival in Illinois. Joe enjoyed seeing the tension drain from her face as she enjoyed his acceptance.

The memory of Maria's smile rode with Joe as he made his way to the Larson farm. All through the ride, he imagined what would happen when he saw Becky for the first time in a week.

He noticed Emma working in the garden, as soon as he rode into the yard.

"Good morning, Emma," he said, once he dismounted.

"I didn't expect to see you today," she replied, as she got to her feet.

"I came out to see Becky."

"Oh dear, I am sorry. Becky isn't here. She's been so sad since you went to town with your parents, Ed thought it would do her good to go over to his place and help with some of the decisions about the house. If we'd known you were coming, I'm certain he would have never suggested it."

Joe felt his spirits plummet. His anticipated reunion with Becky wouldn't happen as planned. If he wanted to see her, Joe knew he would have to go back to the Marrow Place.

"Thank you, Emma. I'll ride over there."

"Do you think you should?"

"Now you sound like Maria. I'm stronger than I look."

"I wasn't thinking about your physical strength. Ed's farm must hold some terrible memories for you. Why don't you stay here and I'll send Ralph over to get Becky. He's up in his room reading the books Tom sent over."

"Don't Emma. No matter what happened in the past, I have to be the one who goes to Becky. If I'm going to convince her about how I feel, I can't do it by sitting on your porch."

Remounting his horse, he turned toward the Marrow Place. Joe's mind spun with memories of the horror of imprisonment. From its far recesses, he relived the night he rode this way as he left Becky behind.

The same voices that assailed him that night echoed in his head as he rode toward the Marrow Place. He couldn't help but wonder if he would ever be free of the memories of the past.

~ * ~

Becky was glad she'd declined Ed's offer to ride with him in the wagon. She hadn't ridden Sugar since the day she'd been thrown. The wind in her hair gave her a lift. If Joe didn't come back, she would have to build a life for herself.

Ahead of her, the Marrow Place came into view. It certainly looked different from the last time she'd been there. The outbuildings had been repaired and now sported a new coat of red paint. The house, too, looked clean with its fresh white paint and new roof. It was hard to believe this was the same place where Joe and the others were held.

"What do you think?" Ed asked, once she dismounted and tied Sugar's reins to the porch railing.

"You've done wonders with this place. Have the Clarks been over to see it?"

"Vince was here yesterday. He asked about you. He said..."

"I don't want to hear what he said. No matter what you and Herman want, I don't love Vince. He'll never be anything more than a very good friend."

"Don't burn your bridges, Little Sister. For all you know, Joe and his parents have returned to Texas. The day may come when Vince's attentions might be welcomed. You don't want to be an old maid do you?"

Becky left Ed's questioned unanswered. Instead, she turned her attention to the flowers surrounding his new home. Lilacs, peonies and other spring flowers needed pruning. Phlox crept across a rock garden its delicate purple blossoms surrounding hen and chicks plants.

As she walked around the back of the house, Becky noticed bridal wreath bushes, which looked healthy. She had to use little imagination to see them full of white flowers.

Across a small expanse of lawn, she saw the remains of a vegetable garden. Someone had taken the time to remove the remnants of last year's vines and dead plants. Although it was too late to do any planting now, next year would be a different story.

At one end of the garden, a tangle of bushes proved to be raspberry and gooseberry bushes along with grapevines. At the other end asparagus and rhubarb had already gone to seed, promising a bountiful harvest next spring.

"I didn't ask you to come here to inspect the garden," Ed commented.

Started Becky turned to face her brother. "You should have. How do you expect to fill your belly this winter when you're living here alone?"

"With luck, I won't be alone. I guess you've been too busy to notice, but I've been courting Lillian Chay. Her parents have a large garden and have been putting up canned goods for us."

"Oh, so it's love that prompts you to bring me here," Becky teased. "You need the house fresh and clean for Lillian."

"I didn't expect you to clean, just make suggestions about the furnishings."

"Before I do anything about furnishings, I suggest the whole place needs a good cleaning. Let me do this one thing for you. It will take my mind off..." she turned away from Ed, leaving the rest of her sentence unspoken. "Now, I need a bucket of water, a scrub brush and a mop. As I recall, I saw you load them in the wagon this morning."

Ed's smile said volumes. He, like the rest of her family, was concerned about her melancholy mood since Joe left a week ago. Becky had to agree, hard work was the best medicine for her.

As soon as Becky entered the house a foul odor assailed her nostrils. It seemed to be a mixture of stale cigar smoke, spilled whiskey and spoiled food. She purposely avoided the parlor and the chilling memory of being alone with Delos. Her cheeks burned as she remembered him running his finger along her jaw line. Becky shook her head to rid herself of the unpleasant memory and went directly to the kitchen.

In the corner, she found a quarter full flour barrel. On closer inspection, she saw it literally crawled with bugs. Wrinkling her nose in disgust, she began filling the barrel with the contents of the cupboards. Even the tinned goods were discarded. As though possessed, she worked to clear away everything that spoke of the time Delos spent in this house.

"Are you sure you want to do this?" Ed questioned, as he set the bucket of water just inside the kitchen door.

"Would you prefer to have Lillian see this mess and smell the foul odor left behind by Delos and his men?"

"I suppose not. What's in the barrel?"

"Buggy flour and garbage. Get it out of here and burn it."

Ed crossed to where she stood and put his hands on her upper arms. "What happened in this house?"

Becky shook her head. How could she tell her brother about the treatment she'd received at the hands of Delos and the others? Instead of words, bitter tears were her response.

"Did that bastard..."

"No," she replied, her voice hardly audible. "It was the look in his eyes and the tone of his voice that frightened me. He knew my feelings for Joe and resented them."

Speaking the words, for the first time, caused her to tremble uncontrollably. She found comfort in her brother's arms, as she buried her face against his chest and shed the tears she'd refused to release at the time Delos had so degraded her in this house.

~ * ~

The Marrow Place came into view and the ghostlike voices in Joe's mind were replaced by a vision of Becky being pulled from her horse by Higgens. The look on her face when she left the house with Courtney made Joe sick to his stomach.

Over the past weeks they'd engaged in one conversation about that time in their lives. Although Becky denied anything happened, he could see a deep hurt in her eyes.

Joe knew what kind of man Courtney was. He knew plenty of men like Courtney. They could rape a woman with their eyes and hurt them with their words. He was certain Courtney had done the same to Becky.

At first glance, Joe saw John working on the roof of the barn and Becky's horse tied to the porch railing. He couldn't help but turn his head to look at the corncrib. It no longer resembled the place where he'd been held. With a new roof, replaced slats, and a fresh coat of paint, it didn't intimidate him at all.

He'd just reined his horse to a halt when Ed appeared in the doorway of the house.

"You're the last person I expected to see here," Ed declared. "I thought you and your folks would be half way to Texas by now."

"Is that what you told Becky?'

"Not in so many words, but it's what she believed when you didn't come back to the farm to see her."

"Of course, none of you bothered to come to the hotel to check on my so called departure."

"We've been busy. Summer means hard work on a farm."

"What about church on Sunday? Surely John and Emma see to it you all go with them."

"They do, but the church is South of our place, not in town. Even Ralph hasn't been to town since Tom brought him out all those medical books."

"You all seem to have good excuses. The same is true for me. After all the time I spent in bed at Emma's request, Maria insisted I remain in bed at the hotel. Today is the first time she's even allowed me to get up."

"So, why have you come here? Surely the trip to the farm to say nothing of the extra distance to get here must have been more than you're ready to do."

Joe felt his anger building. "I don't know why you're so damned concerned. I didn't come here to argue with you. Where is Becky?"

"I don't see why I should tell you. All you'll do is raise her hopes then break her heart. I've seen what you can do to her first hand. I came home to a sister I no longer know, one who's mind has been captured by a Reb who keeps walking away from her."

"I always thought you were too good, too accepting to be believed. No matter what you say, you're no different than Herman. Hatred flows mingled with blood through you veins. None of you will ever accept me so let's stop this game of pretense. Just tell me where I'll find Becky."

~ * ~

To Becky's amazement, the water in her bucket was black with dirt, even though she'd washed only a minute part of the kitchen floor. She got to her feet, surprised at just how tired such a simple task made her.

Leaving the bucket in the middle of the floor, she decided to explore the rest of the house. From the kitchen, she entered the dining room. The solid oak table had been stretched out to accommodate many diners. Had Courtney entertained his men here? She doubted it. Searching her memory, she recalled Joe telling her about how Major Stone insisted they all come to the house for breakfast before they left for their respective destinations.

Becky ran her hand over the fine grain of the wood, making tracks in the dust. As she did, she could see Lillian in this room, lovingly polishing the table until she could see her face in it.

Still ignoring the parlor, Becky mounted the steep narrow stairs leading to the second floor.

Off the hall stood five closed doors. Opening the first, she stepped into a large room with an oak bed, dresser, and washstand. Although the bed was neatly made, she could see a man laying in it, a sheet pulled waist high, his chest bare. To her horror, the man was Delos Courtney.

Come to me, Rebecca, he called, holding out his hand to her.

In terror, she ran from the room and back down the stairs. Once in the dining room, she closed the door leading to the staircase. Leaning against it, she brought her breathing under control.

Did you think you could avoid me by not going into the parlor?

She looked up, only to see Delos standing in front of her, wearing only his britches.

I knew you would come back to me, Rebecca. I only had to be patient. You need a man to love you, not that Reb. Can't you see he's no more than a boy?

"You're only a product of my imagination," she shouted. "You're back in Ohio. Major Stone said so."

Before her eyes two more men materialized next to Courtney. She immediately recognized Teddy, but the second man was a stranger.

This man took his own life rather than face his punishment, the stranger silently communicated. *He thought he could escape his eternal fate by returning to this house. I am your guardian angel. Your brother and I have been sent to take him back to the gates of Hell to face a far worse judge and jury than he would have if he'd allowed himself to be court marshaled.*

Becky felt a chill as Courtney's spirit lunged toward her. *If I'm going to Hell, she's coming with me. I won't be denied a second time!*

A scream pierced the air and Becky realized it came from her lips.

~ * ~

"Are you going to answer me?" Joe asked, when Ed stood, defiantly silent in front of him.

"I don't see why you think you deserve an answer, but..." Ed's words were cut short when Becky's scream sounded from the house.

Joe pushed past an astonished Ed and ran into the house. He'd only been inside once, but he remembered the layout of the place. Ignoring the parlor, he ran to the kitchen. In his haste, he almost tripped over a bucket of water standing in the middle of the room.

Through the door leading to the dining room, he saw Becky. She stood with her back pressed against a closed door, her eyes wide with terror.

In front of her, Joe saw three transparent beings. He shook his head as they disappeared before his eyes.

Becky looked at him, as thought she didn't see him. "Becky! Becky! Are you all right? Did they hurt you?"

The sound of his voice seemed to free her from the trance she'd been in. Allowing him to take her in his embrace, Becky put her arms around his neck.

"Did you see them?"

"Yes, but I hardly believe it."

"It was Delos. He killed himself and willed his spirit to come here and wait for me. My brother Teddy and my guardian angel came to take him to..."

"What kind of nonsense is this?" Ed demanded.

Becky and Joe turned to see him and John standing in the doorway.

"Just what is going on here?" John questioned.

"Oh, Papa," Becky cried, untangling her arms from around Joe's neck. "It was Teddy. He—he came to save me."

"You're upset, Bek," Ed observed, his tone one of a condescending older brother. "Teddy is dead. You only imagined..."

"Imagined what? I've heard Teddy's voice off and on for months. I'm not crazy."

Joe listened as Becky described her encounter with Courtney's spirit. As he did, the memory of Luke's communications over the past several months came to mind.

"You're not a child," John said, once Becky finished her narrative. "You can't possibly believe in ghosts."

Becky began to protest, when Joe felt a chill in the room. Before his eyes, two transparent beings materialized.

Don't question Becky, Papa, the first being declared. *I wasn't ready to die, but I did. Because of my age, I was allowed to come home one last time. I didn't understand why until today. Delos Courtney was an evil man and his spirit is no better. Where he is now is the best place for him, he will pay for his transgressions for eternity.*

"T—Teddy," John stammered. "Is it really you?"

Yes, Papa. I've done what I can for Becky's happiness. Now it's time for me to rest. Tell Mama and Ralph and Herman I love them.

Joe turned his attention to the second figure. It took only a moment for him to recognize his own older brother. "Was it the same for you, Luke?"

The sound of laughter, that Joe knew so well, filled the room. *We all have to earn our places in heaven, especially when we get there the way Teddy and I did. We were allowed to return when Joe got sick and was taken to the hospital. My job was to save Joe's life and Teddy's was to help Becky accept Joe. Neither of us expected you to fall in love, but you did.*

"What will happen now?" Joe questioned.

As Ma has her place in heaven, so do I. The open range and a certain young lady are waiting for me. You and Becky belong together. Love her with all your heart. Just remember, I'll always be watching you. If you hurt her, I promise your life will be a living hell.

The two apparitions disappeared, leaving Joe shaken. He turned to where John and Ed stood. The expression on their faces mirrored his own disbelief.

"Was that really your brother?" Becky asked.

He turned to face her, unashamed by the tears in his eyes. "Yes, it was Luke."

"Did you understand what he meant?"

Joe nodded. "I'll explain it to you, if you'll have me."

"Are you asking me to marry you?"

"That's what it sounded like to me. I promise, you'll never want for anything, and I'll love you for the rest of our lives."

If John and Ed made any protest, Joe didn't hear it. Becky's answer came in the form of a kiss and loving embrace. She would be his forever. Together they would build a life to ensure the future of the Lazy K.

Meet Sherry Derr-Wille

When her sophomore English teacher assigned a handful of students to write for an entire year, Sherry Derr-Wille fell in love. Since then, writing has been more than a hobby. With over twenty books to her credit, she has sixteen contracts for release dates in 2003-2005.

Married for almost forty years to her high school sweetheart, she describes her husband, Bob, as a saint saying, "I doubt of a mortal man would put up the eccentricities of a writer."

Along with her writing, she claims three children and eight grandchildren ranging from infants to adults.

Now that her children are grown, she and Bob enjoy their empty nest and the success of her writing career.

"If nothing else," Sherry often says, "I'm an overnight success after forty years."

VISIT OUR WEBSITE
FOR THE FULL INVENTORY
OF QUALITY BOOKS:

http://www.wings-press.com

Quality trade paperbacks and downloads
in multiple formats,
in genres ranging from light romantic comedy to
general fiction and horror. Wings has something
for every reader's taste.
Visit the website, then bookmark it.
We add new titles each month!